blaze of
silver

THE DE GRANVILLE TRILOGY
BY K. M. GRANT

Blood Red Horse
Book One

Green Jasper
Book Two

Blaze of Silver
Book Three

blaze of
silver

K. M. GRANT

Walker & Company
New York

First published in the United States of America in 2007 by
Walker Publishing Company, Inc.
Distributed to the trade by Holtzbrinck Publishers

Originally published in the U.K. in 2007 by the Penguin Group, Puffin Books

For information about permission to reproduce selections from
this book, write to Permissions, Walker & Company,
104 Fifth Avenue, New York, New York 10011

Library of Congress Cataloging-in-Publication Data

Grant, K. M.
Blaze of silver / K. M. Grant
p.   cm.
Summary: Using principles of their shared Muslim faith to persuade him, an agent of the Old Man of the Mountain convinces Kamil to lead Will and Ellie into a trap, but Kamil repents and seeks a way to save his friends and redeem himself.
ISBN-13: 978-0-8027-9625-7 • ISBN-10: 0-8027-9625-7 (hardcover)
[1. Horses—Fiction.   2. Muslims—Fiction.   3. Knights and knighthood—Fiction.   4. Great Britain—History—Richard I, 1189–1199—Fiction.]   I. Title.
PZ7.G766775Sil 2007   [Fic]—dc22   2006012098

Visit Walker & Company's Web site at www.walkeryoungreaders.com

Printed in the U.S.A. by Quebecor World Fairfield

2 4 6 8 10 9 7 5 3 1

All papers used by Walker & Company are natural, recyclable products made from wood grown in well-managed forests. The manufacturing processes conform to the environmental regulations of the country of origin.

For Douglas and Audrey Grant,
who I wish were still here. —K. M. Grant

Prologue

There was no summer chill in the air but Hosanna was restless. The red horse, veteran of campaigns and crusades, raised his head, then shook it as if to ward off an invisible cloud carrying something he did not like. He sneezed and put down his head again to graze on the lush June grass, but though the grass was fresh and sweet, he could not settle. He turned, nipped a fly from his flank and began to move, rustling up all the other warhorses who had been grazing peacefully as they basked in the sun that jeweled the fields between Hartslove Castle and the river. Some objected, grumpily reluctant to abandon their green feast, but Dargent, the big bay who was Hosanna's constant friend, obediently took his usual place behind the red horse's tail. This was where he was happiest and although long blades of grass hung untidily from his mouth and his lips were stained and frothy, he began, like Hosanna, to trot. Soon, all the horses were trotting for they were fit, and although some were tired because it was the middle of

1

the campaigning season and many had journeyed great distances before being turned out for a rest, their spirits were high. Then they were cantering, making a huge circle around the chestnut tree that sheltered the napping soldiers who had been sent to guard them. One soldier woke, seized his own horse, and shouted. But Hosanna, his tail feathering like an opening fan, just pushed the loose horses faster and faster until, all lethargy abandoned, they were galloping, thundering around the tree as if the hounds of hell were after them.

However, before the soldiers could gather themselves together, Hosanna stopped so suddenly that Dargent bumped his nose and left a dribble of green spittle on the muscled chestnut haunches in front of him. The red tail swung low and the flies, thinking to settle again, were rudely swatted away. When the other horses realized that the game was over, they too drizzled to a halt, some of the older stallions stamping their feet at Hosanna in half-hearted complaint at the pointless interruption. Minutes later, although the soldiers were too rattled to go back to sleep, all the horses were grazing again.

All except Hosanna. The spontaneous gallop had not dispelled his discomfort. In the throbbing of his two crusading wounds he could feel something coming toward Hartslove. To feel this was not unusual, but this time was different for he did not smell the sharp, sour stench of battles to come or sense his master, Will Ravensgarth, calling to him. These things the horse was used to. What he felt now was not so familiar, although he had felt it once before, out in the Holy Land at the height of the crusade. It was a stirring dread, a kind of horror that was quite out of place in this peaceful landscape and on this lovely day.

The red horse walked slowly down to the river but did not drink. The soldiers watched him curiously, his mood infecting them a little. Until it was time to return to his stall inside Hartslove's curtain wall, Hosanna took only snatches of grass and, after carefully looking around in every direction, settled his gaze on the road that ran from the castle gate down the hill and away into the dusty distance.

1

Sitting in the throne room of a rugged fortress known as "the eagle's nest" because of its precarious perch on a spike of mountain, Rashid ed-Din Sinan, also known as the Old Man of the Mountain, was juggling with oranges. Up and down went the oranges. Up and down and across and up and down again the oranges rose and fell with pleasing regularity. The Old Man should have rejoiced at the spectacle. In fact, he hardly saw it. He was looking at something quite else. In his mind's eye he could see only the face of a young man. The face was shadowy for it had been a while since the Old Man had seen it in the flesh, but there was no mistaking to whom it belonged: It belonged to Kamil, the young man whom the Old Man had once ordered to play a crucial role in the murder of the Saracen leader, Saladin. Kamil had not fulfilled his role and vanished soon after, leaving the Old Man raging. The Old Man often raged, but normally his rages subsided into festering grudges. However, his rage against Kamil still burned fiercely

4

every day, fed not only with anger that his orders had been disobeyed but also because he had thought to steal Kamil's love for Saladin and turn it into love for himself. The Old Man had no son of his own, and Kamil, so brave, so impatient of weakness and, above all, so passionate in defense of his own people against their enemies, was the sort of son the Old Man dreamed about. It had been a hideous disappointment when these dreams turned to ashes and Kamil had remained loyal to Saladin. As time passed, this sense of disappointment increased, for the Old Man felt himself growing old. He needed an heir and still he found nobody who could match Kamil. The young man would have been so perfect. The picture of what might have been tantalized and maddened the Old Man until his disappointment turned to a hatred that stung his heart and darkened all his days.

Today the sting was sharper than ever for a spy had arrived bearing news. Kamil, whose whereabouts had been a mystery, had been found in England at Hartslove Castle with the de Granvilles. The oranges flew more quickly as the Old Man's eyes became black smears in the plumpness of his face. *At last,* he thought, concentrating with renewed energy. *At last I shall take my revenge.* One, two, three. One, two, three. He deftly plucked another orange from the bowl at his side. One, two, three, four. One, two, three, four. All was well for a while; then the Old Man threw up his hands and, in complete silence, watched them all roll away.

The fruit was nervously retrieved by the spy, still in travel-stained clothes. He had glowed briefly in his youth but now his skin had set into the color of bleached parchment, giving him the appearance of a mournful albino crow. It was this color and his aptitude that had first brought him to the attention of the Old Man, for men of such color could pass in either East or West without comment. He usually used the old spy for matters of state but now he would use him for a more personal purpose. He would turn him into an angel of death.

Feeling his master's eye upon him, the spy scrambled for the oranges, his wide-legged trousers riding up to reveal bandy legs callused from long hours in the saddle. He had hoped to find enough courage to ask if his age and weariness did not merit retirement among the lemon groves in the comfort of the valley. But even as he framed the words, he knew he would never utter them.

"Sit, sit, Amal," he heard the Old Man click impatiently. Clutching the oranges, the spy hurried to obey, but he could only hover over cushions in the corner. The Old Man was capricious. The penalty for any perceived slight to his dignity was instant execution. Amal remembered clearly that the last time he had been in this very room, a boy who had displeased the Old Man by lolling on a rug had been ordered to leap from the top of the tower. There was no need to look out of the window to feel the boy's breathless drop, the razor-sharp rocks, and the final, appalling crunch. So Amal did not sit. But neither could he stand, for that might be taken as disobedience. So he hovered, half down and half up, very uncomfortable. A small girl came and took the oranges and gave them to the Old Man, who began to juggle again. Again the fruit fell, and when the oranges rolled his way, Amal collapsed gratefully onto his creaky knees once more and gathered them in.

"Kamil has been with William de Granville, Earl of Ravensgarth, for some time, Excellency," he ventured in a voice reedy with nerves. "He's helping him raise the ransom demanded for the release of King Richard, the so-called Lionheart. The king is no longer with Duke Leopold of Austria but has been sold to the German emperor and they say the wagon train bound for Speyer will stretch for miles and miles. One hundred and fifty thousand marks is the price. One hundred and fifty thousand!" Amal coughed, knowing it was unwise to allow the Old Man to see how the amount impressed him. He quickly made his voice more matter-of-fact. "If the earl comes to deliver the money himself, surely Kamil will be with him—"

The Old Man got up and his eyes, no longer smears but gimlets shining bright and fierce, made Amal tremble as he put the oranges carefully into the soft, almost womanly hands that were stretched out toward him. The hands were deceptive. Amal had seen them crush a walnut as if it were a fig.

Almost absentmindedly, the Old Man took the oranges back to his throne and sat down. The juggling began once more. Next to the vision of Kamil, he now had a vision of endless wagons stuffed with treasure. He could already see the dull sheen and his nose tickled with the metallic smell of dirty silver. Amal was right to be impressed. One hundred and fifty thousand marks! Richard must be quite a king that his subjects would give so much to get him back. The Old Man glanced briefly at Amal, wondering what price his own people would give if he himself was captured. But the spy dropped his gaze. A look of genuine sorrow flitted across the Old Man's face. His men would jump out of the window if he ordered it but they would not look at him. If he was captured, they would give nothing for his return. In fact, his capture would be a relief to them. He allowed the oranges to fall again. Kamil would have gazed at him directly. He growled as Amal grovelled; then he began to think and his eyes, changeable as the English weather, lost their gimlet edge and turned coldly beady in their unnaturally round sockets. He would not, for the moment, allow the spy to see how deeply the news about Kamil had affected him. "Forget the oranges," he commanded, "and tell me more about the silver horse you saw in Damascus. Is it really the one that King Richard stole in Cyprus?"

At last, Amal sat down. "It is, Excellency," he said, his leathery cheeks twitchy with strain. "I know it is that horse because I have seen it before, racing across the desert. It was so fleet that even the falcons could not keep up. The Christian knight who had charge of it in the bazaar said that King Richard wanted to gift it to William Ravensgarth's brother, Gavin de Granville, for his part in the Saracen wars but that nobody had arranged for its passage back to England. I found it for sale and at half its real value. It looks very sorry for itself, Excellency, but its silver color is quite unmistakable." The Old Man clicked his tongue again and Amal's palms began to sweat. "I took the liberty of bringing it here in the hope that it will please you."

There was silence. "But if Richard gave it to Gavin de Granville," the Old Man said, his voice like ice, "we must make sure he gets it, Amal. I am not a horse thief."

"No, no, Excellency," said poor Amal. "I just thought . . ."

"You should not think. You are not capable." The Old Man smiled and his face was suddenly that of an indulgent uncle.

Amal was exhausted, trying to keep up with the Old Man's moods, but he could not allow himself to relax, not for a moment. "No," he said. "I will be guided by you in everything, Excellency."

"Good," said the Old Man, and drew his faithful servant to him as a lion draws a lamb. "Amal," he said, his voice melting from ice to oil and his painted, curled nails like velvet claws, "you may rest tonight but tomorrow I wish you to resume your travels and take the horse to William de Granville in England. Show him how you bring it in honesty and peace so that he may give it to his brother and they may ride together, William on his red horse and his brother on the silver. William Ravensgarth will trust you. Stay with him. Help him, if necessary, to collect the ransom for the English king." There was a short pause before the Old Man continued, holding Amal a little tighter. "Commend yourself to Kamil also. Be a brother to him. But be sure, once you have his confidence, to whisper to him that the English king's ransom is to be used by the German emperor to wage war against the Saracens. Even if Kamil has been living in England, he will recognize the Saracens as his brothers. Remind him how Christian knights killed his father. Talk to him of Saladin's wish to rid our land of the Christian scourge and how his people, now in sad disarray, need a strong leader. Flatter him, Amal, and stay with him. You will learn what to do next in due course."

Amal pressed his lips together. A journey to England! Now he cursed the day he had seen the silver horse and thought only of his wife and the increasing frailty of his mother. His sons never bowed to him now, and to his daughter, just flowering into the beauty of early womanhood, he was a distant stranger. Retirement among the lemon groves might be a dream, but surely, surely he deserved to lay his head for a month or two on his own pillow?

Yet he never thought of refusing. It was not possible to refuse the Old Man and Amal's habit of obedience was so strong that he would not have known how. His only protest was to bow so low that he could scrunch up his bleary eyes without being observed and to shake the dust from his feet with a little more vigor than usual when he left the Old Man's presence.

At dawn, he rolled his belongings inside a blanket, carefully placing right in the middle a small, roughly sewn booklet, his most treasured possession. His wife, now snoring in another room, had given it to him in happiness and hope on the day of their marriage when she was still young and beautiful and her new husband the apple of her eye. Amal grimaced. Those days were long gone. But he loved this book. A commendation from the Old Man together with several verses from the Koran were inscribed inside it and, at the birth of his babies, Amal had written their names with pride, each on a different page. Underneath, when they learned to write, he had encouraged the children to inscribe something themselves—anything—that would remind him of them when he was far away doing the Old Man's business. They had obliged him, drawing childish pictures of assassins' daggers and Arab horses under sentiments sweet and dutiful. It was hard to believe that the hearts of the children who had written such things were now, when they thought of their father at all, as dry as the ink.

Amal sighed as he secured the roll, saddled up his own horse and put a halter on his silver charge. The animals were reluctant to leave the horse lines and whinnied to their friends.

From his silken pillows, the Old Man was listening. When Amal had gone, he called for parchment and wrote a letter to the German emperor. At the bottom, he inscribed King Richard's name and, over it, carefully drew a skull. He liked the skull, but it would not do. He deftly changed it to look like a silver piece and found himself so pleased with the letter that he read it out loud. Then he smiled, his smile pretty as a cherub's, before settling himself to sleep as he always did, bolt upright and with a dagger in his hand.

2

In the jousting field at Hartslove, everybody was laughing except Elric, Will Ravensgarth's new squire, who was lying facedown amid the fallen leaves, biting his lip and trying not to cry. It was the fifth time that day he had fallen off Dargent, unbalanced by a lance that was too heavy for him but that he was determined to master. The bay horse waited patiently, as he had been taught, for his young rider to get up. He shook his head as Hal, Will's previous squire, approached and hauled Elric to his feet.

"Don't let the lance drop once you have scored a hit," Hal admonished, his freckled face full of kindly anxiety. "You let it swing about and in the end it pushes you off your own horse. The point is to unseat your opponent, you know." Hal patted Dargent and the horse rubbed his head on his shoulder as Elric wiped his face, spreading the dirt until it hid the redness flushing his cheeks. Hal's last remark about unseating his opponent had riled him. "I know what I'm supposed to be doing," he muttered, "I'll do it again." He seized the stirrup to remount.

Hal looked up at the rough stands erected on the side of the field and saw Will shake his head. Hal nodded back. "But not today, Elric," he said, adding reassuringly, "it's not a disgrace to fall off, you know. We've all done it. When the earl first got Hosanna he fell off dozens of times and he had been riding all his life. You've only been riding for just over six months. You can't expect miracles."

Elric would not be comforted. "But everybody is here, looking. Listen to them laughing. They think I'm stupid. Not Marie, perhaps, because she's nice, and not Mistress Ellie because she's nice too, but that spiteful Marissa and that snooty Kamil, although it won't show in his face because nothing ever does. And then Old Nurse—" The boy groaned. "Oh no! I know just what she'll do. She'll grab me, shove me in a bath, and plaster my bruises with one of her stinking potions so that everybody will point and hold their noses."

Hal tried not to smile. Elric had summed up everything entirely correctly. "Look," he said, "while you ride Dargent back into the courtyard, I'll get Marie"— Hal couldn't help blushing himself at the thought of the sweet girl whose face made his legs turn to jelly—"to distract Old Nurse. You just make sure you are busy until supper. That shouldn't be difficult. For a start, you can brush Hosanna and make him shine, for the earl sets off again tomorrow for Whitby to fetch another chunk of the king's ransom money." He gave Elric a leg up and Dargent tossed his head, preparing to gallop down the lists once more. Hal and Elric both laughed now. "Hold up, Dargent," said Hal, "that's enough for today." The horse seemed disappointed but Hal was pleased to see how Elric soothed him until he could be ridden back up the field with a loose rein.

Hal returned to the stands and Marie hurried to his side. "Is he hurt?" she asked. Marie always expected the worst.

"Of course he's not hurt," Marissa said scornfully, and Hal wondered, not for the first time, how twins could be so different. Marie would never use such a tone of voice. Perhaps it was because of Marissa's limp that she always sounded so bitter. Hal thought it had made her character limp, too. He ignored Marissa, plucked up his courage, and took Marie's arm.

"It's his pride that's hurt more than anything, I expect." Will's deep voice boomed out above those of the other knights standing about in groups. Hal jumped. Will sounded so like his dead father, whose voice had often boomed across this field in those carefree days before the crusade and before the terrible events earlier in the year that had resulted in the death of Will's brother, Gavin.

"That's right, sir, just his pride." Hal nodded.

"He's really very good when you think how little practice he's had." Ellie had left Kamil, who stood slightly apart, and joined the group around Will.

Will was glad to have Ellie by his side. He smiled at her and when she smiled back, his heart sang. "We should get the joiner to make him a lighter lance, though, don't you think, Ellie? Elric's still so skinny. The lance is heavier than he is." He handed Ellie a spare weapon and grinned when she rocked and nearly dropped it.

"Well, he's got to learn," said Marissa tartly, resenting that the smiles and jokes passing between Will and Ellie were not including her. The only time she was truly happy now was when Will was teaching her to ride. Then, she had his undivided attention, and his praise made her glow as much as the ruby brooch she always wore.

Ellie felt Marissa's resentment and forced herself to look away from the brooch. It had once been hers, given to her by Will on hers and Gavin's ill-fated wedding day, and she knew that Marissa wore it to annoy her. With difficulty, she stopped herself from scowling and reminded herself that, at eighteen, she had an unfair advantage. Marissa was still only fifteen and had been at Hartslove for just nine months. Old Nurse, who was the wisest woman in the castle, was always telling Ellie that she should not allow Marissa to irritate her, and Ellie tried, she really did. But Marissa drove her mad, particularly when she clung to Will's side like a leech and even accentuated her limp, just to get Will's sympathy. Ellie began to walk quickly back to the castle before she said something she would later regret. As was her habit, she stopped under the chestnut tree to tidy up Gavin's grave and as she knelt to brush some early-falling leaves from the headstone, her sharp words faded. Gavin's presence was still so strong. It was hard for her to think of him folded into the earth beneath and she could not imagine the day when she would be able to tend his grave without her heart feeling squeezed like an apple in a cider press. Her tears fell onto the stone and trickled down among the flowers.

Gradually she became aware that Will was behind her. She said nothing at first, just dried her tears and tried to show how welcome he was. She knew that he still found his brother's grave a difficult place to be. It upset Ellie dreadfully that Gavin and Will's final parting had been so bitter. Often, from afar, Ellie would see Will here, sitting without moving for hours, with Hosanna grazing beside him. Sometimes the horse would rub his nose on the headstone as he relaxed in the shade, peacefully swishing the flies from his smooth coat. Then some of the lines on Will's face would soften as he murmured to the red horse, leaning on him and touching the star between his eyes before caressing again and again Hosanna's two crusading scars.

That squeezed Ellie's heart, too. She often thought how much Gavin would have liked to see his brother and Hosanna, peaceful and thoughtful in the sunshine. But she never said as much to Will, for part of Ellie's terrible sadness was that it was she who had been at the center of the brothers' last, most disastrous quarrel and it had set up an awkwardness between herself and Will, which she seemed powerless to dispel. She traced the letters on the stone with her finger:

Gavin de Granville, Count of Hartslove
and crusader
died most bravely
21st March 1193

It was Will who broke the silence. "I've had a message from Prince John about King Richard's ransom," he said, watching Ellie's finger but not kneeling down.

"At least one hundred thousand silver marks will have been collected by the end of the year but Richard thinks it would be folly to risk the whole ransom in one baggage train. He suggests that Queen Eleanor, for all her great age, should take the bulk of it and I'm to take three wagons' worth on a different route to Speyer. If there is a disaster at least one of us should get through." Ellie got up. Will's face was troubled. "I'm nervous, Ellie, because it seems that the German emperor's going to make us responsible for the safety of the ransom until it gets to his border." He put both hands on the headstone. "Every greedy prince in Christendom will know that there is a fortune on the move, yet the imperial guards only take it over when the danger is lowest." His brow furrowed. "I wish there was a less risky way to get the silver to Speyer but if there is I can't think of it."

Ellie observed him carefully. "If you are trying to put me off coming with you," she said, "you won't succeed. In fact, I don't see how you can manage without me. People are bound to fall sick on the way—perhaps even you—and I've been studying about herbs and medicines so hard that I think I can deal with even more illnesses than Old Nurse."

"I know, Ellie. I know we need you." Will found that he did not know what tone to use. Sometimes everything he said seemed to be wrong. He wanted Ellie to come to Speyer, not just because of her growing knowledge of doctoring but because he did not like to be without her. Yet the awkwardness that they both recognized got in the way of his ever telling her this. Will could hardly understand what had happened. How could Gavin now appear to be more of an obstacle than he had ever been when he was alive? Where once Will would have been confident of Ellie's feelings toward him, now he was unsure. Perhaps when Ellie slipped her arm through his, it was not because she loved him but because he was the only de Granville left. The thought that he would never, now, be sure, tortured Will. What was more, sometimes he saw Kamil looking at Ellie in a way that made his scalp prickle. Was it Kamil who filled Ellie's dreams? He did not dare to ask.

When they got back to the castle, Hosanna was standing in the courtyard loosely tied to an iron ring. With patient good humor, he allowed Elric to wash his mane, then, when he thought things had taken long enough, delicately undid the rope and took a small piece of the boy's jerkin between his teeth. Elric stretched his hand backward to tickle Hosanna's lips until he let go. Will went at once to his horse's head. "Ho there, Hosanna," he said softly before looking over the chestnut withers at Kamil leaning against the wall. "We'll leave for Whitby at dawn," he told Kamil, trying not to betray any of his thoughts in his voice. "We need to count the ransom silver already there and collect more from towns farther north. Germany before Christmas! Are you ready?"

Kamil immediately went to Sacramenta, Hosanna's mother, who was also tied up outside, and bent over to dig some mud out of her feet using the little triangular blade that he had had the smith fashion and that he always wore at his belt. "I'm ready," he said. Both young men were the same age but Kamil looked older than Will for his face was darker and leaner, and although he had been in England for a number of months, he retained the aloofness of a stranger. If Elric thought this was snooty, Kamil could not help it. It was just how he was, and recently he knew his aloofness had got worse.

For all the Hartslove hospitality, Kamil could not belong and some days he missed his homeland acutely, not just the dry smell of the desert or the warm explosion of fresh figs on his tongue but the chatter of the market and the sense of being wordlessly understood. Sometimes he hated the tolling of the great abbey bell across the Hartslove valley, not because he disliked the sound, but because it reminded him how much he longed to hear the pulsating call of the muezzin. Every day, he felt his Saracen blood running a little thinner. Yet he stayed, partly because, with Saladin dead, it was too dangerous for him to return home, partly for love of Will and Hosanna, and partly because of Ellie. She was the only person to whom he had ever opened his soul. It had happened just once. But he wondered—no, he hoped—there might be another time. Although Ellie gave him no encouragement, he could not shake off this hope and when he stood in the stable with Hosanna beside him and Ellie in front, he could sometimes believe he was happy.

Elric tugged at Will's jerkin. "Can I go with you tomorrow?" he begged. "I may not be good with a lance yet but I can ride and you'll need somebody to tend the horses whilst you count the money."

Will raised his eyebrows. "It's too far, Elric," he said. "I'm not sure you are quite ready."

"But if Hal's going with you, he could carry on

19

teaching me on the way." Elric could be relied upon to argue. "Think how much improvement I could make."

"Well, yes," Will agreed, almost unable to resist Elric's pleading face because it reminded him so much of himself. "I'll think about it over supper."

Elric knew he had won and threw a triumphant glance at Hal, who winked at him as they all began to move toward the great hall. Then Elric found Marissa beside him. "Don't think you are so great," she said, her mouth curled with jealousy. She hated the castle when Will was not at home, and the night before he left she was always at her worst. "It's only because I am a girl that I can't go."

The boy grinned naughtily. "I suppose when you can canter without clinging on to a neckstrap," he said, his voice angelically sympathetic, "the earl might take you over to the abbey. They make honey there, you know, which can sweeten even the sourest temper." He dodged her smack with ease and ran off.

Will sighed. Elric was naughty but why on earth couldn't Marissa be nicer? Her obvious adoration of him was very gratifying but it was also a nuisance since it made her so poisonous. He thought of saying something to her—again—but decided not to. He would never change her and anyway, he had more important things to think about. He had just turned to summon Constable Shortspur, who would be in charge of the garrison in his absence, when an archer practicing his craft from the battlements called down. "Sir," he shouted, "Earl William! There's somebody coming up the road."

Silence fell and the knights stiffened, poised to rush for armor and swords. The porter began to wind up the drawbridge. But the archer, leaning right over, seemed unperturbed. "It's just one person," he called, then after a moment, "and a horse. Yes, sir. One person and a silver-colored horse. The man is leading it and he looks tired."

Will signaled for the drawbridge to be lowered again and with Hal and Ellie right behind him and Marissa pushing forward, he strode out. In the courtyard, Hosanna ignored Elric's proffered apple, stamped one front hoof so hard it drew sparks, and then stood perfectly still.

3

Amal was more aware of the archer than the group at the end of the drawbridge. He had heard about English archers, so he stooped a little lower and shuffled a little more, his cloak, shabby and frayed, dragging its tatters in the dirt. The silver horse beside him was unconcerned. Recovered from the long sea journey and shining with the sheen only English grass can produce, the horse's walk was light and brisk and, every three paces or so, Amal was forced to abandon his shuffle and skip to keep up. Occasionally the horse snatched impatiently at the restraining rein and Amal's arm would jerk. The two looked very ill suited.

Will screwed up his eyes. Something about the horse was vaguely familiar. That color, the kind of silver that can die or sparkle depending on the light, was unusual, as was the concave set of the face, the darker mane and tail and the wide nostrils. The horse was not big—hardly bigger than Hosanna, who himself was small for a warhorse—but it stood tall, its neck rising proud as a swan's and its bearing regal.

In a moment Kamil was in front of Will. "It's an

Arab horse," he said, and his low voice rose until he sounded like the boy he had been not so many years before. A horse from home! "And the man is a Saracen," he added rather unnecessarily since Will could now see for himself the grubby Turkish hat. But despite his excitement, Kamil held back. Friendliness was weakness. Let the man come to them.

Eventually Amal stopped looking at the archer and looked at the group of people barring his way. Ah! There was Kamil. Amal secretly relaxed. At least the journey was not wasted. He saw Will and immediately began to bow and bob until Will thought he must be quite dizzy. Amal halted and the horse stood slightly apart from him as if it found its carer useful but distasteful.

"You are Gavin de Granville, Count of Hartslove?" Amal knew just what to say.

"Who asks?" enquired Will, knowing, without looking, that Hal would be poised, ready for anything, for no man ever had a better or more reliable squire.

"A friend," said Amal, pretending to stumble hard over the language, "who wishes, er, gift, er, er, from king."

Will's face cleared at once. "Of course!" he exclaimed. "I do know this horse! Richard took it in Cyprus on the way to Palestine and wanted Gavin to have it. Do you remember, Ellie? Richard said so in the letter you read to us when we got home."

"You—not Gavin?" Amal drew back.

"No," said Will. "I am Gavin's brother. He died a hero's death in the spring." Amal seemed to retreat but Will moved smartly forward to take the reins. The silver horse ignored him.

23

Amal shrugged. "If one brother is dead, I suppose the other should take the prize," he said deliberately in Arabic. Kamil could not help but betray how good it was to hear his own language spoken again. Amal pretended not to notice.

Now everybody crowded around the horse.

"He's like something out of one of Old Nurse's fantastical stories," breathed Ellie, amazed at the extraordinary reflections she could see. Close up, the silver turned to gray as if the animal were cast from metal. Ellie touched the swan-neck and jumped at the warmth on her palm for the color looked so cold. She moved to the front and tidied the long forelock to one side. The white strands among the dark shimmered like quicksilver and Ellie was dazzled. Then she jumped again. "Oh!" she cried. "This horse has blue eyes!"

Amal shuffled forward and, with more bows, seemed to search for words. He began to speak. Ellie smiled and shook her head before turning to Kamil. "You must translate," she said. Amal began again.

"The man says this horse has a wall-eye," Kamil told her, delighted, "and he is right. It happens sometimes. Look. This eye shows blue and white but the other one is dark, as you would expect."

"And it's not a he, but a she!" exclaimed Will, laughing.

Amal bowed. "Ah, she, yes, she." He reverted back to Arabic with a sidelong glance at Kamil. "We Arabs are happy with our mares. It is only you Christians who prefer the stallion. She is very fine."

Ellie was entranced. "A silver mare. How beautiful and how unusual!" She nodded at Amal to show her approval and became aware, as she saw him droop, that he had not been offered so much as a cup of water. "Kamil, tell the man he is very welcome," she said, looking to Will for his agreement. "He must be hungry and tired after his journey. He needs to wash and be given fresh clothes. Old Nurse will launder his dirty ones and if she makes her usual rude remarks about foreigners, at least our visitor won't understand."

Amal kept an inquiring look on his face, but when Kamil gestured, he glanced nervously up once more at the archer. It was only after Will shouted for the archer to stand down that he seemed happy to cross the drawbridge and follow Kamil into the heart of the castle.

From his place by the wall, Hosanna watched, and when Amal disappeared into the keep, he blinked, and all the nerves shivered down his flanks.

At supper that evening, Amal sat at the top table. The fresh clothes hung from his fleshless bones and with his pale coloring, as unusual as the horse's, he would have looked sinister except that the expression on his face was one of permanent apology, even at rest. Kamil spoke to him, sinking back into his own language as somebody sinks into a familiar bed, unable to prevent questions bubbling out. What was the news from Palestine and Arabia? Like a parched flower, he couldn't get enough and Amal responded with apparent enthusiasm, expanding his answers until Kamil was satisfied. It was some time before Kamil asked Amal about himself. The man was a horsetrader, he learned, and not a very successful one. He wondered about a reward. This brought Kamil up short and his habitual stiffness returned. Then, as Amal prattled on, he grew suspicious. "Why is it, old man," he asked, "that you ask no questions about me? Do they say back home that it is usual to find a Saracen in the household of an English earl?"

Amal was ready for this. "No, indeed, Excellency," he replied quickly. "It is just that I do not like to pry. A Muslim living among Christians must have his own reasons. If you wish to tell me, I wish to hear. If you do not, I will happily remain in ignorance."

The answer amused Kamil. He was certain that Amal did know who he was, for the whole of the Arab world had known Saladin, and Kamil, as Saladin's ward, had been as famous as his master. Nevertheless, he admired a man who could use his wits. However, there was little opportunity for further conversation. Determined to make her mark, Marissa began to bombard Amal with questions of her own, insisting that Kamil translate, and when Marie pressed her arm to stop her, redoubled her efforts. What did Marie know about anything? She would, in time, marry Hal and vanish from Hartslove, leaving Marissa to lonely spinsterhood. If spinsterhood was her fate, why should she not enjoy herself now? "Where have you come from? How did you know the horse had been given to Gavin? Where did you find her? Who told you the way to Hartslove?" She allowed nobody else to speak.

Amal cleared his throat and looked around as if to beg everybody's pardon for being a nuisance. "I am of no interest," he began in his scratchy voice, "but the silver mare, ah! It is said that her father is the wind and her mother the evening tide. You can believe that if you will." He clasped his hands together. "I have seen her race across the desert, a blaze of silver in the sand, and nothing could come near her. She won many prizes. Some say she is Allah's own horse but we know only that after your King Richard stole her, she fell into strange hands and ended up in the bazaar where I found her and was told she belonged here. I had nothing else to do, so I brought her. That's all I can say." He looked at Kamil for support.

"If the mare's so wonderful, why did you not ride her to Hartslove?" asked Marissa, hoping to have found somebody worse at riding than herself.

"The horse is not easy to ride," Amal said simply, "and if the fastest horse in the world takes off with you, who knows where you might end up."

Everybody laughed except Marissa. "She's not the fastest horse in the world," she said, annoyed. "Hosanna is."

Will shook his head as Elric's treble piped through. "Hosanna may be the *best* horse in the world, Marissa, but I doubt that he's the fastest."

Marissa turned on him at once. "Don't be so disloyal," she said loudly, looking to Will for approval and support. "Hosanna has never been beaten!"

"Don't be silly." Elric's voice was taunting. "Nobody races Hosanna. He's a warhorse. That's the trouble with girls, they can't tell one type of horse from another."

Now there was more laughter. Marissa's face flamed at the humiliation.

When supper was over, she cornered the boy. "You think you know everything," she said, "well, you don't. You upset Will by what you said."

"I did not," said Elric, cocky in his small triumph. "Will did not mind me pointing out the truth."

"It's not the truth—and he's Earl William or 'sir' to you."

Elric was unabashed. "Well, anyhow, you're never going to find out who's faster."

"Why not?" Marissa was trembling with fury now. "Are you too frightened that I'll be proved right?"

"No," said Elric slowly, as if speaking to an idiot, "but, as I said, warhorses don't race."

"They could."

"No, they couldn't. Who would ride them? Neither the earl nor Kamil, because they would know it wasn't right. You can only race with racing horses." Elric tried to wriggle past.

"You and I could ride them."

Elric stopped wriggling. "You and I?" His mouth was agape.

"Yes," said Marissa airily. "Why not?"

"Well, for a start, they are not our horses, and then we're all going off in the morning. All the men that is." The taunt was deliberate.

Marissa bristled. "We could do it as soon as it's light."

Now Elric was alarmed. Marissa was serious. "Will—the earl—would be livid. I mean, Hosanna racing? Just before he is needed for important business? We couldn't."

"Well," Marissa was at her most supercilious, "if you're too nervous—I didn't mean race very far, obviously, because of the journey, just once around the jousting field, down to the river and back by the chestnut tree. If you don't think you can do it, though, we'll just take it that I'm right."

Elric hopped from foot to foot. "But you're not right."

Marissa smiled contemptuously. "Well, we'll never

know, will we?" she said as she began to walk away, a victory swing in her limp.

Moments later, just as she expected, Elric was at her heels. "All right then," he said. "I'll meet you at dawn in the stables. I'll get the horses ready—I'll have to find a saddle for the silver but I can probably use Dargent's. Only, if Hal finds out, he'll kill me."

"Why should he find out?" asked Marissa smoothly. "He sleeps in the bakehouse and surely you can find some excuse for keeping Dargent's saddle with you to-night. Something on it must need mending. And by the way, I'll be riding Hosanna of course."

Elric didn't answer. Suddenly, all his bravado disintegrated and, not wanting Marissa even to suspect any such thing, he fled into the courtyard. Once outside, his courage rose again. Hal said his riding was good. The silver horse was used to racing and they were not going very far. What was there to worry about? Without further ado he went to Hal and, mumbling something, took away Dargent's saddle. Then he visited the stables. The silver horse looked placid enough, picking at her hay. Elric grinned as he saw her. He was sure this animal would not prove too much of a handful. He turned to Hosanna. If anything, Elric thought, it was the red horse who looked the more fearsome. Instead of standing steady in his stall, he was pacing around and around and had kicked his straw into lumps. Elric imagined Marissa on his back and her face when the wind began to burn her ears and all she could feel was the pounding of hooves. He smiled and he was still smiling when he curled up in the loft and went to sleep.

4

It was a glorious dawn, with the rising sun giving the summer-parched leaves another chance to shine. Elric soon shook the sleep from his eyes, climbed down, and went to the stables. Marissa was already there, her fair hair tightly plaited and her bad temper banished by determination. She was busy pulling straw from Hosanna's tail. Elric slipped on the bridle and saddle as he had been taught and tightened the girth. Hosanna seemed surprised to be getting no breakfast but did not object.

"Ready?" Elric said to Marissa, and handed her the reins. Hosanna looked around for Hal before following Marissa obediently into the courtyard. His anxiety was apparent and Marissa was alarmed but she could not back out now. Elric noticed nothing.

The silver horse was displeased to find herself carrying Dargent's saddle, even more so when this unfamiliar boy, who was too short to reach, had to climb up the wooden partition and drop the saddle onto her back from above. She struck out at the manger with a flashing front hoof and it took Elric some time to fix the bridle. However, when at last the straps were buckled, she stepped eagerly over the cobbles toward the gate-house, taking no notice of the chickens whose early-morning peckings she rudely disturbed. Marissa caught up and when the horses passed the bakehouse door together, Elric was glad that it was shut, with Hal on the other side. The silver horse felt strange after Hosanna and Dargent. She seemed to stretch up rather than forward and Elric wondered if he would bump his nose on her crest, so high did she hold her neck. Nor did she swing along quite as easily as Hosanna but hung back, holding the bit in her mouth as if it tasted nasty. Nevertheless, when Elric asked the mare to stop so that he could tell the porter, with only a slight blush, that he had been ordered to take both animals to the river to bathe their legs, there was only a slight hesitation before she obeyed. When the porter let them out, a feeling of conspiratorial camaraderie made the two jockeys momentary allies. It gave Elric a pang for he had quite consciously left off the neckstrap that Will always attached to give Marissa extra confidence, and now he felt a little sorry. "Shall I go back and get it?" he offered.

Marissa almost bit him.

Once on the grass the silver mare smelled freedom and Elric felt her change. Now, although still holding her head high, she was almost too willing, surging forward rather faster than Elric wanted. He had thought the race should begin from a standing start but she had no interest in standing still, even for a second, and began to trot faster and faster. Hosanna kept up, one ear cocked back for Marissa's command. But she gave him none, leaving it all to him. If she could just stay on, they would win.

The trot turned into a canter and when he could control the mare no longer, Elric could do little else but shout "Go!" Now the two horses began to match stride for stride, their manes rising and falling. "Around the jousting field, down to the river passing one side of the tree, turn, and back past the other," Elric yelled as his lead increased. "First back to the drawbridge is the winner."

Marissa buried her hands in Hosanna's mane. "You can beat anybody, Hosanna," she whispered. The red horse gathered himself together and in an instant they were flying, a red arrow and a silver, neck and neck around the jousting field, their hooves making glittering dents in the dew. The pace was fast, not wild, and as the mare began to lower her head and stretch out, Elric started to enjoy himself. This was real riding and he was managing just fine. He shifted in the saddle. Immediately the mare shortened her stride and Hosanna drew ahead. Elric cursed but he had learned his lesson. If the silver horse was to win, he must keep perfectly still. Gradually the mare caught up with Hosanna and they were side by side again. Now they were out of the jousting field and heading for the river. It was downhill and slippery but the horses galloped on. Elric could see Marissa's face, her mouth a little open. He wanted to grin, to share the exhilaration, but was too intent on winning to do any such thing.

At the river, Hosanna slowed and turned in a wide arc for he could feel that his rider was not secure enough for anything sharp. The silver horse showed no such consideration. When Elric twitched the rein, she spun around, almost unseating him, and set off back up the hill. Elric began to crow. He could hear Hosanna's hooves behind him but now he could see the draw-bridge. The race was nearly over.

The mare, however, had other ideas. For months she had scarcely been allowed out of a walk, for although Amal had ridden her occasionally, the pace was always slow. She was going to make the most of this and when Elric tried to check her, she began to give him a taste of the pace she had set in her glory days on the Cypriot sands. Ignoring every tug at the reins, clasp of the leg, or squeaky command, she swerved away from the draw-bridge, flattened herself out, and bolted back down the road up which she had come the day before. Now Elric's exhilaration turned into bald terror. Surely nothing on earth could gallop quite so fast? Nor did the mare gallop straight. Instead, she went where she would, twist-ing and turning, sometimes on the road, sometimes off, with Elric's small body snapping helplessly this way and that like a stem in the wind. Every so often the mare's silver neck would arch and Elric's nose would meet it with a thwack. Then she would snake her head in the dirt and Elric would slip farther and farther forward until there was nothing but the unforgiving ground whistling past in front of him. He knew only one thing, that to fall at such a speed would be fatal, so he clung on as the sparkling mane scourged his face and his hands grew raw and numb.

Marissa, halted by the drawbridge, at first watched with smug satisfaction as Elric was carted off. Since the silver horse had never actually reached the agreed finish line, technically speaking Hosanna was the winner. But her smugness died away as the mare rocketed about like a rogue star fizzing through the sky. She began to call out Elric's name. It was quite useless. He could not even hear her. Then she shouted, louder and louder, until her voice carried into the courtyard where Will, Hal, and Constable Shortspur were standing by the water trough. They broke off and within seconds were running across the drawbridge. They saw Hosanna at once. "Ellie said Marissa and Elric had been arguing. I'll bet this is something to do with that," Will fumed as he ran. Then he followed Marissa's pointing finger. "Oh Lord in Heaven!" he cried. "Elric! For God's sake, ELRIC!" He grabbed Hosanna, pulled Marissa off, and vaulted on. The silver mare was now punctuating her galloping with high, bone-crunching bucks. "Sit up, Elric, sit up, try to push her uphill," Will bellowed. It was a waste of breath. The mare stopped bucking and began to rush around in a circle at a speed that was scarcely credible. The gathering crowd gasped as Elric, now more damp rag than rider, finally lost his struggle to keep the reins. As he let go, he seemed to abandon himself to his fate, clutching at the air and attached to the saddle by only an invisible thread.

Will set off. He did not dare aim straight at the mare for fear of making her even wilder but arced around, closing in very slowly. Hosanna and he were as one, just as they were on the battlefield, the red horse second-guessing which way to turn so that Will would have some hope of catching a piece of flapping leather and bringing the crazy flight to a halt. But even as Hosanna drew near, Elric began to tip over to one side. His arms flailed as he tried to right himself, but he did not have the strength to catch even a clump of mane. As the mare thundered on, he began to slide off. Then came something far worse. Elric's left foot, too small for the large stirrup, slipped right through and when he fell, instead of rolling clear, he hung, upside down, his head directly behind a pair of unforgiving iron-shod hooves. "Oh God! No!" Will howled as Hosanna found a new pace, one he hardly knew he had. Slowly, slowly the red horse gained on the mare, until, Will, scrunching his legs into his saddle, let go of his own reins and leaned right over and down. After two unsuccessful attempts, with the iron shoes slicing off some of the hairs of his own head, he managed to seize the scruff of Elric's jerkin with one hand and catch the trailing reins with the other. He could not pull Elric upright and they both hung an inch or so above the ground.

Marissa could not watch, and even Kamil tightened his fists as the horses' legs seemed certain to tangle, bringing them all crashing down. Will could only trust in Hosanna. "Slow her, Hosanna, slow her down." The horse knew what to do. Curving around, he balanced Will's weight against his own, just as he did when they were together in single combat. Now he leaned away, creating a space for Will while he edged his nose in front. The mare was suddenly deflated, as if somebody had turned off a tap. Her legs moved automatically, all pleasure gone. Sobbing with relief, she gradually hooked herself into Hosanna's rhythm. The four-beat gallop became a three-beat canter. Now it was possible for Will to pull up Elric. When the canter became a trot, the boy gave one piercing cry at the jolting and the mare threw up her head as if to go off again. But Hosanna crowded into her, bringing her to a walk, and by the time she halted, she was utterly spent. When willing hands took Elric from Will, she was trembling all over, submissive even, and although her wall-eye gave nothing away, the demon that had possessed the other had subsided and vanished.

Elric's head was already beginning to swell and he was spitting blood. Will was beside himself. "Get a pallet!" he cried, but Ellie was already running toward him with two men carrying a pallet just behind her and Amal behind them. "You idiot, Elric! Oh, you silly idiot!" Will's fury at the stupidity of it all was matched only by his dread, for Elric's eyes were beginning to roll backward. "What can we do?" Will spun around. "Hurry! Hurry! He's going to die, he's going to die!"

Then suddenly Amal was beside him, gesturing and waving a small bottle he produced from a skin bag at his waist. He unstopped it and the smell was bitter but he thrust a few drops down Elric's throat. Immediately the boy jerked up. "Good, good!" Amal murmured.

"What on earth are you doing?" Will hardly knew he was shouting. He wanted Ellie, Old Nurse, or Marie. He trusted them. Amal stepped back. At once, Ellie helped to pull Elric carefully onto the pallet and ran beside it as he was carried quickly to the castle. Amal put his bottle in his pocket, watched, and waited.

Kamil leaped onto the silver horse. "There's only one way to cure a bolter," he said, and turned her once again down the road. Using his voice, his heels, and a hazel switch, he forced the weary animal back into a gallop. Every time she slowed he urged her on until, in the end, long after everybody else had disappeared and she was sweating and grunting, he slid off and looked straight into her dark eye. Her head sagged. When she found the strength to pick it up again, she accepted Kamil's proffered caresses without enthusiasm but also without objection. "Come on," Kamil spoke in his own language. "You are a good horse, but if you are faster than Hosanna, you are certainly not as clever." The mare, weary almost to death, seemed to agree.

As he led her across the drawbridge, Kamil saw that Amal was standing humbly outside as Old Nurse's voice echoed from the great hall. She was denouncing "foreigners and foreign horses." Kamil saw the men turn their backs on Amal and he was ashamed. The old Saracen was not responsible for Elric and Marissa's stupidity. Kamil did not hesitate further but handed the silver horse over to a groom and gestured to the old man to stay by his side.

5

There was no question of Will and Kamil leaving that day, or the next, for overnight Elric succumbed to a fever of such heat and ferocity that Ellie and Old Nurse despaired. "What can we try now?" whispered Marie as Elric's face turned from red to mottled black. She had helped to apply leeches all over his arms and legs and even his cheeks to bleed out the poison, but the boy was burning up.

"Well, deary"—Old Nurse was sweating herself as she wrung out cloths, cursing that the water was not colder despite Ellie's running up and down from the icehouse—"there is only one thing left for us to do. The poor lamb." She squeezed her large, lumpy frame around the bed and dropped herself down onto a stool.

Marie went cold and Ellie found herself clutching the bed-hangings. "Oh no, Old Nurse," both girls whispered, "not that."

Old Nurse took Elric's hand and rocked to and fro. "Look at him, dearies," she said in her most matter-of-fact voice. "There's no real choice. We must get the poison out of his head or he'll die." Marie felt sick. "It will be just a small hole in his skull we have to make," Old Nurse continued, carefully not looking up, "just big enough to let out some of the bad spirits. We can't let Elric's head swell any further, so we'll all have to be brave. I'm going to give it an hour or two, then, if he's no better, with Master Will's permission, I'll call the surgeon."

"Butcher, more like," said Marie, surprising Old Nurse by sounding like Marissa, for Marie was normally so meek. "Trepanning should be outlawed. It's murder— at least I have seen only one person survive. How can making a hole in somebody's head really be an answer to anything? It's monstrous."

"But what else is there?" asked Old Nurse impatiently, shaking her heavy jowls. Her eyes were red for she had not slept, and her legs ached from standing most of the night. "I've never seen anybody with a head so swollen who has lived this long. I don't like to admit defeat, deary, but your lotions and my poultices are just not working. Drilling a hole is the only way."

Marie tried to argue further, with Ellie backing her up by suggesting this herb or that treatment, but Old Nurse would not listen. As the hours rolled past, a curious silence fell over the castle, as if everybody knew that something horrible was about to happen. At last Old Nurse got up, touched Elric's forehead again, then lumbered slowly off to find Will. Although nobody said a word, by the time Hal galloped away from Hartslove's walls, everybody knew where he was going.

He returned in the early evening, and at his side was a cart driven by a man in leather overalls, the tools of his trade open for all to see. Some were still bloody from a previous victim, either animal or human, nobody could tell. Hal had also collected Brother Luke, the monk in charge of the infirmary, from the abbey, and he was perched at the back, clutching a small sack containing holy water and the knuckle bone of St. Hubert, one of the abbey's most treasured relics. "I thought he might help," Hal said to Will. Will did not reply. As the surgeon climbed out and summoned men to help him carry his instruments, Marissa, who had been following Will around like a dog, desperate for his forgiveness, had to close her eyes. "Never mind the monk," Will muttered, wanting to punish her, "we've more use for the coffin maker." Marissa made a strangled sound and fled. Will and Amal both watched her go.

Old Nurse bustled the surgeon up the steps. "I've laid everything out," she said, "and Marie's given the poor child half a jug of wine to prepare him. He didn't swallow much of it but enough, I dare say." Her face was set and her thick forearms bare in preparation. Will and Kamil followed her, with Amal slipping like a shadow behind. Will had no idea how he would feel when Elric's blood began to flow. It would be worse than in battle, for sure, for in battle there was no time to think or to dread. He looked at the butcher and felt his gorge rise. Was this right? Should he stop it? He suddenly grabbed Old Nurse's arm. She understood and sympathized but shook her head.

Will felt his courage leaking away. Would he allow a hole to be drilled in his own head? When they reached the chamber in which Elric was laid out, he held back, unable to go in. He should never have given permission. Certainly, he could not watch. Suddenly and acutely he missed his father. He wasn't old enough for all this fearsome responsibility. When his shoulder was touched, he jumped. "Father—," he breathed, even though he knew it was stupid. The touch was Kamil offering support, one soldier to another. Still, Will could pretend.

The surgeon was a man almost as large as Old Nurse, and the room seemed very crowded. Marie was holding one of Elric's hands, her face registering complete disapproval. Ellie held the other. Despite the crush, the room had an eerie feel for all the daylight was obscured by thick hangings drawn over the window slits and the candles guttered in the draught. It took some time to fix Elric's head in a brace as whenever somebody touched his skin, he shook violently and thrashed from side to side. His eyes, so puffy he could barely open them, glittered in the gloom and the wine, far from calming him, caused a shuddering agitation so that words emerged in bubbles from his blue lips. He could still see but appeared terrified by the shadows. Marie tried to soothe him but eventually it was only with brute force that the restraints were put on and tightened, for it would be a disaster if he moved. When all was secure the surgeon coughed, spat on his hands, and picked up a small spike. Brother Luke closed his eyes and began to pray aloud. The surgeon waited a moment, then he gestured to Old Nurse, who took Elric's hand and squeezed it hard. The spike was lowered onto Elric's skull, just at the hairline.

At the very moment the hammer was raised for the first strike, Amal's voice rang out. His voice was strong enough to make the surgeon hesitate and at once Amal pushed his way to the front, talking animatedly at Kamil and gesturing with his hands.

The surgeon lifted his hammer again. Amal blocked him. The surgeon raised a leg to kick him but Will was in the way. "Just wait, just wait," he commanded. "What's Amal saying, Kamil?"

"He says," said Kamil, listening and speaking at the same time, "that this is madness. If you make a hole in his skull, Elric will certainly die. The black color of his face is not caused by evil spirits and even if it was, if you make a hole, the evil spirits will just retreat further and make his whole body black."

"Well, what does he suggest instead?" Will's voice cracked with strain.

"He says Hippocrates teaches that it is better to use weak medicine than medicine that is too strong. This spike is too strong. He says that Elric should be left alone, that the heat he is generating is boiling off the bad elements inside him. The fever is part of the cure."

"But he is dying," cried Will. "Look at him."

"I'm just telling you what Amal said."

Will bowed his head. Amal patted his arm. "Please to allow?" he said with one of his little bows.

The butcher surgeon began to protest for he was mindful of his fee. "Now look here," he said, brandishing the spike, "we do things our own way here. English people are not like these foreigners and foreign medicine is no good for us. You'll be agreeing with me, Old Nurse."

But although Old Nurse wanted to agree, she was unsure. Now that she could see the spike and could see also how small Elric looked compared to the surgeon's great ham hands, her previous certainty deserted her. Yet if she looked with distaste at the surgeon, she looked with more distaste at Amal. What could an emaciated stick like him know? Nevertheless, in obedience to Will and encouraged by Ellie, she let the old man through.

Amal stroked Elric's face with bony fingers. Immediately, the boy began to jibber. "Unscrew this," he ordered, and Marie willingly loosened the head brace. She looked at Amal with hope. When the brace was off, he produced several folded papers. "Get warm water," he said to Kamil, still smiling apologetically as if he were being a nuisance, "and small bowls with stirrers. Draw back the hangings from the the windows. The boy needs air. And get cushions. He needs to sit up. Later I will need a big bath, something we can lower him into."

Kamil repeated the instructions and even before he had finished, Marie was running to the kitchens. The surgeon stood at the end of the bed, glowering, his arms crossed. He was not going to leave. They would need him yet. Humming to himself, Amal hopped around the bed and indicated to Ellie that she should strip off Elric's blankets in favor of a thin sheet as he set out his folded papers on the window ledge. He avoided the surgeon as he might an immovable tree, brushing past him, always careful not to push. The surgeon wanted to swat him like a wasp.

At last, when all was to Amal's satisfaction, he tipped his colored powders into the bowls. Strange and exotic smells drifted out, of turmeric, ginseng, and cinnamon. Ellie watched, taking everything in, but Old Nurse just sniffed, then sneezed, nearly blowing the powder away. Amal frowned and muttered. He wanted Old Nurse out.

Kamil saw at once. Amal's air of authority impressed him. The man did know what he was doing. He would help him. "Old Nurse, Amal asks what you would normally put on broken bones," he said pleasantly.

Old Nurse was surly. "I sometimes make a paste of comfrey."

"Go and make it now. He thinks it best if you treat Elric's legs," Kamil told her. Old Nurse snorted but she went on her way. Amal and Kamil exchanged glances before Amal turned back to his bowls and told Ellie to prop Elric up. Soon, Amal was expertly pouring liquid down the boy's throat. Occasionally Elric choked but Amal never wavered. He had done this often to injured Assassins. Every so often he met Kamil's eye again, consciously strengthening the bond between them. When the liquid had disappeared, Amal carefully dabbed his lotion onto Elric's heart, neck, and wrists. "To calm the pulse," he explained, glad to see everybody hanging on his words.

Before long Old Nurse reappeared and spread thick, sweet-smelling paste gently onto Elric's shins and covered them with a damp cloth. Amal watched her politely. When she had finished, he settled himself onto a small stool. "Now," he said, "we wait." The butcher surgeon narrowed his eyes and spread his legs a little wider. He still held his spike and made a point of testing the sharpness of its tip.

For at least an hour, Elric seemed no better and despite themselves the watchers grew weary. Kamil fiddled endlessly with his triangular knife. Ellie sat by

Elric's head, rocking slightly, with Marie beside her. Even the butcher surgeon, though he did not put down his spike, eventually found a chair.

Will leaned on the wall. He watched Elric, then Ellie, then Kamil in turn, his thoughts everywhere. Amal alone never moved but observed Elric constantly and carefully. After an hour, the boy seemed to take a turn for the worse. His skin grew hotter and hotter and the whole length of his body shook. Will moved closer to the bed and frowned, but Amal simply nodded and bowed. Only once did the old man get up, and although everybody held their breath, it was just to smooth a wrinkle out of a cushion. The night dragged on. It was not until dawn that Elric's color changed and his breathing quickened. "The crisis," Amal said aloud. But he seemed unconcerned. Now Ellie and Marie huddled together and Brother Luke began to pray in earnest. Marissa could hear his Our Fathers from her chamber and she stopped her ears against them.

It was a dreadful crisis. Far from calling out random words, Elric now called endlessly for his mother. He cried that he could see the pit of Hell and the gates of Heaven. He wanted to go home. "Stop the devils, stop them," he begged. "They're coming for me." Ellie tried to quiet him but he hit out at her as if she were an enemy. Only when Will took his hand did Elric pause for a moment before starting all over again, pushing himself up and down in the bed. Each time he fell back he seemed to fade a little, and Will was frightened that if he let go, Elric would somehow disappear like a flaky chalk.

After half an hour Amal touched Elric's forehead

with the pad of his thumb and smelled the sweat. He sighed, then smiled. "What, old man, what?" Even Kamil was agitated now, wondering if his faith had been misplaced. "How can you smile at such a time?"

But Amal's smile grew broader. "The boy will survive," he said confidently. "His life force is winning against the fever. Soon these cries will die away, then he will sleep. In the morning, he will be weak. We must feed him carefully. In a month he will have forgotten he was ill."

"If you're right, you're a miracle worker." Kamil's eyes never left Elric.

"No, no, no," said Amal, squinting. "You know that is not right. I just practice here the medicines our people practice at home. The real miracle is that any of these Christians survive. Just look at that butcher!" Amal was pleased to see a hesitant smile on Kamil's lips.

It happened just as Amal predicted. Soon, Elric's lips changed from deathly blue to pink and his fingers were no longer plucking at his sheet. Old Nurse, sniffing, touched his cheeks. "Cool," she said loudly, and then repeated in wonder, "quite cool." Marie burst into tears. Old Nurse hugged her and then turned to Amal, rigidly grateful. Amal bowed graciously, acknowledging but not crowing.

It was not long before everybody was surging forward to touch Elric and to gaze at Amal. This foreigner was not so bad. However, having played his role, the old man backed away.

When dawn became day, Will ordered food to be served and Amal sat silently in the hall as toasts were drunk. When the time was right, he searched out a quiet place and beckoned to Kamil. "Allah is great," he said softly.

"Allah is great," Kamil replied, and then the two Saracens kneeled down together to pray.

6

After three days, when Elric's condition had improved enough for Will to scold him gently and Marissa was no longer hiding, Will prepared to leave for Whitby again. Richard's ransom could wait no longer. He was also concerned about the silver mare. "By rights she should be yours, Ellie," he told her as they wandered down to the chestnut tree, "because Richard gave her to Gavin. I know you and Gavin were never actually married, but still. If you want her, I suppose you should have her."

Something in his voice grated. "Do you think the mare would be too much for me to ride, Will?" Ellie asked, annoyed.

"No," said Will carefully, "but I am just wondering if we should give her to Kamil. Look how well they go together." Ellie turned and she could see that Will was right. Under Kamil's control, although her head bent unwillingly to the bridle, the silver horse moved with serene grace. She knew she could not get the better of her rider, but he had not broken her spirit. Ellie was transfixed by Kamil's easy skill and how his hands spoke to the mare's mouth down the reins. She felt a tightening in her stomach. On the silver horse, Kamil looked different, as if he was set for the desert. "If we give Kamil the silver horse, he'll leave." She had not meant to say it, but she suddenly knew it was true.

Will spoke even more carefully, half hating himself, since when they were out hunting or dealing with the inevitable scuffles between armed knights, Kamil felt more like a brother than a companion in arms. Nevertheless, whenever Ellie spoke about Kamil, Will wanted to kill him. "Maybe it is time," he said evenly. "He won't want to live here forever."

They both stopped as Kamil drew up to speak to Amal. Their Saracen voices carried and Will found himself disturbed that for the first time since Kamil had come to Hartslove, he could not understand what he was saying. He turned back to Ellie and tried his best to sound reasonable. "Kamil has said that he'll help deliver Richard's ransom, but even without the silver horse I've a feeling he won't come back here after that unless—" Will stopped.

Ellie pressed him. "Unless?"

"Unless you ask him to." Will colored.

Ellie stared at him. "Do you want me to?"

Will stared back at her, unable to answer.

Hal came past on Hosanna. Brimming with health and eagerness, the horse tossed his head, playfully fighting for his bit. At once the tension dissolved. "He's so beautiful, Will," Ellie said. "What a spectacular pair they make, the silver and the red!" Will relaxed just as Ellie frowned. Hosanna, it seemed, was more than happy to stand close to his new equine companion, but when Amal approached he moved away. "Hosanna doesn't like Amal," she said with some surprise.

"No," Will agreed after a minute or two, "he doesn't. How curious." He watched a bit longer, then shook his head. "I wonder why. But I can hardly turn the man out just because Hosanna wants to avoid him. Not after he traveled so far to bring the horse here and all he did for Elric."

"No, you can't," Ellie agreed, but she was disturbed. "It's just odd. I mean, Amal is a Saracen, but I don't see how he could really hurt us or why he would want to." Yet it was unmistakable that every time Amal put up his hand to touch Hosanna's white star, the horse made sure it was out of reach. "Perhaps Hosanna also thinks Amal will take Kamil from us," Ellie said a little wistfully, "and he doesn't want that either."

Will again found himself at a loss but then Hosanna whinnied at him. Will's mood lifted. "I think," he whispered in Ellie's ear, "that Hosanna might not like Amal because Old Nurse dropped his clothes in some old fish water when she took them to be washed. They stink. Old Nurse said she did it by mistake, but I wonder. 'Really, deary,'" he imitated Old Nurse's voice perfectly, "'you never know where this foreign cloth has been.'" He harrumphed in true Old Nurse style. Ellie's eyes crinkled and she wagged her finger. It had been ages since she had seen Will like this. He had been so serious since he had come back from crusade and it had all been so dreadful after Gavin. But Gavin couldn't want Will to be sad forever. Their laughter pealed out. Kamil and Amal watched them, rather bemused.

"I think I do want to keep the silver mare, Will," Ellie said as she and Will companionably approached the horses. "I don't expect I'll ever love her like I love Hosanna or Sacramenta, but I think we will look very splendid riding together, you on Hosanna and me on—actually, Will, on whom? She hasn't got a name and she can't just be 'the silver horse' forever more."

"You're right, she can't," said Will. Ellie had said "riding together." He liked that picture very much. "Let's think." Will stroked the silver rump. "Ellie wants to find a name for this horse, Kamil," he said before moving to Hosanna, who blew sweet breath into his face. Will murmured endearments and Hosanna gave a rich sigh of contentment.

"Yes," said Ellie, and her eyes twinkled into Kamil's, "a name."

"What about Sanctus?" suggested Will. "It goes well with Hosanna."

But Kamil was scrutinizing the horse carefully. "I think you should call her Shihab," he said, smiling down at Ellie.

"Shihab?" asked Ellie, intrigued. "Does it mean something?"

"It means a flame or a blaze," Kamil explained, "and although the horse is silver, she's as speedy as fire."

"Shihab," said Ellie to herself, then repeated it more loudly. "Shihab. What do you think, Will?"

"It's very unusual," said Will, tickling Hosanna's nose, "and I think it's rather ugly." Ellie looked crestfallen. "But it certainly seems to fit," Will added hastily. He did not want to appear churlish.

"Shihab it is then," decided Ellie, and she tidied the mare's mane.

"It will be strange," said Kamil, addressing Ellie directly. "When I go home I will have Sacramenta, a Chris-

51

tian horse with a Christian name, and you will have Shihab, an Arab horse with an Arabic name." Ellie felt a chill at the word *when,* which had always been *if* before. But at once the silver horse shook vigorously and her mane covered Ellie in a great sheet. "Shihab!" Ellie cried as she emerged. The mare looked around. "She likes her name," Ellie said. "Now, Kamil, you must show me how best to manage her."

Kamil dismounted and helped Ellie on, telling her how the mare disliked too tight a rein and how she must sit for better balance and security. After a while Ellie rode off, alone, toward the castle. Will hesitated, then jumped onto Hosanna and caught up. When the two horses were side by side, Ellie turned and her face seemed lit from the inside. "Oh, Will," she whispered, stroking the proud silver neck, "It is like riding a piece of silk."

"Remember Elric," Will said shortly. "She may feel like silk, but she's dangerous, too."

But Ellie was in no mood for caution. "Of course, Earl William," she said demurely, then her face dissolved into a wide grin, "only last one at the table gets rats' legs for dinner!" At her command, Shihab shot toward the castle, with Hosanna thundering beside her. Once in the courtyard, Will and Ellie tumbled off and Ellie picked up her skirts and ran. When they both banged their fists on the table at the same time, Will took this as a good omen.

The next day, with Elric waving wanly from his window, Kamil, Will, and Hal, together with half a dozen men at arms, left Ellie and Alan Shortspur in charge of the castle. Hosanna and Sacramenta strode out strongly together with Hal on Dargent just behind. Many knights saved their warhorses or destriers only for battle but the de Granvilles were unfashionable and didn't care who knew it. Will always rode Hosanna and this morning, when the last winds of summer were blowing lightly over the heavy leaves, he rejoiced in his horse's supple strength. How lucky he was!

Once they reached the bigger, more well-traveled route that led eastward, Will gave Hal charge of the baggage wagon while he and Kamil abandoned the road for the heathery moor and soon the two red horses were leaping from tussock to tussock like ballet dancers. They would speed ahead to Whitby because the quicker they got there, the quicker they could assemble their portion of the ransom and begin to prepare for the long journey to the imperial court. On this perfect day, with the horses chasing the streaking clouds and racing over the springy turf, Will was suddenly, wildly happy. He and Kamil shared their food and dared each other to leap over the ditches and streams. Though anxious to expedite his business, Will felt sorry when they arrived at the abbey and not only because the abbot fussed about like an old woman, relieved that Will and Kamil, being young and persuasive, would find it easier than he did to part people from their money.

Kamil spoke to Will just as normal, but every day now, and most nights, he found himself dreaming of two things: Ellie and his home. When Richard was ransomed, he would speak to Ellie alone and tell her that his time in England was over.

7

Back at Hartslove, Ellie was busy. There was much to prepare before Will and Kamil returned and they all left for Germany. Marie and Old Nurse, nursing Elric between them, sorted out food and linen while Ellie looked to horses and wagons, armor and weapons and made up a small trunk of the medicines they would carry. It pleased Ellie very much to do this. She particularly liked the rattle of the armory keys. Marissa hung about, getting in the way and pushing Ellie's temper to the limit.

In the afternoons, Ellie went to Shihab. The silver horse resented being left behind and showed it. It did not help that at first Ellie was too busy to ride. However, once the organization took shape, she ordered the groom to saddle up the mare. Their first outing was not a success. Shihab was bolshy and either bucketed about or refused to move at all. The second day, scarcely was the mare ready when Amal appeared as if from nowhere, making Ellie jump. He bobbed and bowed as Ellie mounted. "Brave—alone?" he ventured.

Ellie did not like being patronized. She gave him

a regal look and rode down to the jousting field more quickly than she meant to. Today the silver horse was quite different, pulling hard and always wanting to bend in the direction the others had gone. She was no longer silk but steel, tense and hard. Ellie had difficulty keeping control and wished she had brought a switch. That was what Kamil had said: The mare had to learn who was master. Still, she would not give up and battled on, occasionally fearful that Shihab's sudden, twisting wrenches would unseat her. She remembered Will's warning and unwelcome pictures of Elric flashed in front of her eyes. She was just wondering how long she could go on when she noticed Amal had followed her and was watching her struggle. She clamped her knees tighter into the saddle.

Now Shihab began to buck, great rhythmic heaves, and Ellie was pitched violently up and down. But she couldn't give in now, she just couldn't. Then Amal approached and shouted at the horse in Arabic. At first Shihab took no notice, but as she grew tired, she pricked her ears and listened and, with Ellie's white cheeks pink with humiliation, the old man was at last able to take the mare's reins and lead her about until she was quiet. Ellie did not know what to say, but Amal seemed to expect nothing. He simply showed her how to hold her reins more delicately and then touched her legs, light as a bat's wing, to show her how to use them more effectively. He neither smiled nor spoke. He simply made signs and nodded or shook his head. Despite herself, Ellie began to follow his instructions, and to her delight the mare responded. Soon the mare seemed docile as a lamb and Amal stood back. Yet even as she rode, Ellie remembered how Hosanna disliked Amal and tried to maintain her reserve. It was impossible. With the red horse away, there was nothing at all to keep her suspicions sharp, and by the time Ellie had finished riding, Amal had vanished. The next time Ellie saw him, he was sitting by the fire reading. It would have been rude not to acknowledge him, so she nodded. He nodded back but did not try to be her friend. In spite of herself, Ellie could not help respecting him for that.

The following day, when she took Shihab to the mounting block, Amal was with her again, and again he helped her. They fell into a pattern, which both, by instinct, kept secret. At noon, Ellie would ride far away from the prying eyes of Marissa, a recuperating Elric, and Old Nurse, with Amal riding a courser behind her. It pleased them both when he began to teach her to ride short, Arab length, and to show her some riding tricks. The only thing Amal regretted was getting carried away one day and revealing that even an old man could still throw himself off without injury and how to train a horse to wait so that the rider could vault on again. Ellie loved the idea of this although it took her a few days to muster enough courage to try it herself. She practiced on a chair in her room and then took Amal by surprise by doing it at the walk. It was an inelegant but admirable start and soon she could do it with ease, only occasionally hurting herself. Now she wanted to learn how to sweep somebody up from the ground, something she and Will had once spent a whole summer trying unsuccessfully to perfect with a fat packpony. Amal could hardly not show her.

In the afternoons, when the horses were resting, Ellie

took parchment and quill and made him teach her to write Arabic letters, pointing to various items—saddle, tail, mane, stirrup—and repeating the Arabic word. Amal did not like this at all, for it seemed to spell danger rather than pleasure. But Ellie made it impossible for him to refuse, and it both alarmed and thrilled him when she proved to have a quick ear. One morning, she greeted him in Arabic and his heart leaped, the Old Man temporarily forgotten. Cautiously happy, he began to look less gaunt and his cheeks filled out. He even taught her a little about the medicines of his own people and Ellie drank it all in.

Old Nurse was not fooled for long and scolded Ellie soundly. "It's not right for a good Christian girl to spend time with one of those Saracens," she muttered darkly. "It's not natural." But Ellie ignored her, and at night practiced her letters with meticulous care. She carefully inscribed Shihab's name as Amal had taught her and thought that one day she would show Kamil.

In the great hall, tucked into the space he had made his own, Amal sat up late reading his Koran. Now when he took out his little book during the night, he would turn first to his daughter's page. Perhaps she and this Christian girl were alike. How would he know? It was when he closed the book that the Old Man's dedication would catch his eye. Then his cheeks would grow taut again and he would bury the book away. He was as content as he could be but he knew this could not last. Soon, even though thousands of miles stood between them, the Old Man would send him a message. All Amal had to do was wait.

He did not have to wait long. Just before Will and

Kamil were expected back, a traveling silk merchant appeared. Ellie had him spread out his wares and she, Marie, and even Marissa exclaimed over them as they held the cloth against the light, imagining beautiful gowns. When Ellie sent him away, regretting that she could not buy more, she did not show him to the gate herself, so she never saw how discreetly he slipped something into Amal's sleeve as they passed on the steps or witnessed Amal start with surprise. Only when he was quite alone did Amal unroll the parchment and begin to decipher the crude code. If he had any doubts as to the letter's authenticity, they vanished when he lifted it close to his face. Though it had come through many different hands, it still carried the scent of the Old Man's oranges. Amal brought the candle very close as he worked and one name caused him to blink. He had not expected it. It seemed that Kamil's punishment was to be part of a greater plot, the details of which the Old Man was divulging little by little. As Amal read on, he pulled his cloak more closely around the angles of his frame. He did not like what this task was turning into. But the smell of the oranges lingered, and through it Amal could see the Old Man's currant eyes and hear his voice. He sighed as he went to the fire and watched the parchment smoulder and shrivel into nothing. When all this was over, he would insist on retiring. Vengeance was a young man's game.

8

Toward the end of September, as the horses' coats began to thicken in preparation for winter, Will and
Kamil clattered back across the Hartslove drawbridge.
At once the camaraderie that grew so easily between
them when they were away became a little stiffer. Both
knew it but neither remarked on it. It was just how it was.
Elric was up and about and in among his chatter it was
easy for Ellie to hug her own secrets to herself, not wanting to reveal them just yet. She was grateful that Amal did
not seek her out anymore once Will was back. When they
met she did not slight him, but it was clear to both of
them that their lessons were over.

And Amal had other fish to fry. While Will waited to
hear from Queen Eleanor that he should set off with
the ransom now coffered up and waiting at Whitby,
Amal was exclusively intent on making himself indis-
pensable to Kamil. He made it clear that he had little
desire to return home for, as he told Kamil with apparent regret, there was nothing there to keep him. Deftly
and unobtrusively, he took on the role of servant until
not only would it have been rude of Kamil to reject

him, but Kamil began to like him. Amal knew how to do things the Arab way. He took trouble to spice Kamil's food and to keep his clothes scrupulously clean. Sometimes they discussed parts of the Koran, and Amal recited Islamic poetry to which Kamil listened with rapt attention. Through all this, Amal was careful to avoid Hosanna. He knew the horse mistrusted him, so he scurried about only with Sacramenta and paused, occasionally, to stroke Shihab's nose. He grew almost invisible, so that Will and Kamil, without realizing it, often discussed the route the ransom was to take in front of him. Kamil sometimes wondered if this was wise, but Will did not think about it at all, for it never occurred to him that Amal might understand more than he let on.

When word came that the Hartslove contingent was to leave for Germany without further delay, Will asked everybody to come to the great hall and hand over his or her contribution to the king's ransom. He had put this off until last, but could put it off no longer. Everybody, he told them, had to give what they could, and he stood, stone-faced, as all the de Granville silver was placed in a chest. Nothing was left out, not the chalices and candlesticks from the chapel; not the silver washing bowls that his mother had brought with her for her dowry; not the jewel-studded sword hilts, tankards, domestic bells, ceremonial knives, and all the presents of any value that he had ever received. All were to be given to the German emperor in exchange for the king.

Fighting back tears, Old Nurse gave Will six silver thimbles that his father had given her the Christmas before leaving on crusade. Then Hal and Marie together gently dropped in the rings they had shyly and secretly exchanged. For a long hour, the rings lay haphazardly on the top of the pile, and Will forced himself to harden his heart and not pick them out. The only thing he would not accept was Ellie's green jasper necklace, her last, most precious relic of his brother. When she brought that forward he stopped her. "It is not valuable enough," he said a little lamely, his eyes begging her not to argue. And she did not, but tactfully and gratefully slipped the stones into a little bag at her waist.

Next came Marissa. She did not complain as she parted with the ruby brooch, but she wanted something in return. She waited until Old Nurse had chivvied Elric to his bed after dinner, then launched her assault. It began quite simply. "Why can't I come, too?" she complained to Will. "Why should Ellie be allowed to see something of the world whilst I have to stay here? Please let me go with you. I won't be any trouble, I promise. Please. After all, I did give the ruby brooch and Ellie has kept her necklace."

Ellie looked up, horrified. She would almost rather give up her necklace than have Marissa come to Germany. To her relief, Will refused point-blank. Then Marissa played her trump card. "I might as well go to a convent then," she said dramatically so that everybody could hear. "I shall be a nun. In fact, I want to take the veil at the royal abbey at Fontevraud, and I want to do it now. If I can't deliver the ransom, I can pray for it." Her announcement silenced the hall. A vocation was much to be admired, even if announced in this rather unorthodox fashion. Will heard a small flutter of applause.

He did not applaud though. He laughed. "I don't think you would suit monastic life, Marissa," he told her. "I really can't see you in the cloister. You'd be like a vixen among hens." He meant it as a compliment but touchy Marissa chose to take it otherwise.

"Are you saying I am not holy? That God doesn't want me?" she demanded, pushing her trencher away. Conversation in the great hall, which had resumed, stopped.

"Of course not," Will replied. "I'm just saying that I can't imagine you in a habit, telling your beads and being instantly obedient. You're just like Elric. You argue over everything. Look at you now!"

"Well, I want to take the habit. And, as my guardian, it's your duty to help me."

Will began to lose patience. "Don't be so silly, Marissa. Even if I thought this a good idea, which I don't, I can't take you at the moment. You know I can't."

"Because you have more important things to do, like delivering Richard's ransom!" She made it sound as if rescuing the king was a game.

"Of course delivering Richard's ransom is more important," interrupted Ellie. "You know that perfectly well, Marissa."

"More important than a vocation? More important than settling me in a convent so that I can pray for the king's well-being? More important than God?" Marissa's voice grew louder.

Kamil looked on with detached interest. Although he and Marissa had been thrown together when he had first arrived in England, they had never got on and now seldom spoke. He found her taunting, unforgiving independence too abrasive. Marissa had none of Ellie's sweetness. But he had come to admire her. If she were a man, he would want her on his side.

"Oh, come down off your high horse," said Will, glancing around, embarrassed for the girl. "Fontevraud is in completely the wrong direction for us. It will add weeks to our journey. You can't expect us to trail down to Anjou just for you. Not at this time."

But nobody was surprised when Marissa refused to listen. She went on and on, with no respite. Will tried to reason with her. He even told her that once Richard was home and things were more settled, he would give her such a dowry that husbands would come flocking. Still she refused to give up. "I don't want your charity," she said, setting her jaw. "I don't want a dowry. I want to go to Fontevraud and I want to go now. And if you refuse, Will, you will be disappointing God, so he may well wreak his vengeance on you. How will it be if the ransom goes to the bottom of the sea in a storm cooked up especially to punish you? Wouldn't it be better just to take me, then you can go off and deliver your precious ransom with God's protection and my prayers? Think about it, Will. Can you risk setting your face against God's wishes?" Marissa knew just what she was doing. Will might look completely disbelieving, but she had succeeded in sowing doubt among the soldiers and men-at-arms who would accompany him. For many of them, God's wrath was a real and dreaded possibility. Already there were those who were looking questioningly at Will.

In the end, although it was growing dark, Will sent once again to the monastery, but this time for Abbot

Hugh. He would have to sort the girl out. However, the abbot, when he arrived, was unsympathetic and blinked at Will from under his cowl. "But, my son," he began with what seemed to him was the obvious drawback in Will's argument, "perhaps she really does have a vocation." Will snorted but the abbot was unmoved. "If you think you know God's ways better than God himself, then you are foolish," he said, making his voice unusually stern, "and whilst you are young, I did not have you down as foolish."

"Father Abbot," Will said, losing his temper bit by bit, "I don't profess to know God's ways, but I do know Marissa's. Her sister, Marie, has settled here well but Marissa wants something she cannot have. It's her way of causing trouble to declare, at this most inconvenient time, that she has a vocation and must go at once to a nunnery. If she does have a vocation"—Will's voice rose triumphantly—"it won't disappear before I get back, will it? Waiting could be a kind of test."

"And this thing she cannot have, would it be you?" Hugh asked, his voice deliberately mild.

Will flushed. "Yes. But honestly, really honestly, I've given her no encouragement, none at all. I just teach her to ride on Hosanna."

Hugh considered. "But is that not encouragement? After all, you are not betrothed and she is of an age when girls think of nothing else but marriage—or so I believe," he added hastily.

Will gave the abbot a withering look, which, fortunately, the shadows hid. "I've told Marissa before that she's not to think of me like that."

"Very well," said Hugh, wondering how it was that

Will knew so much about war and so little about women. Will might consider Marissa a child but couldn't he see that Marissa most certainly didn't agree with him? He crossed his hands and made his decision. "I have to say, Will, that a convent really is the best place for her. Quite apart from giving herself to the Lord, she will be off your hands. I am surprised you don't jump at the chance."

"It's a trick," said Will bluntly. "She is jealous of Ellie being able to come to Germany with me. All the talk of Fontevraud is just to make sure she is part of our entourage. She knows how far out of our way it is. We are headed for the Rhine and Fontevraud is on the Loire. I know exactly why, too. She thinks that once we're on our journey, we'll not want to stop, and she'll end up coming with us. Or perhaps we'll get to Fontevraud and she'll change her mind. Believe me, Father Abbot, she's capable of anything. I know her."

"Maybe you do, my son, maybe you do," said Hugh, "but you must serve God as well as your king even if his requests take strange forms and do not fit in with your plans. A vocation is a precious thing. God will not like it to be squandered. Could you not send the girl with somebody else? There is surely no need to go yourself."

"That would never work," Will said, viciously kicking a log in the fire. "Marissa's so difficult and I'm responsible for her. If anybody takes her it must be me. But I can't leave the ransom treasure, either. Where I go, it must go, so couldn't you just talk to Marissa and try to tell her that she must wait?"

"Does she want to talk to me?"

"No." Will could not lie.

The abbot thought for a moment. "Can you be sure

that if she says she will wait, she will spend her time in prayer and contemplation?"

Will shook his head.

"Then you must take her, my son. The king's ransom is important, but so is God's work. Maybe," Hugh suggested, "you could deposit her not at Fontevraud but in the new abbey of St. Martin's at Arnhem? That is directly on your way. They need recruits, and my sister Agnes is the sacristan there. The abbess is a true woman of God. And you may yet be surprised. With the right training Marissa may make a good nun." Hugh got up. With not very good grace, Will kneeled for his blessing. "Hopeless," he said to Ellie after he had sent the abbot, with gifts, back to the abbey. Ellie said nothing. She did not want Marissa to come on their journey, yet the girl's unhappiness upset her. *If only Marissa were more like Marie*, Ellie thought, then chided herself for being so uncharitable. Marissa might be an irritating and even dangerous nuisance but nobody could deny her bravery and bravery was needed, too. And Ellie had never had to face being an old spinster.

In the early morning, Will asked Marissa again to wait and again she refused. An hour later he gave in and received her strange little smile in return. "I'm sure I shall be happy at Arnhem with the abbot's sister," she said, "so long as I can get to Fontevraud in the end. After all, that's the best convent for discarded noblewomen to end up in. They say it is where Queen Eleanor herself will go eventually."

"You are not being discarded," said Will, angrily rising to her bait.

"Well, you don't want me, do you?"

"Oh, for pity's sake, Marissa! I thought we had been through all that."

To his discomfort her eyes filled with tears. "But I have no function here," she said plaintively. "That's the trouble. Ellie's her own mistress, Marie will marry Hal eventually, and I am just the kind of spare girl who moulders away and everybody's relieved when they die. Even if you give me a dowry, who's going to marry me? I've got no land and I limp. Who'll want me, Will? Tell me that."

Will was embarrassed by the look she gave him. "You must be ready to go in two hours," he said shortly, "and remember, Marissa, there will be no turning back." He felt quite out of his depth. Again he missed his father's gruff good sense, and went outside to Hosanna.

After he had gone, Marissa sat in silence. She had got what she wanted. She was not going to be left behind. As she dried her eyes her arrogance returned. Who knew, they might never get to Arnhem, and even if they did, nobody could make her stay. Standing up, she toyed with the idea of rescuing her ruby brooch and was thwarted only by finding the chest locked. *Never mind,* she consoled herself, *at least I am going with it.* And with that she hurried away to pack.

9

Marie cried as they were leaving, which upset Hal. Old Nurse clucked and took the girl under her wing, all the time glaring at Marissa, who was now settling herself in comfort in a covered wagon and looking as innocent as an angel. "I hope you are kinder to the nuns than you are being to your sister," she growled as the wagon lurched forward. "God knows why, but she doesn't want you to go." Marissa didn't answer.

Ellie ignored Marissa and waited to say good-bye to Old Nurse herself. With the more observing eye that comes with parting, she noticed how ancient Old Nurse was beginning to look. Exactly how old she was, Ellie had no idea. For years, the fat lady had not changed at all, but Ellie was conscious that recent events had begun to exact a toll. Old Nurse's comforting plumpness was a little less round; her face a little more withered; and her hands, once so swift and sure, shook and sometimes dropped things. For the first time in her life, it occurred to Ellie that Old Nurse was not immortal and she could see, from Old Nurse's expression, that this thought was shared. The girl stretched her arms as far around the endless waist as was possible and they held each other tight. "Take care of yourself, Old Nurse," Ellie whispered. "Eat lots of meat and get the servants to look after you."

The old lady bent down to kiss the top of Ellie's head. "I'll always be with you, my sweet," she murmured, "just remember that."

When they finally parted, Ellie ran at once to Shihab, telling God, whose judgment she did not entirely trust since it was so often at variance with her own, that if he did not keep Old Nurse safe and well at Hartslove, she would say her night prayers under her blankets instead of on her knees for at least a month to spite him. She mounted and placed herself between Will and Kamil, glad that there was no delay for she did not want to cry. With shouts and whip cracks the carts began to roll, and before they had gone half a mile, with the silver horse obedient beneath her and an autumnal sun above, Ellie began to enjoy herself.

And to begin with, the journey was truly marvelous. A silver blaze between two reds, even Shihab was happy, and although Sacramenta swished her tail if the other mare came too near, the horses were glad of each other. Hosanna liked to keep his nose in front, but when he forged ahead, the two mares willingly quickened. Soon, the three of them left the wagons on the road and were racing on the sheep-cropped grass above. Side by side they cantered freely and easily, their riders laughing as their stirrup irons occasionally clanged together.

Below, the wagons made steadier progress. The first contained the Hartslove treasure and this was surrounded by a dozen heavily armed mounted soldiers, all carrying long swords. Behind them came a dozen handpicked mounted archers. The next wagon contained neatly stacked armor for men and horses, together with spare weaponry and horseshoes. The farrier and his boy drove this wagon, and in a small space on its flat back, the steward tasked with counting the money for the emperor sat singing to the cook, who spent most of the journey clucking at the antics of a couple of excitable pantry boys on small shaggy ponies no bigger than wolfhounds. Then came the wagon of provisions, inside which a fat-armed laundress perched on a barrel of dried beef and teased the steward's clerk about his baldness. It was a cheerful cavalcade.

The last wagon contained all the excess baggage plus two neat bedrolls belonging to Kamil and Amal and a chest belonging to Ellie. On top of the chest sat Elric, whom Will had forbidden to ride until they crossed the sea. Marissa sat beside him. Everybody could hear them squabbling for Elric could not hold his tongue and Marissa, despite flinching when she saw Elric's healing wounds, could not allow him to get away with anything. Soon, however, Elric fell asleep for he was still weaker than he liked to believe, and Marissa got bored. When she was sure Elric was quite unconscious, she amused herself by opening Ellie's chest and rifling through it. She was disappointed when none of Ellie's belongings caught her fancy and moved on to Kamil's roll. It was very meager but in it she found a small bone comb he had fashioned. Its delicate sturdiness appealed to her so she took it. She almost left Amal's roll alone, but as the miles dragged on and Elric didn't wake, she opened that too and the first thing to fall out was Amal's Turkish hat. She tried it on and at once found his little booklet carefully tucked inside. Intrigued, Marissa studied it. Although she could not make out a single word, she could sense that it was important to its owner. The parchment's soft, smooth texture showed that it had been constantly and lovingly stroked as it was read. She turned the pages slowly, liking the feel of it, at once intimate and exotic. Then Elric groaned, and so quickly that she hardly noticed herself doing it, Marissa slipped the booklet in among her own things and pushed Amal's roll away. By the time Elric rubbed his eyes and began to rile her once again, she was sitting back, delighted and horrified at her own dishonesty.

Amal himself was at the back of the party, riding a nondescript brown courser Constable Shortspur had given him. The horse was adequate but no more and Amal spent much of the journey praying that his life would never depend on its willingness to gallop at speed away from everybody else. He thought only of Kamil and, more than he liked to acknowledge, of Ellie, wondering if she would remember all he had taught her.

Though she never looked at Amal, Ellie was aware that she was being observed and did not want to disappoint. In the evenings as she went among the soldiers, dispensing ointment for bruises and sore feet or advising which herbs to boil up for headache, for the first time in her life Ellie felt the joy of being really useful. Amal might have more experience in medicine, but it was Ellie's encouraging voice and her light touch that the Hartslove men found more healing. Ellie glowed in their appreciation as she waited impatiently for chances to show off her new riding skills, praying that Shihab would not misbehave. Already she could see curiosity in Will's face as she rode with her legs bent instead of straight as he did, and she was gleeful when, after a sharp cry of "ditch," she kept her seat as Shihab made an exaggerated leap, fearful of getting her dainty feet wet. Kamil did not hide his admiration. Stunned not only by Ellie's grace and confidence but by seeing her ride Arab-style, his imagination ran riot. Surely this is what it would be like in the future: he and Ellie, two beautiful horses, and nothing to stop them galloping over all the desert plains.

It was on the third day that the almost festival atmosphere growing between Will, Kamil, and Ellie was marred. The three of them were still riding off the road. The wagons were in sight, but the soldiers were reliable and Hal stayed with them, so when Kamil suggested that before they reached the abbey they should gallop off some of the horses' excess energy, Will agreed with alacrity. They began in a line, with the two men soon dropping behind and Ellie streaking ahead. Will did not want to appear concerned, but it frightened him to see how fast the mare was going. He was about to suggest to Kamil that they go after her when she turned back toward them. Will relaxed, then, to his horror, he saw Ellie tumble off. Both he and Kamil cried out and Hosanna leaped at the terror in their voices. But her name was barely out of their mouths before Shihab had stopped dead and Ellie was vaulting back on. At once Shihab set off again. The whole operation had taken fewer than ten seconds.

After he had snapped his jaw shut, for it had dropped wide open with surprise, Kamil began to laugh. "Amal must have been teaching her," he said to Will. "That's a trick from home."

72

But Will was furious. "What kind of an idiot teaches a girl tricks like that?" he stormed, shaking his head violently. "She could have been killed."

"No," said Kamil, "really, no. We do it to fool our enemies so that they never know what to expect. It's all about timing. How extraordinary that she should be able to do it so fast, faster than me even, I think. She must have been practicing a lot since we left." His eyes sparkled as he and Will cantered on together and Ellie circled back between them. Her face was shining, but if she expected praise from Will she was disappointed. He almost refused to acknowledge her. Kamil, however, was full of admiration and grew, for him, quite talkative, telling Ellie how the horse on which he had learned the trick had decided it was much more fun with Kamil on the ground than in the saddle and had taken to throwing him off whenever it felt like it, then expecting a reward when it stood like a rock for Kamil to remount. They discussed techniques and different ways of vaulting. Kamil swung his legs over, ran for a moment beside Sacramenta, then swung himself back on from the opposite side. Ellie wanted to try and suggested to Will that he should, too. But Will shrugged his shoulders and gradually Ellie and Kamil stopped swinging on and off and fell silent. They all spoke civilly to each other thereafter, but things were not quite as they had been. When Whitby Abbey appeared on the horizon, their rejoicing was muted.

The abbey towered over the town spread out below, some of it almost falling into the sea. As soon as the Hartslove cavalcade hove into view, the abbot cantered out to meet them, just in time also to greet three monks, flushed and sweating, surrounded by a pack of hounds. As fat as Hugh was thin, the abbot greeted Will warmly. "Just hunting for the pot," he said, waving his hand at the hounds. "Visitors must be properly fed."

Ellie was shocked. "What a lot of meat they must eat if they keep a pack of hounds! It's quite against the rule!" she whispered to Will. He did not reply. He could not forgive her quite yet.

The hunting monks could not get over the beauty of the Hartslove horses. Hosanna lowered his head and allowed them to stroke his face. Instinctively, the monks touched his star, and Will, climbing off and touching the star himself, felt some of his ill humor blown away by the red horse's comforting solidity. He glanced over at Ellie, wanting her to see that he was recovering himself, but she was on her knees petting the hounds. He watched her, then saw Kamil watching her also and sulkily turned back to Hosanna. He was glad when the carts rolled up and he had something to do.

The treasure was immediately transported down to the harbor, for they would set sail early in the morning. Although a day's rest would have been welcome, it was important to catch what remained of the good weather. Marissa climbed out of her wagon and, much against their respective wills, both she and Ellie were hurried inside the guesthouse by the guestmaster. The advent of the two young women made the younger monks restless and distracted, and it was best to get them out of sight. "Time for Vespers," the abbot declared, clapping his small hands neatly but without much conviction.

Ellie didn't like being bundled along with Marissa. "Maybe the earl's young ward should hear Vespers sung," she said, "but I don't need to. Marissa's going to be a nun." She saw Elric grin and was ashamed of herself.

The abbot turned to Marissa, impressed. "Really?" He looked at her with new respect. "You will be wanting to pray, of course, my sister, so I'll show you where you can stand behind a pillar at the back of the church. We take some pride in our chanting." Marissa almost choked and lashed out at Elric, who skipped away, crossing his hands with mock sanctity.

When dinner was served, the abbot came to sit near Will. According to the Benedictine Rule, the abbot should have eaten nothing, for he had already eaten earlier in the day. However, the venison was too tempting and although he refused a trencher, his pudgy hand kept sidling out. "Just the scraps," he said to Will, his face pink with guilty longing. "It's a sin to let them go to waste." Even Hal had to bite his lip to stop himself from snorting.

With his mouth full, the abbot was full of the gossip his monks had gleaned from sailors returning from Palestine and the East. The Saracens were leaderless and their lands in chaos. "If Richard is released in time to lead another crusade, they say he could sweep all before him." The abbot licked his lips as grease dropped off his many chins. "But for us poor creatures, more war will just mean more money and we have collected so much already."

Amal, disgusted by the abbot as he stood behind Kamil's chair, heard this without moving a muscle. After supper, however, he set off down to the town. Ports were always full of the Old Man's spies. Amal had his instructions but fresh word would also be welcome. As he hung about in the crowd along the quayside watching people gazing with resentful wonder at the heavily guarded ransom wagons, he wondered if anybody would make contact. At first he thought the woman clutching his knees was demanding money. She had the whining voice and ragged clothes of a beggar although a flash of gold at her neck suggested something else. But when she said his name, Amal followed her at once down a side street. Only when she bade him enter her house did he hesitate, fearing a trap. But what trap could there be? Nobody knew him in this place. He went in and was relieved to find the woman did not want to waste any time.

"You received the letter?" she asked, her voice no longer whining but hard and businesslike. She spoke in Norman French. There was no pretence that Amal could not understand.

"I did."

"The Old Man sends word to say that his plans are now complete." The woman looked around her as if the walls might be listening, then she edged nearer to Amal and began to whisper in his ear. She spoke for some time and when she stopped, Amal stood perfectly still. "A strange twist, indeed," he said, his voice low.

"Do you object?"

Amal was frightened and answered quickly. "I do not," he said. "What the Old Man has commanded shall be done. But," he couldn't help adding, "I'm glad Kamil is not my son."

The woman said nothing as she showed Amal out, but when her own boy came home, she kissed him more warmly than usual.

It was not until much later that night that Amal discovered his booklet was missing. He had not looked inside his hat since leaving Hartslove. At first he was just puzzled and shook his clothes carefully, turning his hat inside out. But when he realized the booklet had, indeed, vanished, his long face became quite wild and he rushed back to the wagon, searching it from top to bottom, not caring about the comments and stares. Only when Kamil came and asked what was the matter did Amal try to regain some composure, saying that he was looking for a spare tunic, which he thought he must have left at Hartslove. Kamil commiserated, saying that he, too, had carelessly left something behind—his little comb. Perhaps he could give Amal a change of clothes? Amal had to pretend to be grateful but he could not sleep and, in the dawn, shed bitter tears.

The next morning, as they boarded the ship, Amal was very quiet. Though the loss of the booklet was a personal tragedy, Amal could not believe there was any real danger. Even if somebody found it, who could read it? He did not think Ellie would remember enough now that their lessons were over, and the words she had learned were mainly to do with horses. Anyway, it had most likely fallen out as Amal packed and by now the pages would be scattered. No danger, he decided. But that did not make him feel better. Now he had nothing physical to remind him of gentler times and was completely adrift from everything he knew and cared for. He tried reciting his children's sentiments, for he knew them by heart, but felt himself barely a father anymore. Without his book he was just a cipher of the Old Man's and his face, already shriveled, shrunk a little more.

Marissa was also silent but her silence was nothing to do with her thieving. She was silent with genuine horror. Already she could feel the cloister closing about her, suffocating her in incense and candle smoke. She must tell Will at once, endure Elric's scorn and Ellie's contempt, but say she could not do it. She practiced the words in her head, but when Will was in front of her, his face grim with responsibility, she found herself unexpectedly nervous. He would hate her and she wasn't sure if she could stand that. So Marissa said nothing, only held on to the ship's rail and watched the captain set his course for the Scheldt estuary, the quickest way to Arnhem and then on to Richard and the imperial court. She would have prayed for a shipwreck but with Will and Hosanna on board, even she could not quite manage that.

The others were too taken up with the effort of finding their sea legs to notice either Marissa's or Amal's preoccupations. Shihab, at last tied up and sweating in the hold, had refused to follow Hosanna's steady lead over the ramp. Instead, she had cavorted and plunged about on the rickety planks until Ellie had to shut her eyes, certain that the mare would fall into the sea. Shihab refused to be fooled by the torches emitting a welcome brightness in the dark. She had been inside a ship once before and every fiber of her being was determined that she would never go in one again. In the end, it had been Amal who had persuaded her, taking her from Hal and muttering in Arabic as he slid an arm under her neck. Quite unexpectedly, the mare seemed to cling to him as a child clings to its mother. Kamil was impressed.

The wagons full of silver were soon tied in, one at each end of the hold and one in the middle for balance. Banked with sacks of sand to stop them from rolling, they looked firm enough. Nevertheless Ellie, who went to Shihab's head once all the horses were safely installed, prayed that the restraints would not be tested. It was the first time she had been on a ship and everything excited her, from the creak of the ropes to the swinging of the lanterns. She knew from Will and Gavin's tales that the sea was a most unpredictable friend, yet when the ship finally left the shore, its sail billowing just as she had imagined it would, she could not help leaning over the rail with Elric and waving at the townsfolk who had gathered to watch.

Looking even more threadbare than usual, Amal began the next, the most vital, stage of his work at once. As the ship crept down the coast and Will taught Ellie to play chess, the old Saracen sat with Kamil and mused aloud. What a good thing, he said, for King Richard to return home. Even Saladin had said that Richard was a great man and a worthy enemy. But, Amal sounded almost whimsical, what would the German emperor do with this huge ransom, all those silver marks and jewels? He shook his head and sighed. Perhaps the money would be used to build a fine palace or to give a feast for the poor. But, and he glanced sidelong at Kamil, he doubted it. In fact, he went on, it was rumored that the money had already been earmarked to finance another crusade, the biggest ever mounted, with siege machines that even the gates of Heaven could not withstand. When Richard was freed, he would return to the Holy Land and take his revenge for Saladin's victories. Amal clicked his tongue and looked concerned. Then, so as not to overdo things, he left Kamil to himself.

Much later, as the wind got up and the sea became choppy, he found Kamil again, this time standing beside Hosanna. Most of the horses rested with their heads low, their ears back and their eyes dull with misery at the swell. Hosanna chose to deal with his discomfort by setting his legs at the four corners of his stall and pressing the whole length of his face against Kamil's chest. Next to him, Shihab constantly shifted, always fidgeting, her silver coat slimy with sweat and already stained with tar and green damp where she had been buffeting herself against the partitions.

When Amal approached, Hosanna stamped a back foot and swished his tail. Kamil stroked his neck and said nothing. Nevertheless, Amal did not want to take that chance again. If the horse was always unfriendly, Kamil might grow unfriendly, too. Much later that night, when Kamil was asleep, Amal searched until he found the little triangular knife Kamil carried and slipped into the hold, watching until Hosanna was alone before approaching him once more. The horse whinnied loudly. Amal held his breath, expecting Hal. Nobody came, so Amal held the knife momentarily at Hosanna's throat, then quickly moved and made a neat puncture on the crest of the horse's neck at the point where the heavy fountain of mane was thickest. Into the puncture he rubbed some very finely ground white powder, afterward wiping his fingers carefully on the reeds that were scattered over the floor. The poison was not enough to kill—Amal had been very careful measuring out the quantity—Hosanna just needed to be dozy so that when Amal came near him he did not react. "Kamil trusts those you trust," he murmured into the red ear already beginning to droop. "You must learn to trust me, red horse, until this business is over." Then he patted him, cleaned the knife, carefully replaced it exactly where he had found it, and slept himself.

As they abandoned the coast for open waters, the wind turned into a gale. Several times, the galley was almost driven backward and several times the only things to be heard above the keening gusts and the groaning mast were the prayers of the sailors begging for either respite or early death. Ellie and Marissa, united in misery, huddled into a corner belowdecks and Elric was so sick that Will cursed himself for saying the boy could come.

Deep in the hold, Hosanna fought to keep his feet. The opiate that Amal had administered made every limb too heavy to move and slowed every reaction. With a huge effort, when Amal approached to keep up the dosage, Hosanna would pull away and when Will struggled to his side, would lay his head over his master's shoulder as if to blow some understanding into his ears. But Will could not understand. When Amal commented on how calm Hosanna was, stroked the horse's star, and dabbed away the beads of sweat with a silken cloth, Will was glad to tell Ellie that Hosanna's initial dislike of Amal seemed to have vanished. How could Will tell anything was wrong when nothing felt right in this hideous cataclysm. "Bravest of the brave," whispered Will to his horse as he slithered and slid in the stinking filth, for it was not possible to clear away the horses' waste. It was then that Hosanna closed his eyes, unable to fight any longer.

When the weather eased, Amal found more time to talk to Kamil and made sure to do it when standing close to the red horse. He could see how, when he stroked Hosanna and Hosanna did not object, Kamil relaxed. "Our people will need a strong leader to combat Richard," Amal began to muse, always keeping his voice casually conversational. "After the great sultan Saladin died, Allah keep him, we lost our way. Now the great Christian horde will threaten again and who will save us?" He stroked Hosanna's flanks, his long, thin fingers sliding up and down, making stripes in the grimy coat while Hosanna stood silent and unflinching. "It is the time for all men loyal to Allah, Mohammed his Prophet, and the memory of the sultan, to come home and defend our land. Ah, Kamil! How we need a man of courage, a man people can respect. Without such a man, even I, a poor horse dealer, know that Islam is doomed." He shook his head and then knelt to pray.

He picked up his theme the following afternoon, and as he left the hold he patted the wagons of silver as if he had just remembered they were there. "Such a pity," he murmured sadly, "that every coin, every jewel, and every plate will mark the death of one of our people. That is what King Richard's ransom means for us. It is something, is it not, to know that we are touching the very means by which Christians will be paid to kill Muslims. Your friend Will is a good man, of course, but the rest are dogs."

Over the following days, like poisoned honey, Amal's words began to stick to Kamil's soul. Just as Amal intended, in his mind's eye Kamil began to see himself as the leader for whom his people were longing. Standing forward on the deck when the storms died down and staring into the night sky, he imagined himself entering the mosque at Jerusalem, honored and saluted as the man who saved his people from the Christian menace, a man blessed by Allah and celebrated in song and legend. Soon, he did not just listen, he was filled with new questions, which Amal answered carefully, hesitating just a little so that Kamil always believed he was leading and not being led. And all the while, Hosanna could smell deceit on the old Saracen's breath and feel the treachery in his fingers. But though he stood, his head pressed against Kamil, Kamil never guessed.

By the time they crept into the Scheldt estuary, where they would exchange the ships for barges, Kamil was filled with both dread and exhilaration. Suddenly he saw his choice. This was the moment when he could either meet his destiny or shirk it. And it was clear, so clear he would never be able to pretend otherwise, where his duty lay. He must ensure that the ransom money was never paid. The money must either sink into the river mud or be used in the Saracen cause, and since to sink it into the mud would be a criminal waste, it should be used to unite the Muslim army and push the Christians out of the Holy Land once and for all. In this way, Kamil would save his people.

Yet though his logic was clear, Kamil found his conscience still troubled him. If the ransom was not delivered, Will would be suspected of treachery. He might even be hanged, for nobody would believe a de Granville had lost the ransom by mistake. Moreover, when it became clear that Kamil had taken it, nobody would believe that Will was not complicit. After all, the friendship between Will and Kamil was famous. They were seen everywhere together. People would think that the two of them had made some kind of arrangement from which both would eventually benefit. And if Will suffered from Kamil's actions, then Ellie would suffer, too. Was any cause worth that? *But,* an inner voice was tantalizingly rational, *if Will suffers and even dies, would that not make it more likely that Ellie would return to Palestine with you? Isn't that what you want? Without Will, she would be yours. And she would understand. Wouldn't she? Wouldn't she?* After mooring for the first night in the estuary, Kamil walked alone round the ramshackle village from which they had demanded hospitality. Despite the chill, he felt hot. Logic was all very well but it was not everything. *I can't do it,* he thought. *I can't do it.*

As if by magic, Amal appeared beside him and he knew exactly what to say. "Allah decrees," he whispered, twisting the holy words as he had been trained to do, "that those who fight for his cause cannot stray from the true path for he will always guide them. Things done in his name cannot be wrong. Do you not also remember, Kamil, that Allah loves a noble man and that there is no man more noble than one who sacrifices personal friendships for the greater good? And Kamil"—this was Amal's trump card—"Allah's love for the noble man will surely extend to those Christians whose friendship you value. Do you not trust Allah enough to know that you can act in his name without fear? This is a rare moment, Kamil, an enviable moment in a man's life. I have never had such a moment as is being granted to you. Seize it. If you don't, and this ransom ensures that Jerusalem falls once again to the infidel, what will Allah say then?" He was nervous lest he had overstepped himself, but when Kamil, his face hard as iron, at once prostrated himself in prayer, Amal knew he had won. There would be no need to drug Hosanna anymore. Waiting patiently until Kamil got up, Amal boldly took his arm and drew him into the shadows.

10

Hosanna did not recover at once and was so sluggish and out of sorts that Will grew seriously worried and kept him on the barge, tended by Hal and Elric, when Ellie took Shihab off to ride the travel stiffness out of her joints. The silver mare was skittish. She seemed to know that the watery part of the journey was over, and as they followed the river path in the wake of the ponderous boats, she frisked about and shied, making herself difficult to sit on.

Kamil rode at Ellie's side and every now and again felt the urgent desire to confide. It was mad but he wanted to tell Ellie what he felt he had to do and to explain why there could be no turning back now that he had made his decision. Some of the time, as they gaily leaped over the obstacles they found in their way, he was certain she would understand. Ellie knew so much about loyalty. She would know what the call of his people meant and admire him for taking up the yoke history was holding out to him. The rest of the time Kamil knew she would not understand at all. Like Will, Ellie trusted him absolutely. He knew that by the way she looked at him. It would be the work of a truly bad man to introduce fear and suspicion into green eyes so frank and open. And he was going to be that man. But surely, even if Ellie was bitter at first, in the end she would forgive him. Kamil repeated this over and over. He would believe it. He would.

For Will, every last buzz of excitement had vanished from the journey. Anxiety about Hosanna and the possibility of attack shortened his temper, and even Elric felt the sharp end of his tongue.

Marissa counted the passing miles with increasing dread. She, who was always so full of schemes, could not invent one now. As they inched through the wet October landscape along the muddy banks of the River Rhine, the only thing that sparkled was Shihab.

When attack came, it came at dawn. The wagons had been taken off the barges, for there was a good road and the waterways were becoming so busy with men shouting in a dozen languages that Will thought dry land offered greater security. He was wrong. As the sun crept over the soggy horizon and the damp horses were harnessed up, the whiz of an arrow made them all jump. The first fell short, but the second pierced the spine of the bleary-eyed Hartslove steward as he stumbled out of his tent. Scores of arrows followed and at first it was difficult to see their source. Will shouted instructions as he ducked, scanning the woods and eventually saw, with relief, that this was not a strategic rout but only a band of ragged mercenaries chancing their luck. Yet though their armor was rusty and their horses thin and unkempt, the attackers were all the braver for being hungry. They had heard about Richard's silver and had come to claim it. Wielding jagged swords, they emerged from the trees shrieking their challenge.

But their greed was not matched by their organiza-tion and Will's archers soon killed half a dozen. The ransom was never in danger. Nevertheless, five of the rabble somehow managed to climb onto Marissa's wagon, slaughter the wagoner, and beat the horses into an unwilling trot. The rest of the marauders scattered as Will swung himself onto the wagon as it jolted away. In a flash, Hal was after him, hauling him off. "Sir, don't be foolish," he panted as they tumbled to the ground. "What can you do alone? Quick. The horses are saddled. If we cut around, we can take them from the front."

Elric was there at once with Will's armor, helping him to shrug it on even as he ran for Hosanna. Hal spoke quickly. "No, no sir. Hosanna's still not right. You need speed. You can't risk it." He was holding Dargent's rein, and giving Will no time to reply, heaved him into the saddle. Will did not argue. "Send a dozen archers up the road, Hal," he cried, "but keep the ransom wagons closely guarded, too. This may be just a diversion." He found Kamil beside him on Shihab. Will nodded at him and Kamil gave a half smile. This might be the last thing he could do for Will. "They'll not get away from the fastest horse in the world," he said, and drew his sword.

Will and Kamil, with Hal on Sacramenta following behind, abandoned the track and plunged over marshy ground. Shihab leaped lightly while an eager Dargent floundered a little and Sacramenta followed in his foot-steps. They caught the mercenaries at the next corner. Marissa had been pulled onto the roof and was being used as a shield by the band's bearded leader. She refused to show any fear, though her eyes were wide, but was hissing like a rattlesnake, biting and kicking, scraping her nails down faces, and tugging beards and hair. The man was laughing and his friends were pulling at Marissa's clothes.

"They're drunk," said Will, disgusted, wondering about tipping the whole wagon over.

Kamil took out his knife and it sat, slim and sleek in his hand. "Don't." Will grabbed his arm. "It's too dangerous. You might hit the wrong target." The men, seeing Will shake his head, laughed even more loudly and the smallest of them, crowing like a bantam, grabbed Marissa's long plait, making her scream at last as he dragged her toward him. But his leader would not let go of her arms and soon Marissa was the center of a noisy tug-of-war. Will could wait no longer. Aiming Dargent straight at the wagon, he leaped onto the shaft, simultaneously pulling out his sword and defending himself from a ferocious attack from on high. Hal followed Will just as the Hartslove archers appeared, crossbows at the ready.

In moments, the mercenaries found themselves surrounded, the archers facing alternately inward and outward, an impregnable defence from attack from all directions. Now that they were trapped, the brigands became noisier than ever. Their leader kicked away his rival and held Marissa as close as he might have held his wife. She would be his ticket out. Will hovered on the edge, unable to get near.

Kamil, still mounted, narrowed his eyes. For a moment Will was visible, then the mercenaries stopped fighting each other and turned on him. Though he swung sword and axe, Hal could not hold them off and the wagon rocked, the roof cracking under the unaccustomed weight. However, though they fought like wolves, the mercenaries' fighting skills, dulled by drink, meant they were clumsy and soon, one after the other, they thumped onto the ground, crawling away into the undergrowth until their leader was quite alone.

The man realized at once that he was doomed and, half strangling Marissa, he brandished his dagger. Now Kamil whistled through his teeth and taking careful aim, he let his stiletto fly. It flew true as a dart, the blade almost invisible and Kamil held his breath until a flurry of red spouted from the man's throat, soaking his beard and splattering Marissa's hair. The dying leader's arms shot into the air like a puppet's. Now Marissa screamed even louder and staggered backward, but her captor fell awkwardly and brought her down with him. At once Will was scrambling frantically toward her over wood made treacherous with blood. Kamil called that he could take his time for all was well. But Kamil was mistaken. He could not see what Will could see, which was that the stiletto had fallen from the mercenary's throat and, in the chaos of limbs, had found another mark. It was not only enemy blood that was dripping onto the grass. "Marissa, Marissa!" Will was crying. "Hal! Kamil! Help me! Oh, quickly, for God's sake."

Kamil was off Shihab and onto the wagon in a trice. He hauled the body of the mercenary away and dumped him over the side, uncaring that the last twitches of life were not yet extinguished. Hal already had Marissa in his arms and everybody could see that the blade was lodged between her ribs. The girl's expression was of stunned surprise rather than fear. The only time fear took over was when she saw Will's unsteady hand ready to pull the stiletto out. But Kamil got there first. White-faced, he pulled and when the blade emerged, scrutinized it. 'Thank God,' he said abruptly. "Look," he showed Will, "the blade is almost clean. Marissa is hurt but nothing is severed. We must bind up the hole and keep her still. I have seen men with deeper wounds than this survive." He tried to say something to Marissa but she buried her face in Will's sleeve and held his arm as if she would never let it go.

Though Will hurried as fast as he could, it seemed to take ages to get Marissa back to the camp. She lay on a makeshift stretcher carried by four men, the wagon being too bumpy, but even so, every step caused her eyelids to flutter and her pulse to weaken. Kamil remained obstinately optimistic. "Her silk dress saved her," he told Will as they ran. "Silk helps blades to come out smoothly. If she was going to die, she would have done so already. I know she would." But his face betrayed a terrible doubt.

Will tried to comfort him. "It's not your fault," he said. "You saved her, Kamil. It was still a brave throw." It was true, but Kamil, usually so calm and detached, grew flustered. "I didn't mean to hurt her, Will. You do know that, don't you? I know Marissa and I are hardly friends but I wouldn't want to hurt anybody from Hartslove. Anybody. You know that."

"Of course I do," Will reassured him, surprised at Kamil's vehemence. Glancing over, he caught a look in Kamil's eyes that he had never seen before. Only later

91

did he remember that look. For now, all he could think of was Marissa.

By the time they laid her before the fire, she was so white that Ellie thought her already dead. Elric brought Ellie's little trunk of medicines and she and Amal did what they could. *What a dreadful, dreadful end,* Ellie thought. Kamil hung back, scarcely able to look anybody in the eye. Eventually he went and stood by Hosanna. He approached tentatively, wondering if the horse would sense the darkness in his soul and reject him, but when Hosanna did not, Kamil buried his face in the fiery mane and remained there until Hal called him to some other duty.

As soon as Amal said it was safe to do so, Will wanted to get back on to the river and press on to Arnhem. News of the attack would be everywhere and others would come to try their luck. With Ellie at his side, he conferred with Hal and Kamil. Kamil seemed strangely tense but Will put this down to worry about Marissa. Ellie noticed too and spoke to Kamil privately. When Will saw the way Kamil looked at her, though this was hardly the time, he felt his old jealousy rising. He hated himself for being so childish yet he couldn't seem to help it.

The few days it took to reach the convent were the worst Will could remember. It was a different kind of nightmare from the forced marches on crusade. At least when marching you were doing something. On the river, he stood for hours in the nose of the barge, his legs itching to feel Hosanna gallop underneath him. Never had a journey seemed so slow. And then, on crusade, Will had not been in charge. Any mistakes could be blamed on others. Here, everybody looked to him and though Hal and Kamil were always there to support him, it was on Will that the final decisions fell. Elric's unbounded confidence in whatever Will judged to be best felt like the heaviest of burdens. "How on earth do I know?" he found himself snapping when Elric asked an innocent question and then hated himself for stamping out the spark in the boy's eyes, even though it never took long for Elric's cheeky optimism to re-ignite. Will wanted to confide his fears to Ellie yet he held back, torturing himself as he watched her trying to draw an increasingly silent Kamil back into the companionship they had all once enjoyed. Why was it, he thought, that love could be both the best and the worst thing in the world? His love for Ellie had destroyed his relationship with Gavin and now it was eating away at his friendship with Kamil. He tried to imagine his father scolding him for being so silly and stayed for hours beside Hosanna. Though the horse continued to be worryingly sickly, his velvet breath could still soothe. On the rare occasions that Will slept, it was on the straw at Hosanna's feet.

Marissa was just about conscious when at last the walls of St. Martin's could be glimpsed, rising steeply up about a mile from the river and Will gave orders for the wagons to be disembarked on the wide landing stage. Ellie touched his hand as they followed the horses being led ashore. "Remember that Marissa asked to come," she said softly. "Whether she recovers or not, it was her choice." Will's hand burned though Ellie's fingers were freezing. He did not trust himself to reply.

It was not until they were almost inside the convent

walls that Marissa realized where she was and then she gathered together all her strength, rolled over on her wooden stretcher, and became violent with agitation. "No, Will, no! Don't let them take me."

Will ran to her. "Never mind about anything else, Marissa. The nuns can help you. You're hurt."

But Marissa would not listen. Ellie was quickly by her other side. "Don't be silly, Marissa," she told her, "you'll die if you struggle. You're bleeding!" But Marissa ignored her. "I'm not ready, Will," she begged, her voice high and pleading. "Don't leave me here. Please don't leave me. If you do, I'll certainly die." Her face, already ghostly, crumpled like tissue paper.

"They are just going to look after you, Marissa." Will gave panicky reassurance, almost undone by her terrible distress. "The nuns aren't your enemies."

"They are, they are," sobbed the girl.

They reached the gate where the prioress was waiting with Hal. She was pleased at the thought of an addition to their numbers and cautioned Will. "It is often like this when novices first come," she said, her smile sweet but steely. "Best not to listen too hard. Let us take care of her and patch her up." She summoned six laysisters to take the stretcher from Will's men. "You go to our guesthouse. You can see the young lady again later perhaps, when she is calmer." Before Will could reply, Marissa was gone, her screams fading as the door of the reception hall closed behind her.

They did not see her again for several days for her fever raged high and even Elric looked worried. To steady himself, Will concentrated only on Hosanna. It was still a mystery to him that his horse had sickened so, but he put it down to some kind of ship's disease. Often, when Marissa's cries grew unbearable, he would find Ellie, too, hiding in Hosanna's stable, usually bearing a basket filled with all manner of medicinal herbs. Hosanna stood patiently, eating out of their hands. These moments were inexpressibly comforting to Will. There was something about tending the horse together that smoothed the wrinkles from his heart and, despite Marissa, helped him to feel young and hopeful again. Ellie understood this, but said nothing, though she wanted to. With Marissa so wretched, to speak to Will about their own feelings would have felt like crowing. Though she knew that Marissa would never have shown such consideration had their roles been reversed, Ellie still resisted. There would be a right time, she knew that for sure. One day it would come and she wanted it to be perfect. Nevertheless, with her remedies gradually dissolving the glaze from Hosanna's eyes and with the red horse's coat beginning to shine under Hal and Elric's grooming, she allowed herself, very occasionally, to hum one of Old Nurse's tunes.

Kamil, however, could not be happy and grew more and more uncomfortable within the convent walls. When he should have been planning, his head was filled with images of the mercenary he had killed. At least it looked like the mercenary from behind. But when Kamil mentally rolled him over, it was Ellie's face he saw and his scalp would prickle with dreadful premonitions. At such moments, he forced himself to think of Saladin and even his dead father and mother. Surely he could both save his people and make sure that Will and Ellie were safe?

One morning, as the bells tolled to summon the religious to Matins, he woke Amal. The silver, Kamil had decided, must be stolen before the German guards took over at the border. Will kept his soldiers constantly on alert but he had a limited number. Once over the border, the imperial troops would be many and much more heavily armed. "We will need decent men who will obey orders," Kamil said over and over again. "No blood must be shed. They must meet us just before the border dressed as German soldiers. If Will thinks they are imperial troops, he will hand the money over without any questions. The Hartslove soldiers will then leave. They are not going to travel all the way to the imperial court."

"And the Earl of Ravensgarth and Mistress Eleanor?" Amal sounded as if he really cared, which in his own way, he did.

Kamil clasped his fingers together. "Is it better to take them with us or leave them, bound but safe, for the real imperial soldiers to find?" It was a question of the utmost importance. "They must not be suspected of treachery, Amal. King Richard and the emperor must be left in no doubt that Will is innocent of any wrongdoing."

"I will find a way," said Amal, his voice confident and comforting. He was glad, however, that Kamil could not see his face, for it was full of neither confidence nor comfort. How complicated this task was turning out to be! Enemies should be kept at arm's length, for once you grew closer to them it was impossible for your heart to remain completely cold. Sometimes Amal wished he could slink away. Yet he could not falter now. He had his own family, living under the Old Man's shadow, to consider. "You must trust me, Kamil," he said softly. "Have I let you down before?"

He jumped as Kamil pressed his arm. "You have not," the young man said. "Now, we must also send for a ship to meet us down on the French coast."

"Yes," Amal answered, relieved, "there will be no difficulty. The ports are full of Saracen brothers. I will send ahead for what we need."

But Kamil was still unhappy. "I don't know, Amal. Can we really be sure Will and Ellie will be safe?"

Amal's voice came back, thinner this time. "You must not worry. I know this is not easy. The trouble is that you have been so long among the Christians your loyalty is divided."

The barb stung. "My loyalties are not divided," Kamil said at once, "but I am not a barbarian, who lies and steals without scruple. I know what I must do. But I also know what I must not do." He lit a candle and Amal could see the skin over Kamil's cheekbones drawn tightly enough to tear. It was then that the old Saracen realized just how effective the Old Man's punishment was.

When Marissa was fit to be propped up, the nuns made a sickroom in the visitors' lodgings. Then Will went in to sit with her, with Agnes, a gentle woman glad to have news of Abbot Hugh, as a chaperone. Marissa was very frail. No longer weeping, she seemed smaller, somehow, as if she were crumbling away from the inside. She refused to see Ellie and frequently declared to both Will and the prioress that she refused to take the habit. Will did not know how to answer but the prioress was quite ready. "Men have died to get you here, my sister," she said serenely, with Agnes nodding in the background. "God must want you very much." She took no notice whatsoever of either Marissa's tears or her curses.

By the Feast of All Saints, Marissa was on her feet again and Will knew there was no reason to delay their journey any longer. Hosanna was now fully recovered and Richard would be getting impatient. He dreaded telling Marissa and left breaking the news until the evening before their departure, when he took her to Hosanna's stable, chivvied Elric out, and hung up a lantern. The horse's coat reflected dappled burgundy. To give himself something to do, Will began to brush Hosanna's shoulder with long, sweeping strokes. "We are leaving in the morning," he said. He could think of no way to dress up this news so that it would be less bald. He braced himself.

However, Marissa said nothing, only pressed her palms against Hosanna's star.

Will went on nervously. "We have to get the ransom to Germany as soon as we can." Marissa still said nothing. Will stopped brushing. Nerves were hopeless. He must be bold. "What is it you really want, Marissa?" he asked her, then added quickly, "and don't say me, because as I've told you a million times, that's impossible. I know I said there was no going back, but do you want to go home? Perhaps, if Marie marries Hal, you could go and live with them."

He began brushing again so that he did not have to look directly at her. She made him feel horrible and he couldn't understand why, since he knew he didn't love her except as he supposed he might have loved a sister, had he ever had one. Marissa made him wait but she answered in the end. "I don't want to go with them," she said shortly, "and if I go back to Hartslove, I'll turn into Old Nurse."

"I think that most unlikely," said Will, trying to lighten things.

Marissa began to plait Hosanna's forelock. The horse pricked his ears toward her but shifted away so that she dropped his forelock and started on his mane. The strength of the long, smooth hair as she neatly divided it up and wound it around her fingers made her unexpectedly honest. "I'm just a misfit, Will," she said at last. "I don't really belong anywhere. Even if I had lands, or even if you were to give me a dowry, I still don't want to marry any of the people who might want to marry me. You know the truth, Will, even if you don't like it. If I can't marry you, I don't want anybody else. That's how this whole convent thing began. It seemed the only option—and it meant I could be with you at least a little longer."

Will leaned against Hosanna's flank. "You make me feel so guilty," he said, "and that's not how I want to remember you, Marissa. When you're not goading Elric or being contrary, you're as strong and brave as"—he was going to say Ellie but just stopped himself, and although Marissa knew, she did not want to bark at him now so she let it pass—"as the best of us." Will began to brush again and was suddenly quite sure what he should say. "God needs people like you in places like this, you know. I know I said you wouldn't make a good nun when we were at home, but you could, if you wanted to, and although ordinary nuns may not count for much, abbesses do." He looked directly at her now although he never stopped brushing. "It would make me very proud to think of you as an abbess, running a convent and frightening the bishop." He smiled uncertainly and Marissa smiled wanly back.

"I would like to count," she whispered, "it's just that I don't feel called by God."

"Perhaps the prioress is right and that will come," said Will slowly. "It might, Marissa, if you let it."

Marissa's smile disappeared. "I don't want it to," she spoke loudly. "I want to choose what I do, Will, not just settle for something to make *you* feel better. It's—" she stopped. "What's this?" She peered at Hosanna's neck. "Elric should take more care," she said sharply. "He has nicked Hosanna with a knife." She pushed Hosanna's head around so that the nick caught the light. Then she gave a small exclamation. "How strange! Look, Will. It's the same shape as the scar between my ribs."

Will peered closely. "Are you sure?"

Marissa nodded. "I'm quite sure," she said. "It's that triangle shape, the shape of Kamil's knife. Does Elric have a knife like that, too?"

"No," said Will slowly, "he doesn't." He let Hosanna's mane drop. Outside, the air was suddenly full of the bells for Vespers. The sound disturbed the bats and as one darted down, Marissa seized Will's hand, the scar forgotten. "If I refuse to stay here, will God punish you to punish me, Will? I couldn't live with myself if that happened."

Will did not try to shake his hand free. Instead, he took Marissa's other one. "Of course not," he said firmly. "God's supposed to love us, not just to look for ways to make us pay if we do things he doesn't like."

"But we do pay, don't we?" Marissa was more fearful than Will had ever seen her.

And he could not answer her question. "Look, Marissa, if you hate it, when the ransom is delivered you can leave," was all he could say. "God won't mind."

Marissa gave a small sigh, which Will found harder to bear than anything. "Ah, Will," she breathed, bending her head, "I did not have you down as a torturer. The only way to enter an abbey properly is to close the door behind you." She disengaged her hands, said something to Hosanna, then slipped out, leaving Will feeling unexpectedly bereft.

The admission ceremony took place early the next morning. It was very short and simple. Marissa stood quite still as Will handed over the gold he had brought as her convent dowry. He had been generous but when he looked at Marissa's face, his generosity seemed coarse and unfeeling, as if he were thanking the abbey for taking something unpleasant off his hands.

The girl stood like a lonely flower at the edge of the sanctuary. She did not join in the prayers offered up on her behalf, only kept her mind on the one last thing she had to do. And she knew just how to do it. As the prioress approached to lead her into the cloister, Marissa turned. Will and Ellie held their breath. Was she going to run out, screaming, at this late stage? But Marissa neither ran nor screamed. Making no noise, she walked swiftly to Kamil and plucked the knife that had nearly killed her out of his belt. She held it up high and it's reflection caught the white of her throat. An inarticulate cry escaped from deep within Will's breast. Marissa looked him straight in the eye, then grasped her corn-colored plait, pulled it out behind her, and hacked it off. It was a moment of such violent despair that Will almost doubled up with the shock. Marissa herself remained proudly upstanding and dropped her plait at his feet. It was only as it fell to the floor, stray strands floating free, that tears began to flow and they were not Marissa's, they were Ellie's. The familiar weight of her own auburn braid suddenly felt like a burden of guilt. *I should have done more for Marissa,* she wept, *I should have done more. I could have spoken up for her.* Ellie moved forward, wanting Marissa to see that she did care. It was what Marissa's mother would have done, Ellie was sure. But it was too late. Marissa neatly evaded Ellie; wordlessly handed Kamil back his knife; and, following a porter carrying the small chest that comprised all her worldly belongings, gave one small, almost imperceptible shake of her head, and was gone.

11

For hours Will and Ellie could not stop seeing and re-seeing that little head shake. It dug into their hearts like a needle no matter how many times they told themselves that Marissa would, eventually, be content. Surely she must be. "Even somebody as stubborn as Marissa can't be unhappy all her life," Ellie kept saying, and was angry when Elric said he was glad to see her go. "That's not the kind of thing any squire of mine should even think," Will told him, backing Ellie up. Elric began to argue but Will's face silenced him.

As Will oversaw the silver, stores, and horses being reloaded onto the barges, he almost asked Kamil about the triangular nick in Hosanna's neck, but Kamil was deep in conversation with Amal. Will watched them for some time. His discomfort at not being able to understand what they were saying was now acute, yet eventually he moved on without interrupting. Perhaps Amal would leave once they got to the imperial court. He hoped so. He had reason to be grateful to the old man but he didn't like him. Will found Hal instead and showed him the mark, and Hal asked Elric. Elric thought it was an insect sting. He had noticed it only after they had left the ship. Hal clicked his tongue. "You should have said something, Elric. That's a groom's job." Elric looked crestfallen even though Will made light of it. "Hal's right," he said, "but still, it's probably nothing." Yet he wondered, and wondered more when Shihab picked up a stone in the corner of her hoof as she fooled about and Kamil expertly extricated the stone with his knife. The shape of it, which Will had hardly noticed before, now sent a chill through him.

Early in the morning of the Feast of St. Vitalis, the barges sailed toward the emperor's Rhine border. Although he disguised it well, Kamil became agitated and pressed Amal more and more often for information about the soldiers who were to help him take the silver. Where were they? How many would there be? The whole scheme now seemed harebrained and when Ellie smiled at him and told him she was going to take Shihab off the barge for some exercise, and would he like to bring Sacramanta, Kamil felt dirty and dishonorable. Even the red horse seemed to look at him in a different way. Hosanna knew. Kamil was sure of it. Amal's whispered words began to chafe his nerves unbearably. What must be done should be done quickly. What was the delay?

A mile before the actual border, Will ordered the barges to stop and pull into the bank. Heavy rain was making visibility poor and the river treacherous. "We don't want to lose the silver at this last moment," he told the men as, amid a few protests, he made them roll the wagons off onto dry land and posted a large guard. He was angry with the mutterers. "Look, tomorrow the silver will no longer be our responsibility and most of you will be going back to Hartslove," he said. "You will all be rewarded." There was a small cheer and Ellie's heart gave a great thump. So here they were. Soon she and Will would see the king.

It was before dawn the following morning when they heard the unmistakable thumping and jingling that denoted many men riding in armor and full of purpose up the road toward the river. The Hartslove archers formed a protective barrier and Will was immediately on his guard. They were not at the border quite yet. Ordering the archers to kneel and prepare their bows and his soldiers to set their lances, he told Ellie to stay behind, then called for Kamil and Hal to flank him. The advancing soldiers were soon in sight and clearly wearing the colors of the Holy Roman Emperor. Still, Will did not relax. The emperor was impatient. Will had been told quite clearly that he would be in charge up to the border and they were not at the border yet. He strained his eyes for evidence of a trick but the banner displayed the imperial two-headed eagle, and when a trumpeter in a surcoat of the emperor's household came to a halt in front of Will and presented him with a rolled parchment bearing the emperor's seal, although Will could not read what was written he was reassured. The commander of the force, a thickset knight who rode heavily on his horse, waited courteously for Will to roll up the parchment again. Behind him, his men waited, too. Nobody spoke until Will, satisfied at last, sent Hal to order the Hartslove men to stand back for the new escort.

"My steward, who did the tally of the ransom and should count it out for the emperor, is dead," Will told the commander flatly. "You are welcome to count it yourself. The wagons are not yet loaded onto the barges."

The commander nodded. He did not seem bothered. "Traveling is full of trouble," was his only comment. Will did not recognize the man's accent but the imperial lands were broad and he could have come from anywhere. He turned around but what he saw stopped him in his tracks.

An imperial knight, clearly of some rank, was not talking to his own men or even to Kamil. He was talking to Amal and, from what Will could hear, he was speaking Arabic. Will frowned. What would an imperial knight have to say to an Arab servant? He looked for Kamil and saw him standing nearby. He could read nothing from the expression on his face. Will glanced about. The Hartslove men were chattering as they put away their weapons, only too happy to be relieved of their duties sooner than they thought. Elric was grinning from Dargent's saddle. Hal was holding Shihab. Behind them, the river ran dark. Will began to walk rapidly back, unable to control a terrible shiver running up his spine.

He had just reached Hal when the chattering of the Hartslove men was eclipsed by Elric's high voice. One of the German sergeants had deliberately tripped him and laughed as the boy sprawled in the mud. Livid, Elric scrambled to his feet and squared up, daring the sergeant to fight him. Ellie tried to intervene. The sergeant leered at her and said something in guttural French at which Ellie colored. That was enough. Bleating with fury, Elric launched himself at the German, fists and

106

elbows flailing. It should have been a joke, with tiny Elric against a man who could have swatted him aside like an insect, but the response Elric got was a sword drawn and leveled at his throat. Nothing daunted, Elric drew his own short sword and began to fence, now shouting all the rude words he knew. "Nobody insults Mistress Eleanor in my hearing and gets away with it. Apologize, frog-face! Apologize!" The Hartslove men laughed to start with. Little Elric! What a lion! But when the German did not put his sword down, the farrier spoke up. "Hey, stop that," he said, "he's just a boy, a cheeky boy, maybe, but you shouldn't have insulted Mistress Ellie." The German spat and insulted Ellie again, provoking Elric to yet more foolhardy heroics. Uncertain what to do, the farrier watched until the German suddenly lunged forward and drew blood from Elric's cheek. Then he drew his own sword. "You'll stop that right now," he ordered, pulling Elric away although the boy was still slicing and thrusting. To his horror, this did not pacify the German at all. Instead, he stamped his foot and immediately more than a dozen of his compatriots were in battle mode. Astounded, the Hartslove men grabbed their own arms, and seconds later a vicious scrap had broken out.

Will ran forward. "NO!" he cried. "What are you doing? This is no time to fight! Put away your swords! For the sake of God and King Richard, don't be so stupid." He gestured sharply for the German commander to control his men but the knight did nothing.

In less than a minute, the scrap had escalated into a full-scale riot. The Hartslove men were hesitant at first but the Germans were not. Swiftly, they spread out and with their infinitely superior numbers, surrounded the whole Hartslove contingent, including the ransom wagons. Yet still Will had not drawn his own weapon. Instead, increasingly frantic, he appealed to one imperial knight after another, pulling their surcoats. This was madness. It *could not* be the emperor's wish. But they brushed him off until Will found himself almost trampled underfoot, his voice completely drowned out. Now everybody was fighting, some with swords, some with fists. He could not see either the farrier or Elric. Knocked sideways and having lost all control, all Will could think of now was getting, as fast as he could, to Ellie.

Though the Hartslove men did their best, they had no chance. Many archers did not even have time to set more than one arrow before being cut down with axe and mace. Now it was kill or be killed, and Will found his sword in his hand, hardly aware that he had drawn it. Barging through, he caught a glimpse of Ellie avoiding the German captain by swinging herself onto Hosanna. Though he knew she could not hear him, he bellowed at her to flee. Where was Kamil? Surely he was nearer and could get to her?

There was no time for chivalry. Will fought as best he could, slashing, slicing, tripping people up and knocking them over whenever he saw an opportunity. He hardly realized that he was still shouting "stop" as the twin howls of those fighting and those dying engulfed him. He lunged and parried automatically, wielding his sword like a battering ram, but even now, when he could see the blood, feel the heat, and smell the fear, he could not believe it. He took on every comer who came near yet hesitated before plunging in the deathblow to men he could not consider enemies. There would be hell to pay for this. As one man fell at his feet, instead of finishing him off, Will broke his sword. It was only when the man came for Will again that Will impaled him. The feel of the man's flesh was hideous, quite different from the enemies Will had killed on crusade. This felt like killing his own kith and kin. Will felt sick.

It was only as he increasingly heard the cry "Allah Akbar," and, at last, found Kamil, that Will, with a shock more violent than the blow of a lance, began to understand. Kamil was not fighting. He was being restrained by two men and he was arguing not with the German commander, but with Amal. Amid all the physical tumult, it looked extraordinary. Had Kamil gone mad? But suddenly the word *traitor* rang around Will's head like a bell. *Traitor,* Kamil. Kamil, *traitor! I can't believe it. I won't believe it!* He kicked a German's feet from under him. But amid the heat, the chill he had felt when Kamil had taken the stone out of Shihab's foot and when Amal and Kamil had been conversing alone almost paralyzed him. This was no haphazard quarrel. It had been carefully provoked and Kamil had something to do with it. These German troops were not as they seemed.

Will's paralysis did not last. Instead, an anger grew within him such as he had never felt before. The hurt would come later. He let himself go completely. Now he roared as he fought, every muscle and every sinew filled with rage so pure that his sword, which only moments before he had wielded unwillingly, could hardly keep up with his ferocity. Nobody in his path survived. He wanted to reach Kamil but that would have to wait.

He still had to get to Ellie. At the edge of his vision, he saw Hal forced to abandon a panicking Shihab, and a bemused-looking Elric climbing onto Dargent. The boy had lost his sword but used the horse as a battering ram. Though Will could hardly bear to think of Elric in the midst of this, he could not help him. Dear, brave, impetuous Elric! If only he had not rushed in. But how could Will blame him? Nobody who insulted Ellie should get away with it. He just saw Elric reach down for Hal's arm and Hal's head rising up through a sea of bloody weapons before both disappeared. At least Hal and Elric were together. It was small comfort but the only one on offer.

He could see that Ellie was still on Hosanna and that despite the horse's best efforts as he reared, kicked, and struck out on all sides, he was losing. Each time he shook off one enemy, another took his place. An endless supply of devilish hands were grasping at him. Snarling, Will climbed onto a wagon, then leaped from his perch using bodies and heads as a jagged human carpet in his efforts to reach them. It could never have worked but even as Will sank, he carried on clawing his way through, calling out Ellie's name and urging Hosanna to stand his ground. Then he heard shouting and as if by a miracle the crowd parted before him. He had just a second to look up before something heavy hit the back of his head and everything was black.

It was pain that dragged Will back into consciousness. He was sure there was somebody felling a tree in his skull. When, eventually, he opened his eyes, he could see nothing and, for a terrifying minute, thought he had gone blind. But he had not. Pressure on his forehead told him that he had been thrown onto his front into a cart and it was not only pain that prevented him from moving. He had been stripped of his armor and his arms and legs were shackled together. The cart was not moving fast but every jolt seemed to find new places to bruise for Will's only cushion was the pool of blood in which he was lying. For several minutes he had no coherent thoughts at all until, inside his battered head, the world took shape again. Ellie! Oh dear God! What had they done to Ellie? At once he began to struggle though his throat was burning and he began to choke. Then, as if from very far away, he heard Ellie speak.

"Will, Will," she was repeating, her voice a tiny croak. "Oh, thank God. I thought you were dead, too." She strained toward him. "I can't reach you, Will, I can't reach you," she cried, her voice stronger as she beat her own shackled hands against the side of the cart, "and I haven't anything to help you. They're all dead, Will. Dead. There were just piles of bodies. Piles and piles of bodies. I've never seen bodies like that. How can people do it? They wanted to kill us all." She shook so hard that her chains rattled. "Why did they do that, Will? We brought the ransom. We did everything right. Why did they do that?"

Will scraped his cheeks on the planks as he tried to turn his head to see her. At first his voice wouldn't work at all. He could feel his own blood on his tongue. But he was desperate to speak. "Kamil," he tried to say it clearly. "Kamil."

Ellie heard what he was saying but misunderstood him. "I didn't see Kamil's body," she told him, leaning forward as far as she could. "He must have escaped. He'll come and help us, Will. I know he will." Her voice rose with her certainty.

Will tried to shake his head. "Not help—with them."

"With whom?"

"Soldiers. Not emperor's troops. Trick. Must be Saracen men."

Ellie almost wanted to laugh. The bang on his head had made Will mad. If Kamil was with anybody, he was with them. He loved them in his way. Ellie knew that as well as she knew anything. The idea that Kamil could be behind such a massacre was as ludicrous as believing that Will had engineered it himself. "Not Kamil, Will," she said gently. "Not Kamil."

In the gloom, Will could see Ellie's face shining white but she could not see his, for it was stained dark. His silence was more frightening to Ellie than any words. "No, no, Will. What's wrong with you? What's happened to you? It's wicked to accuse Kamil. He's a man of honor. How many times have you told me that? How can you accuse him, of all people, of treachery?"

For a few moments Will wanted to believe that he deserved Ellie's scorn. Anything would be better than the truth. But the vision he still had of Kamil arguing was too vivid. He knew it was real, as real as the agony in his legs. He made a huge effort to speak clearly. "It's true, Ellie. I saw him just before the attack. Him and Amal."

"Amal? But Amal's just a servant." Ellie's voice grew louder as her nerves began to jump like firecrackers. "I know we didn't like him to start with but he's just a servant, Will. Just a servant." Her eyes seemed to take over the whole of her face as her voice petered out. She was desperately searching her memory for something to show that Will was wrong. But in all the terrible images of the past hour that she could conjure up, she realized that none contained Kamil. He had not come to rescue her. He had not gone to rescue anybody.

"They must have arranged the thing between them." Will knew that she was listening now. "Kamil knew exactly where we would be and how many of us there were." Will was glad of the anger beginning to burn through him again and he fed it. "I wonder when he first began to plan this. I reckon he must have sent for Amal as soon as he knew that part of the ransom was to be delivered by me. They must have organized it together. All for some poxy silver." Will wanted to spit. "I thought Kamil was a better man than that."

Still Ellie would not accept it. "But Hosanna loves Kamil," she said as if that settled the matter.

"Hosanna can be wrong."

Ellie had never heard Will's voice sound so bleak. Everything he had ever believed in seemed to be disintegrating.

"No, Will. No." She so wished she could get to him, to shake some sense back into him. "I can believe bad things of Amal. But Kamil? I just can't."

Will gave a sudden thrust of his boots. It was the only gesture he could make. "Can't or won't, Ellie?"

There was a world of despair in his question. Ellie hunched up. "Can't," she whispered.

"Well, you'd better," Will said. "Maybe I know why Hosanna has been friendly to Kamil. Hosanna has a scar on his neck."

"What does that prove?"

Will spoke slowly. "The little triangular scar between Marissa's ribs is exactly the same. They were both made by Kamil's knife. I think Kamil has been drugging Hosanna."

Ellie had to repeat this to herself before her brain would allow her to understand it. "But if Kamil hates Hosanna enough to do that, he must hate us, too. So why are we here, in this wagon?" she burst out, clinging to her certainties even as they cracked like eggs. "Why are we not dead, like everybody else?"

"He has other plans for us," Will said flatly. "Ransom for you, probably. I don't know what for me. Maybe the same. Or maybe I am to be a slave to Kamil, the new Sultan of All the Saracens." He made the title sound ridiculous.

"I won't believe it," Ellie whispered. "I won't believe it until Kamil tells me himself."

Will shut his eyes.

Ellie did not have long to wait. In the early afternoon, the wagon halted in a clearing and the back was thrown open. As the prisoners blinked in the glitter of a heatless sun, their chains were undone and they were hustled out to find themselves no longer by the Rhine but by a smaller river with the ransom wagons once again being loaded onto barges. Now, although their captors were still wearing imperial uniforms, they could hear more languages than just German and Arabic. It seemed to Will that Kamil had drawn supporters from all corners of the world. This must have taken more than just a few weeks to organize. Maybe Kamil had begun sending messages from Hartslove immediately after his arrival all those months ago. Maybe, all the time he had been under Will's roof, he had been plotting. Maybe, maybe. Will looked back on everything they had done together, every gesture, every friendly glance, and saw it all through the distorting prism of the moment.

He turned to Ellie only to find her transfixed by a vision neither of them would ever forget. Blowing steam into chilled air was Hosanna, and in his saddle Kamil sat giving orders to the bargemen. As if sleepwalking Ellie began to move toward him. Surely now Kamil would explain why this was all a mistake or a terrible misunderstanding. Unable to help herself she cried out to him. "Kamil! Kamil!" Her cry contained everything she had ever believed about friendship, faith, honor, and love and it struck Kamil, already reeling from the events of the morning though he dared not show it, like a hammer blow. It told him at once that Ellie would never understand, that he had stabbed her not in the back but in the eyes and had stabbed her so hard that the wound would never truly heal. Yet even now he knew she was still hoping. Even now, she would still listen if he ran to her. He could see her holding her breath, still believing in him. But he was in too deep and instead, with a groan he thought the whole world must hear, he turned away.

At once Ellie felt something within her shrivel. Her voice deserted her and a vice gripped her stomach. She kept her feet to avoid the indignity of falling but inside she could feel herself shattering.

12

Hours later, Kamil finally sat down to face the fact that his dreams and plans had turned into a chaotic nightmare. Amal had promised him a smooth handover and even now could not explain what had gone wrong. After the dead had been buried, Kamil had shaken the old man like a rat, again and again demanding answers. But what use were answers now? Good Hartslove men were dead. Will could not look at him without hatred and Ellie—Kamil could not think of her at all.

Moreover, Kamil was now boxed into a corner. Amal continued to insist that the quarrel had been an accident, some ill-judged teasing that had got out of hand and then, in front of the listening men, had questioned whether Kamil minded the deaths of Christians more than the deaths of his own people. When Kamil had not answered, the soldiers had begun to whisper and Kamil had had to ride Hosanna, and keep Will and Ellie in chains, to prove himself to them.

Amal had ridden with him, ever the helpful servant. Of course Kamil could mourn the Hartslove men in private, he murmured, and it was right that he should, for some had been his friends. But in public he was now a Saracen leader and must act like one since this was the role he had chosen. What was more—Amal's voice buzzed like a wasp—Kamil must remember that not only his own future but the future of the dispossessed and unhappy Muslims in the Holy Land, depended on him. His people were waiting for both the silver and for Kamil. Amal let that sink in before his buzzing began again. "If you lose the confidence of these soldiers, you know, there will be further suffering. You must show your men"—he carefully stressed the "your"—"that you have not been tainted after months of living in a Christian household. If you do not convince these soldiers that you are a true believer, they will turn first on you and then on the earl and Mistress Ellie."

Amal's words were still hissing in Kamil's head and Kamil knew they were true. He must show nothing of what he felt. Perhaps, in time, when he was leading his people to victory, this terrible pain would diminish.

From the deep shadows Amal watched him with pity in his heart before shaking himself. He could not afford pity. So he concentrated only on drumming into the soldiers that if Kamil suspected they were in the pay of the Old Man before the Old Man chose to reveal this himself, they would be punished in a way that would make them wish they had never been born. Kamil must not get a whisper of the real spider at the heart of this web.

Kamil sensed Amal watching him and although he could hardly bring himself to speak to him, he needed him. Only Amal could understand how important it was to repeat and repeat that it was not the task itself that was wrong, only that carrying it out had been mishandled. In fact, only Amal could provide any balm at all, for Kamil had cut himself off from everybody else.

The following morning, unrested, Kamil went out on Hosanna to reconnoiter the route. It was a long way to the ship on the south coast and Kamil wanted to waste no time. When he returned, Will and Ellie were standing outside their prison wagon, their feet shackled once again. Kamil dismounted and took Hosanna over to them. Will ignored Kamil and hobbled so close to his horse that he could feel the nerves under the skin.

Ellie could not remain silent. Although all hope had really long since left her, she tried just once more. "It can't be as it seems," she said, wondering how she spoke so calmly. "It's just a mistake, Kamil, isn't it?"

Kamil looked at her gravely. The agony of his parents' deaths all those years ago had nearly crippled him but this agony was different. He felt as if he had swallowed a stone. "It is as it seems," he said quietly. There seemed nothing else to say. "I'm a Saracen. The ransom collected for King Richard could never be delivered to men who would use it to kill my people. I am to deliver it elsewhere."

Ellie heard him but all the while she stared at him as if he were a stranger. Should she have noticed something before, she wondered, in his face? She had only seen it as a face full of sadness and mystery. But had the mystery always been leading to nothing more than this betrayal? Had it been written there and she had just been too blind to see it? She stared harder. Could she see it now? But search as she did, she could not. She could see nothing except Kamil's habitually direct gaze and the familiar tautness lurking in the curve of his lips. Her anger was suddenly marbled with appalling grief. She had thought of Kamil almost as a brother, the kind of brother you loved, even if you never really knew him. She broke away, falling over her shackles as she too made for Hosanna. Kamil shut his eyes. When he opened them, Ellie was also crushed against the red horse. They cast a solid shadow, Hosanna, Will, and Ellie, with no crack of daylight between them. It seemed to say everything that needed to be said and Kamil began to walk away.

Will called him back. "What is to happen to us?" He was imperious, indicating he wanted only a minimal reply. He would never again, he vowed, speak to Kamil as if he knew him. Surely even Hosanna would reject Kamil now?

"It was never the intention to bring you with us," Kamil said in a voice flat and dry. "You were to be left unharmed but in such a way that the emperor's real troops, when they came, would know that you were not complicit in the theft. That all went wrong in the fighting. We could not leave you safely and now we must keep you with us until the ransom is delivered to Saracen ships. If I let you go, I think you will lead the imperial troops to us. That's what I would do in your place." He hesitated. Amal and his men were listening. "And if the imperial troops do catch up to us, we can use you to make a bargain. Your horses, Hosanna and Shihab"—only at the mention of Hosanna's name did Will's eyes flicker—"will be returned to you when the ship is loaded at the coast. Once we have sailed, you'll be free to ride where you will." Kamil expected no gratitude for this information and he received none.

Will steeled himself. "Did you see what became of Hal and Elric?" He had to know.

"No. I'm sorry."

"Can I ride to the coast?"

"I can't allow it, Will," Kamil said, "because if you try to escape, my men will be obliged to come after you. You and Ellie must travel in a wagon. But I promise the horses will be well looked after."

Will had little choice but to hand Hosanna over and for a brief second, he and Kamil held the red horse together. Then Will let go and had to watch Hosanna walking obediently away. It was hard to understand why the horse did not object and Will put it down to some spell woven by Amal. Ellie could offer no explanation at all. Nor, as they were pushed back into their prison, did she notice that the leather thong of the pouch at her belt broke, tipping her green jasper necklace into the mud. Amal saw and went to pick it up but as he passed by, he could feel Ellie's hatred as much as if she had spat at him and just left it where it lay. When Ellie finally noticed her loss, her heart sank further than she thought possible.

Using the river network as best he could, Kamil pushed south as fast as the wagons could go. They had hundreds of miles to cover and winter had set in. To begin with, he daily expected to find the rutted roads blocked as the real imperial soldiers realized the trick that had been played on them. But it did not happen. This disconcerted Kamil, who sent scouts out into the foggy dawns to scour the valleys and wooded hilltops. The emperor surely cared more about the ransom than just to let it go. However the best scouts returned having had no sight of any large group of soldiers flying the imperial pennant and with no rumors of any rippling through the village markets. Kamil found this hard to believe but let it pass as he pressed on, right away from the Rhine, over which the emperor would surely be keeping watch, heading in due course for Rhone. Yet even though he commandeered barges at will, throwing money at merchants whose manners were as rough as their dialects, the route south was not easy, particularly when they had to go by road and the land broke and rose in stiff climbs before them. Nevertheless the men, fresh and well disciplined, made good time, setting their shoulders to the carts when the horses strained and remaining reasonably cheerful even through squally weather and endless gray, finger-chilling hours in the saddle. Days turned into weeks. The air was crisper and sometimes even pleasant but now Kamil found it harder and harder to cajole weary men and reluctant animals down unmade tracks in desolate forests, across swollen streams with treacherous banks, and below hilltop towns over whose walls men peered in an unfriendly fashion. Sometimes the road was crowded with shivering pilgrims returning from visiting the shrines of saints. Huddled in cloaks they pushed resentfully against the wagons until Kamil and Amal had to brandish their swords to get them away.

Will could not be sorry that the journey was hard. Every day he spent peering out of the wagon, whether on the road or on the river, praying to see a glint of armor. Surely, if somebody had survived, they would even now be leading a rescue party. However there was no sign of anybody and after a fortnight Will gave up hoping.

As they drew farther away from the imperial lands,

the soldiers removed the emperor's livery and dressed as European merchants and merchants' clerks. Though a few spoke Arabic, many carried on speaking German and Kamil was glad, for this made them less conspicuous, it being common to hear German in these southern parts. When they passed too close to busy castles, he ordered the three ransom wagons to separate, then meet again, thus courting less attention. Kamil allowed no rest days and utilized all the hours of light, pushing well into the dusk, not only worried about attack but hating every moment Will and Ellie spent in chains.

Each evening when Amal came to pray with him Kamil put away his heartache and spoke only of how best the silver might be used when they got it home. Afterward he would read the Koran. Hunched into a thick blanket either by Hosanna or in his wagon, he sometimes managed to cease thinking about anything in his past or his present and look only to his future.

Under the furs provided to warm them, Will and Ellie, too, thought about the future, but only the immediate future, spending dreary hours working out how long it would take them to get back to the imperial court, and to Richard, once they were eventually released. Sometimes they were allowed to walk and eventually Kamil relented and even allowed them to ride, provided the horses were led. They did not complain of their treatment but at night, in his dreams, Will shouted and raged while Ellie lay sleepless.

Yet, it was strange. Once Will was allowed back onto Hosanna and saw Kamil praying and carrying out his duties as a leader with quiet authority, it became impossible not to understand a little of his former friend's motivation. Understanding was certainly not approving. Yet Will's experiences on crusade meant that he knew something of being caught up in a cause so important that you would sacrifice everything for it. When he had been in the Holy Land he himself would have done anything in the name of his God and his king. Now Kamil was simply doing the same. Will resented his understanding but he could not deny it.

It was Ellie who could not bear even to think of Kamil. If she found him looking in their direction as they walked or rode she would demand to return to the wagon. Once, in the middle of the night, she peered out and saw him standing in the moonlight with Hosanna. The red horse's head was low and Kamil was leaning with his face pressed against the chestnut withers. Ellie wanted to throw something, anything, to get Hosanna to pull away from Kamil and despised herself that, instead, she simply watched as Hosanna raised his head and turned, shielding Kamil with his mane. It was a gesture not so much of comfort as of protection and Ellie retreated as if stung. She did not want to see that. Furious with herself, she lay down and dug her nails into her palm as a punishment. The next day, she railed against Kamil to Will. He had hypnotized the horse. How else could Hosanna still bear to be near him? Will tried to explain some of his own feelings, which would, in turn, explain Hosanna's, but Ellie wouldn't listen.

After six grueling weeks, they gained the hospitable lower reaches of the Rhone, and the barges sped easily along. By the week before Christmas, they could see the sea. Just as they reached the estuary however, Kamil, directed by Amal, ordered the ransom wagons be dragged from the barges and harnessed up once more. The ship would be waiting not in one of the ports, but in a less conspicuous inlet. The wagoners cursed and swore as the soldiers hacked routes down paths so stony that the puffing carthorses stumbled and often fell. When two lamed themselves badly enough to be left behind, the wagoners almost mutinied. But Kamil persuaded them to keep going and, soon enough, mud gave way to meadow, which, in turn, gave way to chalk. At the cliffs, the pack animals, squatting onto their haunches, began the hazardous process of slithering down to the shingle below. The soldiers cheered as they found caves offering shelter. They would wait in these until Saracen sails appeared.

After the immense effort he had made to get the ransom safely to the coast, Kamil was at first glad to rest bones weary from constant movement. The caves, though damp and cold, were spacious and in them it was possible to light inconspicuous fires and hide the ransom. Will and Ellie were loosely shackled near the horses and after Kamil had made sure that they were as comfortable as possible, he slept, awaking rested and slightly more at peace. Soon this would be over. After a day of doing nothing, however, with no sign of a ship, he was nervy. After two, he grew anxious. The men seemed less respectful here and sometimes he saw a few conversing animatedly with Amal, conversations that came to an abrupt halt when he approached. When he enquired as to their concerns, Amal just gave a troubled smile and said that they were impatient to get home.

Will too was impatient. "Where are your great ships?" he demanded contemptuously when Kamil came into the cave to check the ransom. He could not resist, just wanting to get away from Kamil and away from his own confusion. "Are you sure your people really want you back? Perhaps they will just leave you here."

Kamil tried to blank out Will's anger and did not look at Ellie at all, for he did not want to see how her face had become like that of a statue—no, harder even than that. It was bitter to him to know that he would never again see that open and welcoming smile or hear any delight in either her voice or Will's. He was taking much needed treasure to his own people but he had destroyed treasure of his own.

It was of enormous comfort to Kamil, and not a little surprise, to find that Hosanna continued to bear no resentment. "Perhaps you alone really understand why I have to do this," he murmured as he ran his hands over ribs growing more pronounced, for, while the people were sheltered, food for the animals was short down here. "When the ships have sailed, red horse, bear Will safely back to Hartslove and remember me kindly sometimes." He caressed Hosanna again and again, warmed by the notion that the horse seemed as reluctant to let him go as Kamil was to leave him. Holding onto Kamil's sleeve with more intensity and determination than usual, Hosanna would not open his teeth when Kamil tickled his lips and when Kamil eventually prized himself away, he left a small scrap of cloth behind.

On the third day, just as dusk was falling, Amal spotted something on the horizon and the men lined up along the wide beach, shielding their eyes as they tried to make out whether this was, indeed, their relief. There was excited chatter as a slim ship eventually slid close in under the cliffs, testing the depth all the way. The pennants were undistinguished, deliberately open to misinterpretation, but as the galley eased into the safety of the inlet, the watchers saw splashes in the ship's wake as if giant, faintly discolored snowballs were being hurled from the deck into the water.

It took some time to realize that these were not snowballs but pigs. The wretched animals had been kept on deck during the long journey to disguise the ship's Saracen origins, for only Christian ships tolerated pigs and, now that disguise was no longer needed, they were being tossed overboard to a great chorus of bellowing squeals and piteous shrilling snorts. Like a gaggle of chubby babies, they desperately paddled about, their snouts high in the air, imploring Heaven to help them to find solid ground. Heaven did not hear them. As they succumbed, one by one, to exhaustion and the freezing water, their cries became weak gurgles and finally just air bubbles. When even the air bubbles vanished, the corpse would disappear for a moment before bobbing up again and floating back toward the ship as if determined to take some kind of revenge. Then the Saracen oarsmen, disgusted, would push the dead pigs away. However, it was not so easy in the current and as the ship anchored offshore, it was soon surrounded by small hillocks of mottled pink flesh. Ellie, never moved by the annual slaughter of the Hartslove swine, had not seen anything quite like this. Revolted, she clapped her hands over her ears to block out the last feeble cries. In her head she could hear Old Nurse deploring the pigs' watery deaths as a waste of food, but even Old Nurse would have found the sight of the animals washing about in the tide horrible. Ellie turned to Will in her distress but Will was not looking at either the ships or the pigs. He was looking at Kamil.

Standing at the end of a jag of rock sloping out into the bay, Kamil was watching a small boat being lowered from the ship's stern. The boat contained five people, three passengers and two oarsmen, and was soon heading for the beach. Kamil was staring at only one of the passengers, and as he stared a trembling began, right in his core. It was just a tiny thing at first, a kind of vibration, but the vibration took on such force that he felt as if he was caught up in an earthquake created just for him. His arms crossed over his chest and he found it difficult to see. Blindly, he began to turn, almost slipped, but then recovered enough to break into a faltering run back along the rocks to the shore.

Amal's breath came quickly. Now that the final moment of revelation had arrived he felt no triumph. Indeed, never had he felt so old as when he watched Kamil's entire world disintegrate and the young man's proud bearing collapse. Nevertheless Amal stood as upright as he was able, kept on his feet by the knowledge that the Old Man would be watching him. He stood his ground as Kamil ran toward him. Only his tongue moved, flickering over dry lips.

At first Kamil could hardly get a word out and when words did come, they were a jumble of Arabic and Norman French. The color, he babbled, the color. Could Amal see the color? Though the clothes of the passengers in the boat were perfectly ordinary, their beards were dyed a strange shade of red, not deep red like Hosanna, but a pale kind of crimson. Could Amal see that? Could he also see that the color of their beards clashed against the color of the oranges that a small, round man with a jeweled turban on his head was juggling? "Amal, Amal," Kamil cried finally, "do you not know who it is?" He peered back toward the rowboat through a fog of incredulity. It could not be. Yet it was. He may have met the Old Man only once before, but like the Old Man himself, he had never forgotten it and prayed such a meeting would never happen again. Yet now the Old Man was here, arriving at this lonely beach as if expected. The fog began to clear as Kamil looked at Amal. He took hold of the old man's arm and found no resistance. He looked into his eyes and found no shock. Kamil shook his head and stumbled backward. "No, Amal, no. Tell me this is not your doing, you with your prayers and your great schemes. Tell me it isn't. Oh, please tell me." He stumbled forward again. "Tell me I have not done everything I have done for— for—" Kamil could not bring himself to name the Old Man. He grabbed the old spy, then hurled him away, frightened he might snap him in two.

Amal did not protest at his rough treatment, and in Amal's silence Kamil finally saw what a dupe he had been, seduced by easy admiration and childish visions of his own importance, visions now dissolving like sandcastles in the tide. What a dirty, dirty trick. Why had he not remembered that real saviors were humble men of courage and discernment, not men like him who dreamed of riding through the desert like heroes of myth and legend? He wanted to tear not at Amal but at himself, to slash a knife through his veins. Yet he did nothing. He simply stood in place because behind Amal, in the mouth of the cave, hovered Will and Ellie and at the sight of them, at the thought of what the Old Man might want to do to them, Kamil was turned to stone.

As soon as he could, Amal tried to slip away. He could already hear the oarsmen calling for the soldiers on the beach to throw ropes. But Kamil grasped him as he brushed past.

"What's this, Amal?" Kamil forced himself to sound reasonable in these last few moments before the Old Man took complete control. Already Amal's eyes were veiled but Kamil had to try. "You told me that we were going to use King Richard's ransom to help our people in Palestine and to drive the infidel from our lands. Now I see that the man who has really come to collect the ransom has no interest in that at all. Yet that is for your conscience to deal with. But I must ask just one thing. Is it really for this that we have abused Will de Granville's hospitality and scattered Hartslove blood in the dirt? Is it for this that Will and Ellie are prisoners?" Amal's mouth twisted into a grotesque smile for he could see the Old Man getting out of the boat. This was too much for Kamil. He swayed and broke down. "Oh, what have I done?" he cried out. "How could I have been taken in by somebody like you? How could I have listened to you and not seen? Oh, how clever you must think you are, coming to England with your gifts and your holy sentiments when all the time you are just the miserable slave of a murderer and a robber. Curse you and the Old Man! I hope the Christian silver destroys you all." Kamil lunged forward, raking his hands round Amal's scraggy neck before forcing them back to his sides and looking Amal full in the eyes instead. A great well of bitterness broke. "Perhaps some of this silver is even destined for your pockets. How much did the Old Man pay you? How much was I worth?" He sagged.

Amal squinted up at Kamil, his face working furiously to hide his emotions, and his bones sticking out like prickles. "I do my master's bidding. That is reward enough. This is more your doing than mine. My master thought of you as a son and you let him down." He spoke faster and faster as the Old Man pattered toward them across the sand. "The Old Man is like a falcon, Kamil. If he sees a rabbit and the rabbit gets away, he hovers above, a speck in the sky, until the rabbit comes out to play again. Then—" Amal banged his right fist into his left palm, bruising his knuckles. "This time, you are the rabbit."

Kamil ignored all this and concentrated only on one request. "Amal," he implored, "I will take what's coming, but Will and Ellie have no part in this quarrel. If you do nothing else in your miserable life, let them go. Hosanna and Shihab can be ready in seconds. Do that, Amal, and Allah will bless you. Give Will and Ellie their horses and let them go free. It's the right thing to do. You know that."

Amal's palms began to sweat. "Oh, no," he replied, keeping his tone conversational for as the Old Man drew nearer and nearer he felt his servitude winding itself about him like a shroud. Compared to the Old Man, Kamil was a fly and Will and Ellie like grains of dust. "Alas, I cannot let them go. The Old Man wants so much to meet them and he has come such a long way."

Kamil opened his mouth, but a tinkling laugh made

him shut it again. The Old Man had arrived. "My faithful servant," he said, patting Amal's shoulder, "you have done gallant service and I shall reward you as only I know how." He twinkled and scraped his nails down Amal's arm, leaving five small scratches. The scratches split the skin but Amal knew better than to wince. The Old Man tiptoed around to stand directly in front of Kamil, his beard shining where it had been heavily oiled. "Well now," he said, "this meeting is a long-awaited pleasure, Kamil. I cannot tell you how much I have looked forward to it." He looked up into Kamil's face, then, monstrously, he winked.

13

Hundreds of miles to the north, two horses were trotting very close together, their riders deep in conversation. At least one rider was talking and the other had not much choice but to listen. Elric had scarcely paused to draw breath for hours and even Hal's patience was wearing a little thin. Yet he could hardly be cross. Elric had, after all, saved his life, parrying sword thrusts and blows as best he could as he pulled Hal up behind him instead of fleeing as he must have so badly wanted to do. Both were injured by the time Dargent had begun to gallop aimlessly away from the ambush with the last of the terrified pack animals. They did not see Will being knocked unconscious and by the time Hal fell off, dragging Elric with him, they were several miles from the battle scene and quite alone, deserted even by the loose horses.

They had lain overnight in the grass until Hal had felt his legs being pulled and kicked out in response. "Ouch!" came a voice from above and, opening his eyes, he found himself staring at the familiar mop of brown hair. Elric was trying, very inexpertly, to bind a wound in Hal's leg. "It's not too bad," Elric said. Hal pulled himself up. His head was thick and muzzy and he could remember almost nothing. Elric, white and his voice tense, had to repeat himself several times. "We must get back on Dargent and find them. That's what we've got to do, Hal." The boy's eyes were glazed. These new blows to the head, added to his old ones, had set him back.

"Dargent?" Hal, still bemused, could taste blood on his tongue.

"Dargent's here. He's fine. Can you mount by yourself? We MUST go back."

Hal's head began to clear although he could not yet understand what had happened. It seemed easier to agree. "Yes," he said automatically. "We must."

Elric helped to haul him into the saddle, but it was only after Dargent had jolted along for a good few miles that Hal began to remember what had happened. Then he turned as white as Elric.

It took longer to get back to the ambush spot than they thought for they had no idea where they were, but at last they arrived at the river and followed it up to where they had camped. There they found nothing living at all and Elric, finally, broke down. "It's my fault," he sobbed, "my fault. That man, he insulted Mistress Ellie but I shouldn't have drawn my sword. They're all dead because of me."

Hal was too shocked to offer any comfort at first and, as memory piled in upon memory, he had to confront his own crippling guilt. "I left the battle scene with Will and Ellie still in danger." He slumped to his knees in front of the mass grave Kamil had caused to be dug. "What sort of a squire am I? I should have died here with all the others." He could not at this moment think about how the fighting had broken out. All that mattered was that Will and Ellie were almost certainly either dead or captive, and Hosanna gone. He thought hard. The emperor's soldiers—and Hal had no reason to believe that they were not—would surely not leave Will and Ellie alive? Much better if they were dead and then the emperor could spin what tale he wanted about the slaughter. He could even blame Will, so that his own troops would be completely innocent. Hal felt dead himself.

However after a long while, Elric's tears disturbed him. The boy was still his responsibility and he got up and put his arm round Elric's shoulders. "We both failed them," he said simply. "I don't know how we will ever get over it. We can't stay here, though." He whistled to Dargent, who was grazing nearby.

"Do you think they really are dead?" Elric clung to him.

"I think so," Hal could only whisper.

"Where shall we go?" wept Elric.

Hal thought for a moment, trying to keep his composure. "We ought to go home," he said doubtfully, "to tell them."

Elric clung to him again. The thought of Old Nurse's face was unbearable. "No," he cried, "we should at least try and find Hosanna and Sacramenta. Surely they can't be dead, too? We must find them. Isn't that what Will would want us to do? And what about the silver?"

Hal frowned. He knew he should care about the silver.

All his training told him that matters of state were more important than personal losses. But he could not care. He did, however, care very much about Hosanna and Sacramenta. He looked about him. The cart tracks were still visible. Hitching Elric onto Dargent, he climbed on himself. Elric was right. They should find the horses. It was the least they could do.

If Dargent found carrying the two of them hard, he did not object. They dismounted often to try and tease out the ransom cart tracks from others. Hal was puzzled greatly by the southerly direction the ransom seemed to be taking for surely the imperial troops should be heading east. At the river, when the cart tracks disappeared entirely, they had to guess which way to go. Neither Hal nor Elric thought about Kamil, presuming him dead with Will, or about Shihab. They thought only of Hosanna and Sacramenta and Hal had a hard job keeping Elric from despairing self-reproach.

It was through luck on the third day that they found Ellie's necklace. Lying down for the night having stolen rabbits from peasant traps, Elric shifted and groaned until Hal suggested they move to somewhere more comfortable. Elric mumbled and put his hand under his back to pull out what he thought was a stone and tossed it away. It landed under Dargent's saddle and, in the thin dawn light, it would have gone unnoticed except that the leather thong caught on the stirrup and suddenly, in front of Hal's eyes, the green jasper trickled out in a glowing stream. Hal was not quick enough to catch it, but Elric was. It dropped into his filthy hands and at once the boy began to jabber. "God in Heaven, Hal, it's Mistress Ellie's necklace! And here in this place! She must be alive! The men who've got the silver must have taken her with them."

But Hal could not believe it. "They've stolen it from her," he said, but he quickly finished saddling Dargent.

Elric refused, point-blank, to accept that. "This necklace is full of luck," he declared confidently, his old chirpiness returning fast. "If we found it, it's a sign. I just know it, Hal. I think at least Mistress Ellie is alive. Perhaps Will, too."

Hal did not dare believe it, but he didn't want to knock Elric back. "What's the necklace telling us to do, then?" he asked gently, forbidding himself really to truly share Elric's hopes. "Should we go on following the tracks or not?"

"Yes, follow them," said Elric. "Come on."

Hal frowned but did not refuse.

But the tracks kept on disappearing and when they asked people they met if they had seen a cavalcade of heavily armed men surrounding wagons, the people shrugged, unable to understand Norman French and not very impressed with two ragged creatures on an increasingly ragged horse. Deeper and deeper into unfamiliar country they went, crossing borders unknowingly and occasionally hiding from men wearing strange armor and flying unknown pennants. The forests seemed thick and endless and nothing about them inspired confidence. Once, some jobbing stonemasons told them, in a gutteral dialect they could just about grasp, that wagons had gone south, and for a week they rode faster, expecting every day to see Hosanna's red tail or, by some miracle, to hear Will's or Ellie's voice. But most of the time they both knew they were going around in bigger and bigger circles though neither said a word about that. At night Hal stared at the stars as if they could help him but they never did.

After a month of utter frustration, even Elric's optimism was fading and one morning, Hal saddled Dargent and turned the horse to the North. Elric argued, as was his habit, but though Hal listened, he was not deflected. This was no good. As they made their way slowly back along roads they had already traveled, Elric fell silent. Only in the evenings, as he held fiercely on to Ellie's necklace, did he tell Hal that he knew, he just knew, all would be well. They had not found the necklace for nothing. Hal let him prattle but he himself felt leaden as he sat in front of their makeshift fire trying to think, trying to work out what Will would do in his place. Never did he come up with the same answer twice. He needed somebody else to talk to.

Hal did not tell Elric at once that they were going to Arnhem to tell Marissa what had happened, and to see if the nuns had heard any news, for convents were hotbeds of gossip, and by the time Elric realized, and objected violently, Hal was exhausted enough to be sharp. "At the very least the nuns will give us another horse," he snapped, "and maybe they know something. Nobody may care about dead Hartslove men but if Richard's ransom has gone missing they'll care about that."

"Why do we have to go to Marissa's convent, though?" Elric muttered furiously. He couldn't bear the thought of her triumph when she knew the trouble he had caused. He pressed Ellie's necklace into his palms. "She'll just shout."

"If Will and Ellie are dead, she has to know, and it's

our duty to tell her," Hal retorted. "And if, as you believe, Will and Ellie are alive, then perhaps we'll learn something that might be helpful. Why did the ransom seem to go south, for instance, when we know Richard is at Speyer? I don't know anything anymore, nor do you. We need to talk to other people, preferably people whose language we can understand."

Their arrival at Arnhem was not a happy one. Marissa, pale and very thin under her ugly habit of undyed wool and with her short hair still shocking, was astonished, then devastated to see them. As Hal told his tale she would not look at Elric, which crushed and humiliated the boy more than any shouting. She spoke exclusively to Hal, begging for every detail, gazing at Ellie's necklace with dread. She did not wait until Hal had finished before jumping up, her distress making her mind very clear. "The nuns will give us horses. If Will is dead, we must get to Richard—or at least you and I must, Hal—" She glared dismissively at Elric. "We can't tell what's happened to the ransom but suppose it's been stolen?" Hal gave a small exclamation. It was possible, of course, but stolen by the imperial soldiers? It made no sense. Marissa did not stop, however. "Richard and the emperor must know that Will had nothing to do with it," she said, pacing up and down. She couldn't bear the idea of Will's name being dragged through the mud any more than she could bear the thought that despite the fact that she had remained in the convent, God had sent down this appalling punishment. "And then we've got to look for Hosanna and not give up, ever, until we find him. Never, you understand? Never."

She ran to the prioress but though she begged and pleaded the prioress would not allow her to leave. The refusal was calm and measured and she looked to Hal to uphold her against Marissa's hysterical rage. No nun from St. Martin's could go rampaging around the country when there were two perfectly good men to perform such a duty. At this Hal looked very uncomfortable and Elric sat up a little straighter. It was enough. Marissa turned on the boy with the full force of her scalding grief and frustration. She hated him. He was wicked and dangerous. What was more—she chose her insults with cruel care—he lacked all the qualities necessary to be a knight like Will. Even Kamil, a foreigner, had been a better friend to Hartslove. Will had taken Elric in because he felt sorry for him and had been repaid with mayhem and death. Marissa spared Elric nothing and the boy's ears were still ringing with venom when he mounted the horse the nuns lent him. The horse was not as fine as Dargent, but for once Elric made no comment. Indeed, it was only by chattering hard to Hal as they left Arnhem headed for Speyer that he could drown out Marissa's words and carry on clinging to the certainties he prayed were embedded in the green jasper necklace that he had tucked into his shirt.

After they had gone, the prioress sat with Marissa for a long time. The girl was silent now; then abruptly she got up and ran into the abbey church. She knelt right at the front as she railed against God. The wise prioress watched her from the back, frowning slightly, and when, three days later, she found Marissa, her belongings, and the laundry pony gone, she did not become agitated or send out a search party as Agnes and the other nuns expected. Instead, she sat in the abbey church herself, praying that God would look after this troubled child and do with her as he, not the prioress, thought best.

14

An hour after the Old Man's arrival, he sat dressed in the finest gold and silver samite under a jewel-encrusted canopy held by four shivering slaves. Four more slaves, equally chilled, held flaming torches aloft. Darkness fell quickly and the ship was swallowed into the black with nothing to reveal its presence save occasional tiny pinpricks from lanterns and the surge of voices carrying clearly across the still waters. Under the flares, a feast of exotic splendor had been laid out. The Old Man was not eating. Instead, he had swapped his juggling oranges for walnuts, which he cracked between his thumbs, a favorite trick and one he had learned from a slave who had afterward been put to death so that he could teach nobody else. Amal had been summoned to sit at his side and the place opposite was empty until Kamil was brought from the tent in which he had been confined. The Old Man gave Kamil a long, hard look, then broke into a beaming smile. His whole face danced though his eyes were glacial. "Sit, sit." He nodded. *Crack, crack, crack* went his thumbs. "You must be tired from all the traveling. Sit. Eat."

Kamil sat but even had he been starving he would not have taken food from the Old Man's table. The Old Man threw down the nuts and reached for some figs. "You will have missed all our lovely fruit," he said as if Kamil was a young relation who had been away on a holiday, "and we have missed you, Kamil." He chewed slowly, over and over, and occasionally his teeth snapped together. A long silence followed. From the beach in front Kamil could hear the murmur of soldiers gathering driftwood and from the caves behind he could hear horses stamp and sneeze at the swish of grain pouring onto the floor for their evening feed. All the time he felt the Old Man's eyes on him, and eventually, in his own time, met his gaze. He wanted to look fearless but it was hard to stop his cheeks from quivering.

The Old Man paused and licked the sticky fig syrup from his fingers, each in turn. "Well, Kamil, this is a strange place to meet," he said, darting his tongue in and out of his mouth like a lizard. "Our last conversation took place in the mountains and here we are at the sea." He bared teeth stained yellow with saffron. Amal shifted his bones. "At the sea," the Old Man repeated softly and picked up more walnuts. He splintered one shell effortlessly, then threw the kernel away. "Do you know," he said, "had I really set my mind to it, I could have had you killed anytime over the past two years? Several times I nearly gave the order to find you, but then it occurred to me that you should be given a chance. After all"—his currant eyes were wide with false tenderness—"at the time we last met, you were only young, only a boy. So I said to myself, let's see what kind of a man Kamil turns out to be. Let's see if he is worthy of his father and his ancestors. Let's see how he develops as a warrior. Let's see exactly what he is made of." He popped another fig neatly into his mouth but it was large and some of the purple juice ran down his chin and into his beard. The tongue emerged again and only after it had finished its business did the Old Man continue. "The thing is, Kamil, I still don't know how you have turned out, so I hope you'll forgive me but I've taken the liberty of devising a little game to test you." He gestured around. "Here we are in this delightfully secluded spot and, do you know, I find myself longing to see a tournament. Your new friends, the Christians, are keen on tournaments, are they not? I know you have seen a good few at Hartslove." He paused and his tongue slid about. Amal could not take his eyes off it.

"We also have the perfect ingredients," the Old Man said when his tongue had retreated once again. "Two knights, one Christian and one Saracen. What could be better? You see my game? There will be a contest between yourself and the Earl of Ravensgarth, and the prize"—his eyes were like fireworks—"will of course be the king's ransom." He rubbed his hands together. "But we must make it more interesting than that, must we not? So I suggest that if the earl kills you, the ransom should be returned to the imperial court. If you kill the earl, the ransom will go not to me—why would you fight for that?—but, and here is such a clever twist, it will go to those for whom it was intended when you stole it. What could be fairer? Each man fighting not just for his life but for his cause?" He waited for Amal's ecstatic praise to die away before turning back to Kamil. "And just in case either of you decides not to fight, I better say that if that happens, I will keep the ransom myself, as I shall, of course, if you both die." He sighed at the thought, then cracked three walnuts in quick succession.

Kamil had to speak now. "And Ellie?" He could hardly breathe. Immediately he knew he had made a mistake.

"The girl?" The Old Man held his hands in the air.

Kamil could only nod.

"Oh, I didn't realize she mattered!" The Old Man looked craftily from under his eyelashes and considered. Then his face cleared. "I know! We'll make her part of the prize. She can't be left out, can she? Let's see. If you kill the earl, you can have her to do what you like with. But"—he plumped himself back into his cushions—"if the earl kills you, I think perhaps I should take her back to Syria with me. Yes. That's what I'll do. I'm sure I can find a use for her." He smirked. "And what about the horses? Now what have we got? Those two chestnuts and the silver?" He pondered, then chuckled. "Whichever one of you is dead won't need one, of course." He pondered some more. "I think the horses should be my prize. I particularly liked the look of the one you were riding when I first met you. Hosanna, isn't it? I'll take him. My men can draw lots for the others. Or perhaps I should give that silver mare to Amal? He really has earned something nice." He turned and his arm, cobralike, wound around Amal's waist.

Kamil kept his voice low. "I abhor the rules of your game," he said. "Whatever you say or promise, I know you will do exactly as you please."

The Old Man pulled Amal closer to him. "Maybe I will, maybe I won't," he said, his lips like razors, "but not knowing quite *what* I will do is all part of your punishment." His eyes were opaque. "You cannot see into my heart, Kamil. If you could, you might find things that surprised you." He waited for a second, then let go of Amal and clapped his hands together. He was suddenly tired and being tired made him petulant. "Prepare my bed," he ordered his servants. Then he dismissed Kamil. "Go away now. We will finish our discussion in the morning. The contest will be in the afternoon and by dusk the winners, whoever they are, will have claimed victory."

Kamil got to his feet. The Old Man held up his hand for he had one last thing to say. "Now, Kamil, I put no guard on you but if you leave this camp, within five minutes the blood of all those you care about will flow freely into the sand." He waved as Kamil walked off. The young man was almost at the caves when he heard his name called once again. "Kamil," shouted the Old Man, full of joy because his bath was steaming, "may your dreams be sweet!" Then he cackled.

Kamil began to run but the entrance to the caves was barred by two brawny soldiers. "Out of my way," Kamil ordered. They did not budge. Amal slunk from the shadows. "There is to be no conversation between you and the earl," he said staring at his feet.

"What has Will been told?"

Amal shrank away. "He has been told nothing. The Old Man is going to speak to him in the morning, but alone."

"So I will not know what's said?"

Amal shook his head. "You will never know," he said, "just as the Old Man never knew why you would not be a son to him."

"May I speak to Ellie?"

"She does not wish to speak to you."

"Will you tell her of the Old Man's game?"

Amal looked terrified. "No," he whispered, "of course not. I can do nothing I am not told to do. My family . . ."

Kamil turned away, then turned back. "Will your family be proud of your part in this?" he asked.

"They will be alive," was all Amal could say, and Kamil, shaking his head, left him.

The night deepened. Had Kamil not been pacing about, the scene could not have been more peaceful. Well-fed soldiers snored by fires while those on watch wrapped themselves in blankets, thankful that tomorrow this charade would come to an end. Even those guarding the silver-stuffed wagons were dozy as they trod slowly back and forth across the cave entrance. Some quietly told stories. There was, for this moment, no fear in the air, for the servants of the Old Man of the Mountain were frightened of nobody except their master and he was asleep.

Will and Ellie sat close together, their backs to the wall. They had recognized the Old Man because his reputation as a treacherous Assassin, an implacable enemy to all rulers in the Christian West and a rival to many in the Muslim East, was well known even in England. But why Kamil should have agreed to deliver the silver to him was a mystery. Kamil was not just a traitor, Ellie declared, but a wretch, his allegiance not to the Muslim people but to a common criminal. Will let her rail on. It seemed better that way for at least Ellie still seemed to believe that once the ship was loaded Kamil would keep his word and let them go.

But Will was full of trepidation. It did not seem possible to him that Kamil, having been so loyal to Saladin and the Saracen cause, had stolen the ransom silver for the Old Man. The more he thought, the clearer it became that Kamil himself had been tricked and that he was no longer in command. Will leaned hard against the wall and his head pulsed. If Kamil was no longer in command, he and Ellie were unlikely to be freed. He jumped as a guard kicked more driftwood onto a dying fire. In the dancing light, Will saw images of Ellie and the Old Man, vile images that dried his mouth and sickened his stomach. At dawn he began to pray. Was God not supposed to help those who believed in him? But though he listened hard for God's answer, Will heard nothing at all.

In the early hours of the morning, Kamil walked along the bottom of the cliff. It rose, sheer, above him, a wall of blotched white grooved by shadows. Outside the furthest reaches of the camp, about half a mile away, the shingle grew rougher and Kamil slithered over the stones as the ground dipped, worn down by a small stream flowing bumpily toward the shoreline. Without thinking, Kamil began to follow the stream upward to where it disappeared darkly into the rock. The rock looked completely solid from below but at close quarters it was evident that it had cracked, forced open thousands of years before when the stream was a torrent driving its way to the sea. Now that the water was just a gentle trickle, its steep descending path would be possible for a man, or even a horse if it was brave, to climb up. Kamil's heart beat hard. Had he been on his own, his escape route was right here in front of him. He could vanish in a trice. But he never even thought of it. Will and Ellie might hate him, they might never trust him again, but he would not desert them to save his own skin. He retraced his steps and went back to the caves to find Hosanna. He did not know where else to go.

The horse was half dozing, his head between his knees, and Shihab had lain down beside him. When he heard Kamil, Hosanna blinked and roused himself, shifting so that the young man could put his arms around his neck and rub his face against the horse's mane. *What shall I do, Hosanna?* Kamil begged silently. *Help me.* Hosanna stood for a while, providing a rock to lean on, until eventually Kamil left him.

15

As Hal and Elric woke to continue their journey to Richard at the imperial court, so the camp on the beach began to stir, although quietly so as not to disturb the Old Man. Only when his personal servants emerged from his tent, rushing to satisfy their waking master's ever-changing demands, did they dare to raise their voices. When the Old Man at last appeared, dressed this morning all in crimson, there was a shiver of expectation. It was the Old Man's boast that if his crimson tunic was laid in water, the blood of thousands would seep from it. He wore it jauntily. It suited him.

Men were at once put to work to create a jousting arena. It was to be situated some way away from the caves, on the sand near the water's edge. The Old Man, juggling oranges again, was scrupulous in asking Kamil about the rules. Was there a special way the jousting list should be set up? How many lances should each knight have? How far apart should Kamil and Will be when mounted? If they did not kill each other with the lance, the Old Man had a fancy for swords. Was that in keeping with the spirit of the game? And then, was it customary for competitors to bow to the audience? He had heard that a lady's favor was often sought. Was that right? Kamil would not answer but with each refusal the Old Man's smile grew tighter and Amal's face grew paler. "Oh well," the Old Man said eventually, with studied carelessness, "bring out the girl. We'll see if you remember the rules better when she is here to remind you." Amal gave a strangled cough. The Old Man inspected him and, with new malice in his voice, asked if his faithful servant was unwell. He was in a peppery mood.

Kamil intervened. "There is no need to bring Ellie out," he said, and at the sound of his voice the Old Man metamorphosed at once into a kindly grandfather listening to advice from a grandson. "You may institute any rules you wish," Kamil told him, sounding as sarcastic as he dared. "Will and I should be at least twelve ships' lengths apart. Before we begin, we will bow to the audience and Ellie should give a token to whichever one of us she wishes. Then we will take our places and when the trumpet sounds we will advance. When one of us lies dead, the winner will take off his helmet to receive his applause."

"Applause!" Now the Old Man looked genuinely delighted. He dropped his oranges and began at once to clap. A dozen servants rushed toward him. He looked at them with some amusement. "No, no"—he flapped his wrists—"I don't want anything. I'm just practicing. These Christian tournaments are full of fun. We have a rare treat in store." The servants, not sure how to respond, fell to their knees. The Old Man looked sorrowfully at them. "They never laugh unless I tell them to," he complained. "I wish I had people about me who were less servile." He leaned forward and pinched Kamil's arm conspiratorially before turning to Amal. "How many years have you served me, Amal?" he asked.

"All my life, Excellency," Amal answered.

"And do you like me?"

The terror on Amal's face was almost comic. In different circumstances, even Kamil might have laughed. "L-like you, Excellency?" Amal stammered. "I am a servant. It is not a word I know." He could not hide his dismay.

"You see?" The Old Man blinked. "It is a great burden."

"I will go and see that the horses are made ready," Kamil said shortly. He could bear sitting here no longer.

At once the Old Man was sharp again. "You will not. When it is time, your horse will be brought to you. Until then you will sit here, beside me, and as we sit I can imagine to myself how well we would have got on together had you chosen a different path." Kamil had no choice but to obey.

The day dragged by. The only time Kamil was alone was when the Old Man went to speak to Will and Ellie. He had them brought out of the cave and showed them the preparations under way. Kamil could not see their faces but he could hear as the Old Man, most politely and in perfect Norman French, told Will that in the interests of fair play, he was to be allowed a chance to kill Kamil and regain Richard's ransom.

"Why?" asked Will at once. "You hate my king and you want all the silver. Why should you give it back to me?"

"Indeed," said the Old Man, and his smile was brilliant, "but you see I don't expect you to win. Kamil and I came up with this idea because Kamil tells me that he wants to bring that red horse back to Arabia and that he cannot do that if you are alive. He has some honor left, you know. So he will be fighting to the death. Not only that"—he glanced lasciviously at Ellie—"but our little tournament will sort out the fate of this delightful girl. You, madam, are to form part of Kamil's prize. He seems to like that idea very much. Now"—he turned back to Will—"it only remains for you to accept the challenge."

Ellie was too shocked to move but her voice did not desert her. "We were promised our freedom once Kamil had delivered our silver. Is it not honorable, even for a Saracen, to keep promises?"

"Oh! Is that what he told you?" The Old Man seemed full of remorse. "I am sorry he deceived you. But," he added more cheerfully, "we will have a splendid time."

Ellie began again. The Old Man listened for a moment, then grew bored and tapped his fingers together. Ellie's voice trailed off. "So will you fight, Earl?" the Old Man inquired, "for this girl, for your horse, and for your king's ransom?"

There was only one answer Will could make. "I will fight as a Christian knight against a foreign traitor," he said coldly. "I do not know what treachery has brought us here or where the treachery begins or ends. But I know one thing: that you are an evil man, perhaps the most evil of all men. Come, Ellie, we will not listen any longer."

When the Old Man returned to Kamil, all pretence

152

at benevolence had vanished. Sniping at his servants, he juggled his oranges high and with venom. When the time came for Kamil to prepare himself, the Old Man let him go without a word.

An hour before dusk the bugler raised his instrument and blew one long, strong note. The scene could hardly have been more picturesque. The tournament list was ready on the beach and, midway between the cliffs and the sea, two makeshift thrones had been set on a dais, their yellow silken canopies billowing gently in the breeze. On the larger throne sat the Old Man and on the smaller sat Ellie. On each side, and forming a semi-circular human fence reaching down to the water's edge, the Old Man's followers were crowded together, all pushing to the front so that nobody should miss out on the spectacle. Quite a distance behind, outside the mouth of the cave, the packhorses and riding horses were tethered, with Sacramenta among them. At the bugler's note, Shihab and Hosanna emerged, Shihab decked out in silver and Hosanna in gold. Sacramenta threw up her head and whinnied at them but neither horse replied. The unfamiliar hands that held them made them uneasy and Shihab, particularly, was very agitated. Her skin quivered as if a thousand tiny insects were biting it and she barged about, pushing against Hosanna and nearly knocking her handler over. Hosanna was calmer but held his head high so that the grooms struggled to settle the headpiece of his bridle in place.

Will had been given back his armor, cleaned and oiled, and had been helped to put it on by two servants who treated him as if he were an honored guest rather than a prisoner. Will knew why. Knights going to their death had an aura about them that all civilized people respected. These men, though followers of the Old Man, were not savages. They spoke courteously and were at pains to ensure that Will was physically comfortable. It was almost enough to make him smile. But he could not smile, not with Ellie sitting so close to the Old Man that she was reflected in the jewels of his turban; not with the Old Man playing nonchalantly with his dagger. Then there was Amal, folding his hands over and over, obviously wanting to say something to him that Will did not care to hear. Amal was a villain. Taking his helmet, Will turned on his heel.

Another bugle blast bounced off the cliffs and as it drifted out to sea, Will was invited to step forward. He did so at once, for he did not want to appear reluctant. He heard Sacramenta whinny again and bid her a silent farewell. Ellie heard her too, and, much as she tried not to, she could not stop herself echoing the mare: "Will! Will!"

Now Will was torn. He and Ellie had not said a proper good-bye in the cave. Yet he did not want to look at her, even though not looking at her was worse. In the end, he could not help himself.

Ellie had risen to her feet, her arms slightly raised, and the expression on her face rocked his heart. She glowered, half defiant, half pleading, at the Old Man, and when she got no response except a slight quickening of the plump fingers running over the dagger blade, she took a hesitant step forward. There was no reaction so she ran, stumbling down the steps of the dais and across the sand, her feet sinking and her dress dragging behind her. Will caught her in his arms. It was difficult to hold her without hurting her, for his mail surcoat kept him locked inside its steel webbing, but his soul could not be locked away and neither could hers. "I'm ready, Ellie," Will whispered, although he had never felt less ready in his life, "I'm really ready." Ellie, determined not to sob, just held him tight.

As she returned to the dais, she saw Kamil waiting, armed just like Will. With her head held rigid, she walked past him with queenly disdain. Kamil's eyes sought hers but she would not notice. Whatever had happened, whatever Kamil's story, whatever the crippling pull of divided loyalties, it was an outrage of Kamil's making that Will should end his life here, in this mock tournament on a wintry beach in a hostile country. This was what he had done. Ellie knew Kamil wanted to speak to her and she knew too that Will would not have thought ill of her had she been willing to listen. But she would not. She could not. To address Kamil at all, she felt, would kill her. So she walked blindly on and resumed her place next to the Old Man. His fingers slowed on the blade, now stroking it like a cat.

The trappings of the horses and the armor of the two knights sent lightning flashes across the bay and the Old Man moved his head so that his own baubles added their glitter. His crimson robes rippled and his men, who had been murmuring, fell silent. Even the sea seemed to hold its breath as the Old Man raised a hand. At once the horses were brought forward, Shihab nervy and unwilling, Hosanna obedient but his flanks trembling. The jingle of their trappings seemed unnaturally loud and made Shihab jump. Having never taken part in a tournament before, she was thoroughly alarmed. Hosanna, on the other hand, knew at once the exertions that were to be demanded of him and prepared himself. Under his mane, he felt the tiny triangular wound still pricking. He twitched his head just once, then, as he had been trained to do, he fixed his attention entirely on the task ahead.

It was time to mount. At the signal, Kamil and Will walked out and handed over their helmets, each to his designated groom. Two wooden mounting blocks were brought forward and both men climbed up. Once settled on Hosanna, Will somehow felt better. Even through the thick saddle, he could feel the horse warm and supple underneath him. Hosanna took one step back to balance himself, then lowered his head briefly into his chest as if chasing the reins. The familiar movements were very dear to Will at this moment. Once the horse was satisfied, his ears flicked back in a salute, waiting for his master's instructions.

Kamil settled himself too, even though Shihab was determined not to help. Jostling and jibbing, her eyes full of peevish anxiety and her back unused to the full weight of an armored man, she chewed her bit until her mouth was a mass of froth. Kamil tried to reassure her, both in Arabic and in Norman French, but she would not listen. Her ears were flat back, deliberately deaf.

Once more the bugle. Hosanna jogged to the end of the list, where the man in charge of Will's lances was waiting. Will made to put his helmet on but before he did so an order came from Kamil. "We must bow to our patron," he called out, "and take our favor from the lady present."

"Why?" Will's voice was loud and angry. "Let's just start quickly, before the sun vanishes."

But Kamil was insistent. "It's the custom," he said. "We must perform all the customs. It is the Old Man's particular wish and you must obey him since he is our master of ceremonies."

Will flushed at the humiliation and turned back. He would stand in front of the Old Man but he would never bow. Without protest, Hosanna retraced his steps. Kamil was already waiting, his helmet tucked under his arm. Shihab, relieved to see Hosanna, shoved her head against him and flecks of spit speckled his neck. Kamil's left knee brushed against Will's right.

The Old Man was happy as a boy with a new toy. "This Christian chivalry really is full of formality," he crowed, "just as I have always been told. Do we stand up for this honor? Do I give you my blessing?"

"Ellie must stand up," said Kamil clearly. "She must come down and give a token to me."

Ellie started. "I will not," she declared in ringing tones. "I would rather give a token to this old man than to you." Her knuckles were white against her dress.

The Old Man arched his eyebrows. "That would be an honor indeed," he said softly. Ellie shrank back into her seat.

Kamil's knee brushed against Will's again, and through the armor, Will could feel an insistent pressure although Kamil never looked his way. "Come down, Ellie," Kamil repeated. "Come down and give me a token." Kamil would not allow Shihab to move from Hosanna although the mare snorted and banged a front hoof on the ground.

Every nerve in Will's body began to tingle. Through the corner of his eye, he saw Kamil's lips twitch nervously. But though Kamil ordered Ellie again and again, she continued to refuse to come down and the Old Man grew impatient. Only then did Kamil look Will full in the face. "Perhaps she would prefer to give a token to you," he said, his eyes boring into Will's. "One of us must have one. We cannot leave this spot empty-handed."

Without taking his eyes from Kamil's, Will slowly inclined his head. "No," he said hesitantly, trusting where there should have been no trust. "Ellie, come and give a token to me."

"These are just games," cried Ellie wildly. "Why are you playing their games, Will?"

"We must play this game, Ellie," Will said, slightly raising his voice. "It may be our last. Let's play it properly—you know, like we used to play in the meadow at Hartslove when we were small. Do it, Ellie."

For one moment, Will thought that Ellie was not listening. She was crammed far back in her seat and was shaking her head from side to side. He almost gave up. But the pressure on his knee from Kamil was intense. The Old Man began to complain. Fed up with the delay, he stamped his foot. This made Ellie jump and Will opened his eyes so wide at her that she stopped shaking her head and was entirely still. Then, just as the Old Man reached boiling point, she rose.

"Yes," Ellie said, though her voice was cautious, "like when we were small. I remember." Kamil's knee jerked. Ellie looked at him for the first time. "I need a token," she said, then she turned around and snatched the Old Man's knife. The Old Man gasped but Ellie took no notice. With a small flourish, she simply cut off the tail of her belt and tossed the dagger back. The Old Man caught it and looked at Ellie with new respect. What curious people these enemies were turning out to be! This was going to be some show.

Ellie walked down the dais steps. Will's breath was coming quicker now and he was already drawing off his right gauntlet, following Kamil, who had drawn off his left. The horses parted and Ellie found a path opening up for her. With the end of her belt clutched against her breast she found herself forced to go down the middle. For courage she brushed Hosanna's star lightly with her fingers as she passed. Shihab would allow no contact but blew out, scattering foam, her ears still flat back. But at least she was obedient now and when she felt pressure on her left rein, asking her to turn her head to form an arc around Ellie, she did as she was told. Ellie held up her arm, not sure what she was expected to do next.

Kamil moved with lightning rapidity. Dropping both gauntlet and helmet, he seized Ellie around the waist and swung her up behind him. There was no time for her even to cry out, for at once Will crowded in and both he and Kamil drew the swords with which they were supposed to kill each other. Just once, they clashed, with a sharp, metallic slice, then raising the swords high above their heads, both men galloped straight for the wall of spectators.

The Old Man leaped as if he had been stung, biting his tongue and stabbing himself in the palm of his hand. The unexpected pain and the sight of his own blood seemed momentarily to mesmerize him, but then he was shouting and screaming like a banshee. The devils! The devils! He rushed down the steps. Nobody must break ranks. If the human fence remained intact, the horses would stop and Will and Kamil would be trapped. "The man who moves even one muscle is a dead man!" he howled, "and his flesh will be meat for the vultures." But seeing Hosanna and Shihab wildly spurred on by their riders, the spectators began to shift, then waver, until, at the last possible moment, they cracked and splintered. The horses never hesitated but plunged straight through them, Kamil and Will using their swords like scythes, mercilessly sweeping away those who remained in their way until the sand around them was red and the Old Man's roaring was drowned out by the wails of the wounded.

The Old Man cared nothing for his injured men. His howling became more and more savage. "Stand firm, you dogs! If these people escape, I'll cut off your useless arms and roast your children." But it was no good. With sword thrusts raining from above, blinded by sand and blood, crushed against each other and under the weight of those thrust backward, the Old Man's followers could hardly hear him. Still howling, their master tore off his turban and stamped it into the dirt.

Ellie had to cling to Kamil to prevent herself from falling off and Kamil could feel Shihab scrabbling to keep her feet. By a miracle she kept going, pushed on by Hosanna, but Kamil knew that she could not carry two people at speed for long. The second they broke through the crowd, he veered her toward the caves and sliced through the rope that kept the packhorses tethered together. Most of the animals fled at once but

Sacramenta, already excited by the noise and the thundering hooves, hardly needed to hear Kamil shout her name to follow him instead. Within seconds, she was thundering behind as Kamil turned again and set off along the bottom of the cliff face.

Close on her tail, Will bellowed his delight. Oh, clever Kamil! Yet even as he punched the air, his heart was sinking. On their left was the sea and on their right, a stern, unyielding wall of limestone. Though they could gallop to where the cove rounded off into a sharp promontory, after that there was nowhere to go except into the waves. He told himself that at least dying all together would be better than dying apart. But very quickly he began to fear that even that would be denied them. They could not keep up this pace. The sand sucked each hoof down and only reluctantly let it go. It became a fight to keep up any speed at all. Shihab was already sweating and even Hosanna began to flag. The shingle might save them. But it was deceptive. Even as they heard its welcome crunch, they found themselves slipping about like drunken skaters, every moment in danger of tearing precious ligaments and tendons. "Kamil," Will cried, "we can't go on! The horses' legs will be wrecked. They will fall!" Kamil said nothing, only gritted his teeth. It seemed an age, far farther than he thought, until he heard the splash of the stream and turned sharply to the right. Will, in an agony of apprehension, turned, too. But now they were just heading straight at the rock. "God help us all," he whispered to Hosanna as the horse stumbled over the deadly terrain. "May he have mercy on our souls."

Once under the cliff's lee, Will could barely see

Shihab's tail. Then both she and Sacramenta disappeared and, a moment later, Will too found himself no longer under the shadow of the rock, but inside it. His shock, then shocked delight, was short-lived. Within seconds, the light had vanished and the air hung thick and slimy. The narrow streambed was even more treacherous than the shingle, for the stones were unstable and the gradient became steeper with every step. The riders' legs scraped along the jagged rocks that enclosed them like a tomb and the horses' pace slowed to a clamber. The water, though not deep, sounded like a torrent in the compressed space. Occasionally, a foothold would completely give way and Shihab, losing courage in the lead, began to slide backward, threatening to push them all down again. Only Hosanna, a solid bulwark at the back, kept them from disaster.

Squashed within the fissure, it was impossible to see what might be going on behind but the fugitives could imagine it all too clearly. By now, mounted men with lowered lances would be pushing up the opening. Soon they would be in full cry, using flaming torches to flush out their quarry. Kamil did not even have the comfort of knowing what lay in wait for them all at the top of the streambed, if they ever made it that far. Nevertheless, there was nowhere to go but on. They all tried to help the horses as best they could, but it was impossible to prevent their joints and bones being banged and raked while the stream tumbled and burbled, mocking and uncaring.

An endless twenty minutes later, their legs a patchwork of scrapes and tears and their coats dank and steaming, the three horses made it back into the fading light and hauled themselves onto the clifftop. Shihab was sobbing from her double burden and as soon as he could, Kamil leaped off. He discarded his armor and Will at once followed suit. Lightness meant speed and speed was more important than protection. Kamil grabbed Sacramenta's rope. They could give the horses only a moment of respite. "They'll send others by the track," Kamil said tersely. "Quick. We must go." He vaulted bareback onto the chestnut mare. Ellie, stroking Shihab's trembling neck, said nothing and Kamil did not look at her. "Ready?" he asked Will.

"Ready."

But Ellie was not. "How can we trust you?" she burst out, holding Shihab back. "Why should we go where you tell us?"

"I don't know," Kamil said to her, "but I know that when they catch up to us we will have more chance of escaping if we are together."

Ellie did not listen. "Why did you do it, Kamil? Why did you do it?"

"Please, Ellie, we've no time."

"I can never forgive you, Kamil. Never."

Now Will was pushing her from behind. "Come ON, Ellie."

Ellie moved off. "Keep close to me, Will," she begged, and he nodded as they sped away.

The better ground raised the horses' spirits and soon they were among the trees, galloping along a path that had been cut through for logging carts. It was wide enough for the three horses to travel abreast and Hosanna and Sacramenta flanked Shihab in the middle. Their riders were silent, straining backward to hear sounds of pursuit, but it was difficult to hear anything apart from the flapping of leather; the quick, gasping breath of the horses; and the snapping of twigs. They cantered on for roughly a quarter of a mile and Will was beginning to hope that their pursuers had given up when arrows suddenly showered over them, not from behind but from the side. The Old Man's followers had found another way into the wood and were hell-bent on cutting them off.

Immediately, Kamil wheeled to the left and the three horses plunged off the path, into untamed forest. It was impossible now to keep together and each horse had to take its chance, tripping over tree roots and weaving underneath low-hanging branches, its rider's legs snagged by briars and stunted saplings. Ellie's dress was soon ripped to shreds and she could feel Shihab, hating it all, thinking of refusing to go any farther. Seizing a branch, Ellie had to use it as a switch. Now they did not need to listen, they could clearly hear the Old Man's men pushing through the forest using the last of the light to follow the trail. Will kept glancing behind him. "We'll have to stand and fight, Kamil," he panted.

But Kamil pointed ahead. Will could see nothing except that the ground fell away and disappeared. "A river," Kamil breathed, crouching low over Sacramenta's back. The mare's ears were flat but she never faltered. "We'll turn upstream and hope it bends out of sight." An arrow thwacked deep into bark above their heads. At once, Kamil and Will crowded over Ellie. The three horses plunged forward and before another arrow could be loosed had almost fallen over a muddy ridge. The river was not wide and the bed was smoother than they had dared hope. Kamil forced Sacramenta back into a canter. But there was no welcome bend. Once the Old Man's soldiers themselves reached the water, their quarry would be easily in sight. The only thing that might prevent this was the swallowing shadow of the night. The dark horses might sink into it but not Shihab. Her silver tail would gleam like a beacon through the gloom.

Kamil scanned the banks rising on each side of the water and, just as the pursuers themselves fell into the river, spotted what he was looking for. He did not hesitate. "Ellie!" He spoke quickly. "Ellie, swap horses with me. I can make Shihab go faster. Do it right now. Right now." Ellie turned just as a second arrow sliced past her shoulder. It did not knock her over but was close enough to tear her skin. Shihab heard the swish and leaped sideways. Ellie felt no pain at first, just a tremendous sense of heaviness, as if her arm were made of lead. She folded over.

Will was beside himself. "Ellie! Oh God help us, Kamil. She can't do anything now."

"She must, Will, she must." Kamil bent forward and said something to Sacramenta in Arabic. The mare flicked up one ear. Kamil prepared himself. "Ellie! Ellie!" he urged. "Remember those beautiful days before we got to Whitby? Pretend we are there again. Ellie! Ellie! Are you listening?" Shihab had her head right down and her legs were dragging. She did not like the dead weight of her rider and she did not like the lap of the water. The only thing keeping her going was Hosanna, hard against her side. Ellie was listing and her arm hung uselessly. Kamil hissed in her ear. "Come ON,

Ellie. One last effort. Come ON." Ellie raised herself a little and Kamil forced her to look into his eyes. They had so little time and they could not afford any mistakes. "Remember our game. Follow exactly what I say. Get rid of the stirrups. Hitch both legs up. Come ON." He could barely see what Ellie was doing. "Now, get your left leg onto Shihab's neck, let go of the reins, and, if you can, grab Sacramenta's mane." He could see her moving. "Well done, Ellie. Well done." The horses slowed. Another arrow landed in the water and the men behind were yowling like dogs in anticipation of success. "Hurry, hurry, Kamil," urged Will. "Oh, Jesus Christ help us!"

Kamil waited no longer. Slipping backward, he seized Ellie. "Push with your left foot NOW and whatever you do, hold on tight, Ellie, just hold on tight." He gritted his teeth, took a deep breath, and yanked her off Shihab, swinging her over so that she ended up in front of him on Sacramenta. As soon as she was steady, he wound her hands into the thick red mane as best he could and let go. With one smooth movement, he slipped off Sacramenta himself and vaulted onto Shihab, catching the mare's reins just before they flew over her head. It had worked! But there was no time for exultation. "Grab Sacramenta's lead rope, Will, and turn left in five paces," Kamil whispered urgently. "There's a gap in the banking. Trust me. You'll get up there into the trees and they won't see you."

"And you?"

"I'll keep to the river to give you a bit of a start and then get out farther on."

"Kamil . . ."

"Go, Will, go."

Will did exactly as Kamil ordered. With Ellie clinging to Sacramenta's neck, both horses scrambled up the bank and disappeared. Kamil waited until he heard the bloodcurdling cry that meant that the Old Man's men could see Shihab's silver tail, then he urged the weary mare forward. She did not want to go and once he was sure Will and Ellie had got away, Kamil pushed her no further. The Old Man wanted him, not them, and the Old Man would have him. He felt a fierce joy that at least Will and Ellie would be safe as he deliberately allowed Shihab to slacken. He prayed that they would make it home. He prayed that they would one day forgive him. Then he prayed to Allah that he could meet what was coming like the man Saladin had trained him to be.

16

As soon as they were hidden, Will almost fell off Hosanna. The baying of the men made him terrified for Kamil, but Ellie was his priority now. Her arm was wet with blood and she could not ride much farther. Tripping and cursing, Will led both horses until he found a small clearing. This would have to do. He caught Ellie as she slid to the ground and laid her down as best he could, peering to see how badly she was hurt. He could see almost nothing and panicked when he thought what he might find when the dawn came, his only comfort that everything was suddenly quiet. All their pursuers had vanished. Occasional sudden noises still made him jump but they always turned out to be only owls or vixens. He loosened the horses' girths, then huddled next to Ellie, trying to stop her shuddering although he couldn't stop shivering himself. She kept whispering words that Will could not catch. "I'm here, Ellie," was all he could say, "I'm here." He kept his eyes open, for whenever he closed them he had terrible visions of Ellie dead and Kamil's body being torn apart. It was the longest night of his life.

At the first thin fingers of light, he heard something lurching as though drunk along a path leading toward them. He crouched down, fearful, then stood up, alight with hope. Kamil! Perhaps it was Kamil! Into the clearing stumbled Shihab. She made straight for Hosanna and Sacramenta, who whickered at her in greeting. But Will's greeting stuck in his throat. Though the mare herself was unhurt, her saddle was empty and all down one side her coat no longer gleamed silver but was streaked red with blood.

Will was still staring when he heard Ellie call his name. He ran to her at once. She was pale as a ghost but at least she was not delirious. He sank down on his knees and took her hand. "What's happened to me?" she asked.

"You were hit by an arrow."

"Is it bad?"

"I don't know," Will told her truthfully. "It was so dark. But at least you can speak to me, Ellie. Thank God for that. Can you move your fingers?" He would not tell her about Shihab.

Ellie shifted slightly and grimaced but she moved her fingers without difficulty. "That's a good sign, Will." Her voice was weak. "I am trying to remember," she said, "but I'm so thirsty, and the horses must be, too."

"I daren't go back to the river," Will told her. "I'll find a ditch."

Keeping Shihab's bloody side away from Ellie, Will took the horses. It was not hard to find what he was looking for and all three animals surged forward and drank gratefully. Hosanna and Sacramenta never raised their heads until they were finished, but Shihab snatched a mouthful or two at a time, her flanks quaking and her nostrils flaring. Will tried not to think of the horrors she must have seen. Quickly, he rinsed the blood from her side. He could feel guilt creeping up on him. He should never have let Kamil go off alone. Harder and harder he splashed Shihab's side as if he could wash away the terrible tide of self-reproach. Yet what else could he have done? He wanted to shout Kamil's name, to shout it over and over. But he knew he must remain silent.

Instead, as the horses drank, he tried to think. The Old Man would have learned by now that he and Ellie had escaped and Will could not know whether they would still be included in his revenge. Maybe getting Kamil was enough, maybe not. But Will knew, with overriding certainty, where he would go now. He would go to Richard. He needed to see the king, not only because Will felt the king to be the nearest thing he had to a father, but also because, just as Marissa had also worked out, he knew what would happen if he did not. Few would sympathize with Will over the loss of the ransom. Instead they would whisper that the loss was too convenient and that, in all probability, at least some of the silver was even at this moment somehow making its way back to the Hartslove coffers. The word *traitor* would be used. In many ways it was unimaginable to Will that Richard might believe that one of his most faithful supporters would sell his loyalty for money, but Will also knew that in troubled times people tended to believe whatever they were told. If Ellie could travel, they would head straight for the imperial court. If Ellie could not, he must find somewhere safe to leave her, then go himself.

He half carried her to the ditch and helped her to drink, then bound up her wound with Hosanna's saddlecloth and a leather thong. There was no way of knowing if gangrene would come. The thought sat like a toad at the bottom of his stomach and he knew it would be the same for Ellie.

"Do you think you can ride?" he asked, desperate to move away from this awful place.

"I can try."

He took Shihab's saddle and put it on Sacramenta, feeling more confident of the red mare than of the silver. Shihab immediately lay down and rolled. Ellie frowned. "Where is Kamil?" she asked.

Will, busy with the bridles, braced himself.

Ellie asked him again. "Should we wait for Kamil?"

"Kamil's not coming with us," Will said shortly.

"Not coming with us? Has he abandoned us? Where's he gone?"

Will secured the girth.

"What is it?" Ellie's voice was worried, then bitter. "Did he just go off in the night?"

"Don't you remember?" Will could stand no more.

"I remember he betrayed us."

"He thought he was helping his own people."

"But we were his people!"

"We weren't, Ellie," said Will. "You don't know, but when we were on crusade Kamil once told me that we could never truly be friends because our worlds were too different. Now I know what he meant. He loves us but in the end he had to choose. You must forgive him, Ellie, or at least try to understand."

"I can't forgive." Ellie's voice was bleak. "I can't,

Will. All those deaths. All this horror. Hal and Elric—
that tournament—"

Will looked at the ground. "Kamil made a mistake in
trusting Amal. And we all trusted Amal. Look at what
he did for us, with Elric and everything. And look at all
those riding tricks he taught you. If it hadn't been for
Amal we would never have got Shihab. If Kamil was
taken in, so were we all. Amal poisoned him against
us." Will tried his best.

But Ellie just shook her head. "Well, where's Kamil
now then?" she asked again. Then her face changed.
"Was he too ashamed to stay?"

"Ellie . . ."

Suddenly she was crying all the tears she had not
shed since their capture. Everything was jumbled in her
mind. She wanted Kamil to be there so that she could
beat him with her fists, beat him for betraying them and
deserting them. She felt as if he, more than the arrow,
had taken a great chip out of her. "He should be here,"
she wept, "he could at least have given us that."

Will stood straight in front of her. He must tell her
now. He could not let her go on without knowing. "He
did give us something, Ellie," he said. He did not want
to say the words aloud but he had to. "He gave his life
for us, Ellie."

It was as if Will had slapped her. "His life, Will?
What do you mean? I thought you said—"

"I said he wasn't coming with us."

She sank into the ground, a picture of disbelief, and
Will knelt beside her. "He's dead, Ellie. You were hurt.
He made you swap horses, then he carried on riding
Shihab up the river. He knew that the men would be

able to see her, even in the dark, but that Hosanna and Sacramenta would be invisible. Then Shihab came back this morning. She was alone." There was a short silence before Will blurted out, "She was covered in blood." He took Ellie's hand. She said nothing, only squeezed his fingers like somebody in childbirth biting a stick. They remained like that for some minutes before Will gently extricated himself. "We've got to move," he said. "I'll help you onto Sacramenta."

"Did you see his body?" Ellie felt her voice was very far away.

"I didn't need to."

"Then maybe—" Ellie tried to say more but Hosanna suddenly threw up his head and they heard the sound of voices. At once, Will put his fingers to his lips and pulled Ellie and the horses deeper into the trees. "Kamil," Elli murmured, but Will shook his head. One voice was familiar. It was not Kamil's.

Less than a minute later Amal appeared, together with a couple of soldiers looking this way and that. Now Ellie clutched at Will and fought not to scream for in Amal's belt, clearly visible, was Kamil's triangular knife. Ellie could not take her eyes off it. The men drew to a halt and the two soldiers began to talk both at once.

At first Will too was mesmerized by Kamil's knife, but soon something quite different caught his attention. It was quite a time before he realized what it was. The men were not speaking Arabic as he expected but were still speaking German. It was odd since there was no need to pretend anymore. He leaned cautiously forward, straining his ears to make sure he was not mistaken. No. They were definitely speaking German and they were speaking it as if it was their native language. He drew back, wanting to whisper to Ellie, to see what she made of it, but before he could do anything Shihab stirred. She resented standing still and restlessly swished her tail. At once Will put a hand on her nose, thinking to warn her, but she shook him off and, as if to spite him, raised her head to grab a few dead leaves from an overhanging branch. The branch pinged down and immediately the soldiers' eyes sharpened. Dismounting, and with Amal in the vanguard, they inched forward. Shihab sneezed.

"You stupid, stupid horse!" Will was frantic. There was only one thing to do. He smacked her rump and sent her straight out so that she emerged from the thicket like an apparition. Amal yelped and caught her reins as they swung past. The men, chattering noisily, gathered around her, pointing to her back. Where was her saddle? Amal seemed as confused as they were but instead of ordering a search of the clearing began to explain, occasionally punctuating his narrative with actions that would have been comic had not their meaning been so appalling. Though Will, peeping through the undergrowth, could understand very few words, the gist of the old spy's tale was only too clear. He seemed to be telling how Kamil, struck by several arrows, had fallen and how his throat had been cut with his own knife and then how Shihab, frightened by the crash of the body, had run away. The girth must have come undone, Amal said, when Kamil's corpse was dragging through the water. To illustrate his story, Amal drew out Kamil's knife, brandished it about, inspected it and, when the story was over, shook his head a little as if genuinely sorry. That shake of the head, so neat, so economical, was more chilling to Will than any description. It smacked of the truth.

The men soon lost interest in hanging about and after a few more words Amal, with unexpected spring, pulled his skeletal frame onto Shihab's back. Will expected all the men to ride off together but they did not. Instead, once again Amal drew out Kamil's knife. Once again he gave that little shake of his head, only this time the name he mentioned was not Kamil's, but Richard's. The men nodded. This was something that had clearly been spoken about before. There was a hurried farewell and without any more ado, Amal clapped his heels into Shihab's sides. For one breathless moment, Will thought the mare was going to turn around and give them away, but although she scowled in her habitual complaint, she obeyed her rider. The soldiers waited until she had vanished, then whipped up their own horses and made their way back to the sea.

At once he was pushing Ellie toward Sacramenta. "We've got to get to the king," he said, "we've got to get to Speyer before Amal. He's going to kill Richard. I know it."

But Ellie could not think about anything except Kamil. She clung to Will, the pain in her arm temporarily forgotten. "What did they do to him?" Horror gouged cavities into her face.

Will avoided her eyes. "We've got to get to Speyer before Amal," he kept repeating. "He is going to use Kamil's knife to kill the king." But Ellie would not get up. She beat one fist into the soil and groaned like an animal. At first Will felt helpless, then he could bear it no more. His voice rose as he seized Ellie and shook her, forcing her to listen to him. "Jesus help us! Can't you see what's going on? The Old Man's revenge isn't finished yet. Not that he's going to chase us. Of course not! He's not interested in us and never has been. But he's not yet finished with Kamil. Kamil's body may be dead—I can hardly think Amal would have dared to leave him alive—but the Old Man now wants to destroy his reputation. Amal will kill Richard with that triangular knife and make sure to leave it behind. Anybody who knew Kamil will identify it at once. Kamil will then be both thief and murderer and the Old Man will claim that he was an Assassin all along. It's diabolical." He set Ellie down and quickly began to prepare the horses for mounting. "We've got to ride now, Ellie, not for ourselves but for Richard and Kamil. Can you do it?" He did not know what would happen if she could not or would not.

But Ellie was already hauling herself on. Her arm throbbed unmercifully yet she was glad of the physical pain. Perhaps if, when they had emerged at the top of the cliff, she had not wasted time, Kamil would not have been caught. He may have done wrong but he did not deserve to die like a dog. Perhaps if she had condemned a little less and understood a little more, as Will had, she would not be seeing, in her mind's eye, Kamil's body lying untended for the vultures to pick at.

Will did not try to comfort Ellie. He simply urged Hosanna into a gallop and took some comfort of his own from the sound of Sacramenta's hooves behind. He too mourned for Kamil with his whole heart, his old jealousy forgotten. Unlike Ellie's, however, his mourning was not full of regrets, it was full of promises. Whatever the cost to himself, he vowed to avenge the man he still thought of as his friend. He knew the vow would involve sacrifices but he knew too that he could not live with himself unless the sacrifices were made. God would surely ensure that such sacrifices were not impossible to bear. He had to believe that.

A mile ahead, Amal sat on Shihab, a shrunken old man with too much on his conscience. But he had the knife, he had his orders, and there was nothing else to do except carry them out.

17

Returning to his ship, the Old Man of the Mountain sat on his golden cushions and mused. His revenge on Kamil may have suffered a glitch, but the glitch had turned out to be nothing for Amal had assured him that the boy was dead and now only the final destruction of his reputation remained. The Old Man had, on the whole, recovered his temper, cheering himself with the thought that by the time Amal had finished, Kamil's name would be so blackened that when history came to be written, nobody would have a good word to say about him. That was just the kind of revenge the Old Man liked—the kind that lasted. His musings were not, at this moment, concerned with Kamil. Instead he was wondering whether he should or should not go after William de Granville, Earl of Ravensgarth, to punish him and the girl for their insolence. He did not believe that even if Will got to Richard he could prevent the king's assassination. A knight was no match for an Assassin. Yet it went quite against the grain for an Assassin to allow any slight, even the smallest, to go unpunished. So the Old Man could not decide. Will and

Ellie were not really his enemies and, now that Kamil was no longer under their roof, they had nothing that he wanted. But they had not been polite. He began to crack walnuts, then changed his mind and clapped his hands to send, as usual, for oranges. A flunky scurried up from below with a bowlful. The Old Man chose three and began to toss them. Up, up, up they went but when he caught them in his round white hands they dissolved, one after the other, into a sticky mass of pulp and discolored juice. They had gone moldy on the journey. The Old Man let out a piercing shriek and drummed his small heels on the deck. The whole ship rocked with consternation. Men stopped their ears. When the Old Man shrieked, they knew he would not desist until he had made somebody else shriek louder.

The orange-bringer trembled the most. He ran for a bowl of warm water but, in his terror, spilled some of the water and soaked the Old Man's towel. Desperate, he shook out his hair and offered it instead, crouching low and trying not to moan as he felt those sharp fingers curling, twisting, and pulling. It took him some time to realize that the drumming was less insistent and even longer to realize that the hair tugging had, in fact, ceased and the Old Man's shriek had faded into a hum. Eventually, he felt two fingers lift up his chin. "Hair," said the Old Man dreamily, his face like that of a fat round robin. "Do you know, my good man, I suddenly have a fancy for hair."

The orange-bringer gave praise to Allah. He was only going to lose his hair! He made cutting signals but the Old Man batted him aside. "No, you clumsy idiot, not your hair," he said, "but that girl's. That's what I want. I want you to go ashore and follow William de Granville and his little friend. You must find them and when the girl is asleep you must cut off her hair as close to her scalp as possible and bring it to me. They must not see you. They must suspect nothing. When they awake, it must be as if the devil has visited them. That's the way to punish them! For ever after, my shadow will hang over them, day and night. If they see you neither come nor go, they will never sleep easy in their beds again."

The Old Man was so pleased with this plan that he patted the orange-bringer's head, carefully wiping into it the last of the pulp. "Go now," he said, "and don't return here until you can lay the girl's plait at my feet. You have some time. Storms are predicted. We shall wait until they pass before sailing home." The orange-bringer began to crawl away. The Old Man stared at the horizon, then suddenly called him back. Now he was showing his teeth and the orange-bringer's heart sank. "I've thought of something to make your task even more amusing," the Old Man said. "At the same time as stealing the girl's plait, steal that red horse's tail. I have a fancy to use it as a fly whisk." The orange-bringer breathed again and ventured to give the Old Man an oily grin. "It's a pity Will de Granville is clean-shaven," he said, and when the Old Man jokily wagged his finger at him, the orange-bringer's spirits soared and he ventured to stand up straight.

As soon as the Old Man heard the splash of the row-boat over the side, he began to tap his fingers. He had held off inspecting the ransom silver, saving it for a treat. Now, he felt, he deserved such a treat. His fingers stopped tapping and began to itch. The anticipation was gloriously unsettling. When the itch moved along his fingers, up his arms, down his body, and even into his toes, the Old Man rose in a surprisingly graceful movement. Half an hour later, he was sitting in a sealed cabin that stretched half the length of the ship. The darkness was absolute, pushed aside only directly over the wagons by huge round lamps that swung slowly back and forth with the wash of the sea. The ransom wagons, painstakingly emptied, then floated on rafts to the galley before being hoisted aboard and refilled, were open and the Old Man was entirely alone. He climbed up onto the first, lowered himself into it, and lay down. The bed of stolen Christian silver felt better than the best goose-feather mattress. He buried his arms up to the elbow and his legs up to the knee. He trickled the coins over his palms and even juggled with a few silver artifacts, enjoying the dull clink as the precious objects dropped back into the great pile. He stood up and dropped handfuls of treasure over his head. Then he climbed onto the side and leaped lightly over, now landing in the wagon containing the Hartslove contribution. This the Old Man inspected with added interest because it was full of beautiful things, and when he came across the ruby brooch that Marissa had so reluctantly given, he took it carefully between his thumb and first finger. The red horse's head glowed gently as the Old Man held it this way and that. He read the inscription with Hosanna's name and inspected the ornament again. This was a fine piece. He liked it. He would wear it himself. Deftly, he undid the catch and pinned it to his tunic. Digging deep, he found a circlet of gold given by an Anglo-Norman duke, carefully crowned himself, and began, in his delight, to dance. His shadow on the wall danced with him even though it wavered slightly. A squall was blowing in from the east. When the Old Man had finished dancing, he locked the wagons up again and went back to his golden cushions to wait for the squall to pass.

Once Marissa had fled from the convent, it had not taken her long to decide that she did not like her pony and also that in her determination to follow Hal and Elric to Richard she would not bother with any niceties of riding. Using her heels and a variety of threats, she kept the pony scrambling along, hating its rider but unable to get rid of her. Marissa's woolen habit was both a drag and a boon: a drag because when it got wet, which it did almost at once, it weighed her down, but a boon because when they saw it, nobody accosted her.

And Marissa spoke to nobody. When she wanted food, she held out her hands like a pilgrim beggar, and when she wanted shelter, she presented herself at farms and cottages, where her habit was treated with reverence rather than disdain. She did not need to ask for directions since she knew that Speyer was on the Rhine. If she just followed the river, she would surely get there in the end. This was more difficult than it looked, for though the river was bigger than any Marissa had ever seen in England, sometimes she had to leave it when the road veered away or when it had collapsed and become impassable. When she found the river again, she was nervous lest she had mistaken it and it was another waterway leading elsewhere. All the time she was not worrying about the route, she rehearsed what she would say to Richard when she found him. This was all she could do for Will now and afterward, when Richard fully understood that Will was a hero beyond criticism, then she would begin her search for Hosanna, a search that would not finish until she either found him or dropped dead. She dwelled only briefly on Ellie and even more briefly on Kamil. Amal never entered her head at all.

When she first saw the gathering of nuns, loosely guarded by lay monks, moving slowly along the same route as herself, her heart rose. The gathering was so large that she was sure that their destination must be one of the large convents set somewhere along the Rhine's banks. Today she could ride with them and not worry about getting lost. They would hardly notice her.

There she was wrong. The abbess was soon alerted to the unknown novice traveling in their midst, clearly a runaway. Nothing was done at first but when dusk fell and Marissa tried to leave the nuns behind, one of the monks seized her pony's bridle. "Get off!" Marissa was suddenly horribly aware of her stupidity. "I'm on my way to my motherhouse." The lie came easily. "They're expecting me." The monk took no notice but hauled her off the pony and marched her to the abbess. Marissa kept her head. If she struggled and swore, she would give herself away. She must be haughty but dignified if she was to persuade these busybodies to let her go.

But she met her match. The abbess listened politely to Marissa's explanations, even encouraging her in her lie. Where was the motherhouse? In Speyer, Marissa said, not knowing the name of any other large town.

The abbess seemed pleased with this answer and for a moment Marissa thought she had won. Then the abbess smiled. "We too are going to Speyer," she said brightly, looking Marissa straight in the eye. "You must travel with us and we will hand you safely over to your new home. I'm surprised that you have been sent on this journey alone. Where did you say you came from? Clearly not a convent of any merit." She glanced up and down at Marissa's grubby clothes.

"But I must hurry," said Marissa, clenching her fists.

The abbess looked at her. "Are you going to hit me?" she asked.

Marissa could not bear it. "Please," she begged, "please let me go. You don't understand."

"I think I understand perfectly," the abbess answered shortly. She had humored this runaway long enough. Then she added, with what she thought to be kindness but to Marissa was maddening complacency, "We'll get to Speyer soon enough, my sister. I'm afraid we are to make many stops on the way, so you will have plenty of time to learn the virtue of patience. But once we get to Speyer you can face the proper authorities." Though the unhappy girl argued and argued and even tried to tell the abbess the exact nature of her business to stress its urgency, the abbess's ears were deaf, and very soon Marissa found her pony had vanished and she herself was loosely bound to another sister, who, taking very unkindly to Marissa's tugs, kicks, and stream of invective, returned every blow and insult in kind. Marissa tried every trick in her considerable armory to free herself. None worked and though it nearly choked her to accept that she must get to Speyer slowly or risk dying of fury and not getting there at all, she had little choice. The abbess watched her carefully. In her day, she thought, girls who were told to be nuns just accepted it, even welcomed it. Now she met many more girls like Marissa. The world, the abbess decided, was not moving in the right direction.

18

For the first few hours, just as Marissa had done, Will thought that he and Ellie would find the journey to Speyer relatively easy. He knew the town was hundreds of miles away, but with so many rivers to use, it was not impossible. He cursed when they had to stop for food and thought ruefully of all the ransom silver. Now he didn't even have enough coin for a bowl of pottage. With false promises he persuaded peddlers and pilgrims to give them bread and oats. The effort of riding made Ellie feverish and Will knew that her wound was still bleeding. He steadfastly refused to look at it, however, terrified to see the discoloration that would spell Ellie's end. It was better not to know. "If the weather holds, we'll make it to Speyer in a month—five weeks at most," he repeated endlessly as they headed back to the Rhone. Even as he said it, he realized what an impossible task they had. Five weeks! Anything might happen to them in that time. Hosanna and Sacramenta would tire and Amal was on the swiftest horse in the world. Whenever he thought of Shihab, Will ground his teeth. He could not think of her with any affection at all.

Though Kamil had tamed her and Ellie loved to ride her, he wished her ill.

The orange-bringer had no difficulty in following their trail. Like all the Old Man's servants, he was adept at changing his appearance and could speak several languages. Mingling unobtrusively with the peddlers and pilgrims, he elicited information without causing any suspicion. It was less easy, however, to maneuver himself into a position where he could do what the Old Man asked with no risk of discovery.

It seemed to take ages to get anywhere. Miles felt farther here than they did in England. The sky seemed higher. Now that it was just Will and Ellie, it was not just the impossible dialects that made the place feel alien. The wind felt bigger and more menacing than it ever was at Hartslove, as if it wanted to remind them all the time that they were friendless and far from home. They rode past slope after slope of straggling vineyards and sheltered under trees he could not name. Villages were unexpectedly set out and houses unfamiliar shapes. At night he scarcely slept because he could not quite place all the noises. He feared wolves.

Once at the river, Will managed to negotiate a lift on a barge transporting skins. The skins smelled but this was not the time to be fastidious. The horses, hating it, nevertheless stepped obediently onto the rickety wooden slats, holding their heads high to breathe in fresh air. The bargeman, heavy of jaw and with a gypsy countenance, saved all his breath to drive his oarsmen hard. Will exulted as they rowed, bare-armed despite the cold, their muscles knotted and their hands like leather. This was better. Now they were really moving. The orange-bringer watched them embark, then found himself another barge bound in the same direction. The crewmen hardly noticed him for the man seemed to be exactly what the Old Man so often told him he was—nobody.

Will and Ellie stayed with the barge for many days. The temperature dropped and they feared that the water might freeze. But though the wind turned tears into icicles, the river remained free. Sometimes it cut a swathe under giant, tree-topped cliffs. Other times it rolled through endless valleys bounded by hills shrouded in winter fog. Will tried to be patient, reassuring himself that Amal was also in an unfamiliar land experiencing the same conditions and that a horse galloping alone seldom goes as fast as two traveling together. "We will be in time," he said confidently to Ellie, "I know we will."

Ellie didn't reply. To stem his terrors Will began to talk. He spoke of their childhood, of all the things at Hartslove that he loved, of his brother, of his father, of Old Nurse, of Kamil, of Marissa, and of himself. He scarcely knew what he said or how long he sat. As night fell his words were punctuated with sleep, and sometimes the bargewoman, who fancied herself a healer, came and plastered Ellie's bandage with potions, each more evil-smelling than the last. Will did not object, only talked on and on, speaking more quickly when Ellie's temperature was high and more slowly as it sank. He had no idea how many hours had passed by the time he noticed that Ellie was actually listening. Then he talked more gently and more guardedly, finding himself quite suddenly, when the fever left her and she looked at him again, afflicted by his old doubts as to whether he would ever know whether she could really love him. He was amazed to find these thoughts surfacing at such a time. Would they never go away?

A week later, after the bargewoman reassured them that the danger to Ellie had passed, Will's relief was enormous. When the barge stopped to replenish food and water stocks, he took the horses off and stretched their legs along the river valley, encouraging them to pick at what grass they could scrape through the snow that fell sporadically. There was no goodness in what they cropped but they enjoyed the temporary freedom and when Will brought them back, Ellie told him that their flanks looked rounder and their thick coats less dull. Will also used these excursions to listen for news of Amal and Shihab. Shihab was too distinctive to miss. But they heard nothing and Will slowly began to allow himself to hope that something had befallen them miles back and that the race to get to Richard was already won.

All the while the orange-bringer followed on close behind, but now he was nervous. Time was passing and he did not want the Old Man to sail without him. He would have to act soon. His moment came when the barge could go no farther and Will and Ellie mounted the horses again. At once, the orange-bringer bargained for a mount for himself and pressed hard behind them.

As far as the orange-bringer was concerned, the first night ashore was a failure for Will hardly slept and kept jumping up at unexpected intervals, disturbed by Hosanna, who would not settle. However, the second night, when Will had pushed the horses hard all day and sleep felled him like a giant stone, the orange-bringer managed to creep very close. The horses were loosely tied outside the deserted herdsman's shelter into which Will had pushed Ellie, making a bed for himself in the doorway where he lay, his hand on his sword, as dead to the world as a marble knight atop a crusading tomb. The orange-bringer slid up to Hosanna, slowly drew out his dagger, and grabbed the red tail. Two seconds later, he had been kicked unceremoniously backward and Sacramenta, jerking up from her doze, heard a great and furious rumble emerge from deep within Hosanna's chest. It alarmed her and, tugging on her rope, she freed herself. Fearing Will, the orange-bringer limped quickly over to the safety of a rock as the mare barged past him. He cowered into a cleft but though Will murmured and his hand clutched his sword hilt, he did not wake. Beyond exhaustion, his senses were dead. Inside the cave, Ellie heard nothing and turned to the wall.

The orange-bringer waited a moment or two, then tried again. Again Hosanna made a racket and the man knew at once that he would never be able even to touch the horse's tail. Yet he could not afford to come away with nothing, so he held back until Hosanna quieted down, then slid forward once more, this time avoiding the horses altogether. Crawling on his belly, he slithered past Will and only once inside the shelter did he stand up and flatten himself against the rough stones. With senses sharp as a cat's, he could tell at once where Ellie was and in what position she was lying. Now he grinned. With her face to the wall, his task was easy. Crouching down on all fours, his dagger between his teeth, his fingers slowly crept over the blanket until he found what he was looking for. The plait, so long and heavy, was curled like a thick auburn rope in the dirt. It felt soft and strong and the orange-bringer stroked it gently. How many years must it have taken to grow? What did the girl look like as she shook it out? His eyes narrowed and flickered quickly up and down as Ellie shifted in her sleep and he felt the sudden hot dart of temptation.

Then he heard Hosanna stamping outside. At once he focused only on his task. Ellie's skin twitched as he delicately touched her neck and pushed his hand farther up until he was right at the root of her plait. He tested his knife's sharpness with his tongue before, with one fluid movement, he sliced. The plait came away so quickly that he was caught off balance and nearly dropped it. Quickly he scooped it up before it could begin to unravel, extracted a thong from his pouch and tied it tightly around both top and bottom. His grin returned as he backed away, stepping quietly over Will, who slept on. At the sight of the young man's unprotected face, the orange-bringer's hand prickled. Success made him bold. It would be so easy to cut that Christian throat. What a pity the Old Man had wanted both Will and Ellie to remain alive. Yet . . . Suddenly inspired, the man turned the tip of his blade into a pen and deftly carved the dagger mark of the Assassins onto Will's cheek. His touch was like a feather. Will felt nothing. The orange-bringer's grin grew wider. He did not bother to approach Hosanna again and Sacramenta had disappeared. He shrugged. Maybe he could have got the tail hair from the mare. Never mind. He would get the Old Man his red fly-whisk from another source. It was the girl's plait that was the real prize. He felt it, folded it into his pouch, and felt it again. What a thing of beauty was a woman's hair. Then he shook himself, cast one more baleful look at Hosanna, and vanished.

Will woke with a great start. Surely he had been asleep only for a second? He pulled himself up, hardly noticing the stinging in his cheek. He saw at once that Sacramenta was missing and that the ground around Hosanna was scuffed and trampled. Exclaiming out loud, he made sure that Ellie was still lying asleep before racing to the track up which they had ridden the evening before and gazing down it, praying to see the mare. He saw nothing and rushed back to check Sacramenta's rope. It had not been cut. Now he felt a fool. This was his fault. He must have tied the rope too loosely, simply trusting that the mare would not test it. He did not want to call out for he wanted to find Sacramenta before Ellie woke. Instead, furious with himself, he untied Hosanna, who stamped his foot, edgy and troubled. "Find her, Hosanna, for God's sake, find her," Will begged. Surely she would not have wandered far? He let the horse go and Hosanna obediently moved off, but only yards. Will was right. Sacramenta had not wanted to leave the camp. She was grazing behind a tree, easily visible had Will looked in the right direction. Will sagged with relief. When he whistled, she ambled slowly toward him. He swiftly retied her and turned to find Ellie standing in the doorway of the cave.

He could not, at first, decide what was so strange about her. Her face looked different but the features were the same, except that they were expressing a degree of such shock that Will automatically moved toward her. "It's all right," he called, "Sacramenta's here. She must have just got loose in the night." Ellie glanced over to the mare briefly but without seeing her. She had no idea the horse had ever been missing. She opened her mouth, trying to say something, and when nothing emerged, slowly turned around instead.

Will's mind simply refused to take in what he saw although his hand flew to his lips. He stood right in front of Ellie for almost a minute. "Why did you do it?" His voice, when he found it, rose high. "Why on earth did you do it?" He dared not touch her. Something in her expression frightened him. What desecration! Her hair! Her beautiful hair! He wanted to shout at her. After all, what good did she think such a sacrifice would do?

Before he could say anything more, Ellie raised her own hand and touched his cheek. Immediately, Will was aware again of the stinging. He tried to push Ellie's fingers away but she caught his own and made him trace the thin lines of the dagger. "Do you think I did that, too?" she asked softly. Will felt black dread descending. As it folded around him, it changed from black to crimson, the same crimson as the Old Man's beard, and Will gave a terrible groan. Now he ran his hand over the ragged remains of Ellie's plait as if they were wounds and took her in his arms. In response, Ellie pressed her cheek against his and when they finally parted, her skin was blotted with his blood.

Will went almost off his head, crippled by what had happened and what might have happened. He cried out that he had slept like a boy when he should have been awake like a knight. His cries were loud and unremitting and Ellie could hardly persuade him to leave her side and saddle the horses. At every shadow, every noise, he rushed back, convinced that she was about to be murdered, then he ran back to the horses, convinced that they would be murdered, too.

It was Ellie who broke the spell. "Will," she implored over and over, "Will, Will." Eventually, she had to grab his arm and pinch it. Her voice betrayed no panic for she felt none. In fact, although the loss of her hair had given her the biggest fright of her life, the lightness of her head, now she tossed it about, was not unwelcome and although she waited for a great sadness to well up within her, it never arrived. Her hair had been beautiful but it was only hair. To her surprise, Ellie found that she did not really care. "Will, listen to me. You have to pull yourself together. Amal will have done this and I don't think he wants to kill us. He's just warning us, trying to frighten us away from Richard. He must have passed by. We must only concentrate on catching up to him." She ran her fingers through the crop she had left. It stood up on end, forming a kind of halo. Then she made a funny face. "At last Marissa and I have something in common," she said, and smiled the old smile Will had not seen for months.

The smile calmed him a little and he desperately wanted to believe her but he could not think the intruder had been Amal. Shihab would surely never have arrived and left again without creating a scene. Ellie, however, displayed an endearing obstinacy. "I am going to believe it was Amal," she said decidedly as she helped to tighten Sacramenta's girth, "and I refuse to be frightened. You know, Will, I have felt so sorry for myself, since Kamil"—her face darkened and her voice dropped before rising again—"but we can fight back, can't we? Amal and his Old Man may be able to do what they like and maybe we can't guard against them as easily as we can guard against snakes but we can refuse to be turned into mice. Say we can, Will. Say it."

"How can I say it when I don't feel it?" cried Will. "If I were to lose you, what would be left for me?" He couldn't help it. He had never felt so helpless, so in the grip of forces against which he had no weapons.

Ellie came over and took his face between her hands. She made him look up but he didn't want to for he could not get used to her new appearance. Without her hair she was a little girl again while he felt so old. Nevertheless, he did not move away. "William de Granville," Ellie said, forcing him to meet her gaze, "you are a knight of England. Your king needs you. Hartslove needs you. The memories of all the people you have loved and still love need you. Old Nurse needs you. And"—she looked straight into his eyes—"I need you. Don't you see? You are doing just what the Old Man wants. He doesn't care about killing bodies. He wants to kill souls. This dread is his victory. Throw it off, Will. If you can, then I can, too. We can do it together. We have the horses and we have each other. If we can't be brave now, then we really are lost and I don't want to be lost, Will, and if I don't want to be lost, you can't be lost either." As her words died away she held his face tighter, took a deep breath, and kissed him. It was a kiss filled with everything they had ever shared, filled with their present fears and their future hopes. It was not delivered as a reward or in expectation of gratitude: Ellie gave it because it felt as natural as breathing.

Will never forgot that moment. It was not a moment of joy or of triumph or of reassurance. He did not realize at once what it really was. The kiss was not fleeting, nor was it passionate. It was firm, almost severe, and was full of something deeper and more durable than a sudden impulse. It seemed somehow at odds with Ellie's new, almost childish looks but he knew it could only have come from a heart that beat for the same things as did his own. It did not dispel his worries about either Ellie's feelings for him or their situation yet he no longer felt helpless. The kiss gave him a new kind of courage he had not felt before. He no longer felt alone.

Afterward, they did not speak but mounted quickly. Hosanna set the pace and the two horses sped on, side by side. Occasionally Will looked over at Ellie and saw her face set with the effort of keeping up. But he did not need her to look at him. Even as they galloped, though his fears were as sharp as ever, the crimson pall of dread began to lift from his shoulders. Hosanna felt strong underneath him and when the horse flicked back his ears to hear his master's words, Will found his heart glowing.

It did not glow for long, for almost at once the weather became their enemy. Struggling against gales strong as a slamming door, the horses were battered half to death. At night they shivered and more than once even Ellie's new hopefulness was not enough to keep them cheerful. Sometimes Will imagined Amal already at Speyer and Kamil's knife already lodged between Richard's ribs. Sometimes he could already hear men muttering Kamil's name and his own with loathing. Then he depended on Ellie's encouragement and Hosanna's keenness as never before. On many icy dawns, humans and horses would gather together, leaning on each other to pool their collective strength.

Then the weather changed again. Now they traveled through countryside turned eerily magical by a winter sun sparkling with an edge unknown in England. The snow was pristine and the trees star-studded with frost. The vista was so bright that it stung Will's and Ellie's eyes. Life was difficult for the horses as the snow balled in their feet. Will endlessly had to climb on and off to dig it out. At first they preferred this to the slush, but as the days dragged on, the brittle otherworldliness of it all sickened them and they longed for something duller and less piercing. As the clouds once again began to gather they at last heard news of the silver horse. Seeking hospitality from a farmstead, they learned that she had passed through two days before. Will began to panic again. They must go faster. It would be worse to be nearly there and still to fail. He asked more of the horses, hardening his heart as Ellie and Sacramenta visibly drooped. When they finally reached the Rhine and found another barge for the last lap, they all collapsed onto it with gratitude.

This river journey, however, was far from peaceful. The bargeman asked questions all the time and Will had to make up increasingly evasive answers. Indeed, the bargeman's questions were so pointed that Will and Ellie feared that he was another of the Old Man's spies. Once this thought had taken hold, they could stay on the barge no longer, and early one morning they slipped overboard and were away.

It was lucky they did, for through the dawn mist the following day, Ellie saw Shihab's tail, unmistakable as it swung away through trees in the distance. Ellie called out to Will, who had been conscious of nothing, his face dead with the monotony of the pace. He stood up in his stirrups and came back to life, whooping, hoping that the mare would hear and slow down. But a brisk breeze blew his words back to him and though they hurried on, they did not catch her. In the next clearing, however, in front of a rough forge, they found a farrier, his arms folded and his head full of gruff complaints. Yes, he had seen a silver horse and the rider had not stopped even though the animal had lost a shoe. He felt insulted when Will did not hide his joy at this news. "That animal'll be hopping lame soon enough," the farrier said sourly.

"Poor Shihab!" Ellie whispered, but she could not condemn Will's glee.

They pressed on and on but, much to Will's frustration, never caught sight of Shihab again. Soon Will stopped asking for he reckoned they must have fewer than a hundred miles to go. "If we go as fast as the horses can carry us, we can get to Speyer in under two days," he said to Ellie. "We will have to push them very hard but it will just be for that short time. When we get there, they can easily recover." He found that he himself could not rest at all. All the time he saw Amal raising the dagger for the fatal thrust. Even the slightest delay was unthinkable.

About three hours after dawn on the last day of

January, they at last passed through the gate of the town. Neither Will nor Ellie had any strength left to cheer and while Hosanna was still sound, Sacramenta was limping badly as they ground to a halt in the shadow of the great cathedral. Bone-tired, the horses' hooves dragged. Will slumped off, his ears still reverberating from the endless galloping beat and his muscles throbbing. But even as his body tried to readjust, his mind was asking why their haphazard arrival had been completely uncontested. The town seemed sleepy, and not just with the sleep of a winter's night. Where were the soldiers, the retainers, the wagons and horses, and all the great gaggle of imperial hangers-on who should have been jostling for space in the streets? Where were the men from England and from the Angevin lands who had made the journey to see Richard? Where was Queen Eleanor, who must surely be here by now? Big as the cathedral was, they could surely not all be living inside it? Will gazed about him, uncomprehending. Any moment now, the place would come alive. It would. It must.

But it did not. Nobody appeared until a group of women emerged from a small door. Their heads were covered and they walked with that special gliding movement that marked them out from field-plodding peasants. Will stared at them. Nuns. He shook his head. He didn't want to see nuns. Maybe he had made a terrible mistake and this wasn't Speyer after all.

The women stared back disapprovingly from under their veils. They too were expecting visitors but of quite a different nature. They instinctively moved to the other side of the road and would have passed by swiftly and in silence if Ellie had not addressed them directly. When the girl called out, the nun at the head of the small procession jumped, pretending that she had been too cocooned in prayer to notice the dirty travelers for she did not like to be thought lacking in Christian charity. But she need not have worried. Ellie was too tired to feel anything other than relief when she spoke French and was understood. "We are seeking King Richard of England." Ellie was suddenly very conscious that she looked like a gypsy. She could not imagine what these women made of her hair or her shaking legs. "We must see him. Where is he?"

The nun was taken aback. She had been expecting demands for food or money. Such a question could be answered easily and at once. "Why, he's not here," she said. "All the imperial court has moved up the river and the prisoner king with it."

Will fell to his knees. "But he was to be here!" His voice was a wail. "He was to be here."

A young nun standing behind her superior and wanting her breakfast, shrugged and began to walk on, pushing her sisters before her. "Come on, Petronilla," she urged. "You have answered their question."

"Just wait, Hersende," said the older woman, clicking her tongue. "Our breakfast will not run away." She turned back to Ellie, a little more expansive now, thinking to teach the greedy nun a lesson. "King Richard *was* here," she said, "but there was trouble—squabbling—and the emperor decided to reconvene the court in Mainz. It was the English king's men who wanted this," she added, sensing that Will was about to say something unflattering about the emperor, which she did not wish to hear. However, Will could think of only one thing. "But now we must carry on," he cried, "and our horses are so tired."

"Not only tired, but lame," Hersende observed tartly, looking at Sacramenta.

Ellie began to sink. Her blood felt thick and her skin raw, as if she had been turned inside out. Her eyes rolled back. Now Petronilla abandoned all her reserve. She could not let a girl, even a filthy one, collapse into the gutter. "So many people wanting to get to King Richard," she observed as she caught Ellie in her arms. "It's said that Queen Eleanor has even sent for the pope. Certainly, he would not be the strangest person who has passed by." Petronilla was surprised to find Ellie jerk up.

"Has a man on a silver horse been through?" Her green eyes were now huge black holes. "You must tell us."

Alarmed at the intensity of the question, Petronilla was more careful with her reply. "Well, the men we have seen have been mostly knights and bishops," she said brightly. "The church always sends its sons onto the road."

Will lost his temper. "She asked if you have seen a man riding alone on a silver horse. It has a wall-eye. It is unmistakable. Now, please answer." His words echoed around the square.

Petronilla hesitated, but Hersende, her mind on only bread and milk, responded immediately. "As a matter of fact, yes," she said. "Only an hour ago—"

"That's enough," said Petronilla sharply. Nuns were not supposed to admit to staring at strange men.

Will dropped Hosanna's reins and ran forward, taking hold of Hersende's sleeve. Though thin and unkempt, he would not be resisted. Some of the other nuns clucked. Petronilla intervened. "Now, young man, there's no need for that. We did see a person such as you describe as we went into our prayers. He's gone now. That is the answer."

Will let go and at once hauled himself back onto Hosanna. Ellie stumbled over. "I'll have to go on by myself, Ellie," Will croaked at her. He was doing no more than state the obvious. "Sacramenta can't go any farther. If Amal has only just left, I can still get to Richard first."

"And if you don't?"

Blindly, Will gathered his reins. "I will," he said, trying to shake some last drops of energy into his folding legs. "I will if I waste no time. At least Shihab must be tired, too." Deep lines etched themselves around his mouth. He knew he should have stayed and bargained for a fresh horse, but where, at this time, would he get one? And he did not feel he could manage without Hosanna. "Stay with the nuns," he ordered Ellie. "Don't go anywhere. Promise me that. When Richard is safe, I'll be back for you." He needed to believe it.

And so did she. She pulled herself up. "I won't say good-bye, then," was all she could manage as she brushed her fingers over Hosanna's star and his crusading wounds. Will met her eyes and because of what he saw there, bent down and touched her cheek. Then he was gone and Ellie could hold herself upright no longer.

The last part of the journey, so cruelly unexpected, was the worst. "It's only fifty miles at most to Mainz, Hosanna," Will kept repeating. "We can easily make it by nightfall." The red horse responded to his master's voice by stretching out a little more. Fifty miles! It would have been so easy had they not been in almost ceaseless motion for so long already. But after five miles or so, Will, to whom Hosanna's motion was as familiar as his own, sensed his horse's breathing grow jagged and could feel the great heartbeat occasionally stall and flutter. "But we've got to go on, Hosanna!" Will cried softly, and knew the agony of being understood. Leaning forward, he tried to make himself as small and still as possible, lifting his weight up onto his creaking knees to ease the pressure on the saddle. He knew that Hosanna appreciated the gesture but knew too that it did not help.

There were no mountains and the terrain, though hard and unyielding, was not difficult to transverse. Yet the horizon never seemed to get any nearer. Will set his sights on markers in the scenery—a tree, a small shrine, a few peasants trying to light a fire, or even just a corner in the track. He shut his eyes, hoping that when he opened them again, the marker would, miraculously, be behind them. It never was. Sometimes they looked barely to have moved forward at all. He missed Ellie's presence behind him. His loneliness was acute.

Then he saw Amal and the dregs of adrenaline were like a kick in his chest. The man was standing by the side of the road, his clothes so filthy he could have been wearing a mantle of dust. Shihab stood beside him, one leg raised. There was no defiance about her now. She looked as deadbeat as her rider, who had finally stopped to have her fitted with new shoes since the hard winter roads had worn the mare's foot down to nothing and her pace had been reduced to a hobble. Will never took his eyes off them. Amal was trying to bargain for a new horse, but in light of Shihab's condition, nobody seemed keen to sell. Will clenched his fists. He would kill Amal there and then. He would just clench that scrawny neck between his hands and break it as he might break a chicken's. But as he drew nearer, he knew this would be the action of a fool. First, he could not be sure he had the strength. A man, even a man as desiccated as Amal, always fought for his life harder than you imagined. Then, the small crowd would seize on him as a murderer. If he was in a dungeon, how would that help anybody? No. He turned Hosanna off the main road and picked out a new track behind a group of straggling thorn bushes. They would offer enough cover until he was well passed. If he never saw Will, Amal might imagine he could finish his journey at a more leisurely pace.

Shihab, however, had a different idea. Smelling Hosanna's scent on the wind, she threw up her head. Suffering and miserable, she whinnied loudly and persistently. Will quickly put his hand on Hosanna's neck, warning him to be silent, but Amal was already roused from his torpor. He glanced about, not even needing to see Will to know he was near, and exhorted the farrier to hurry. Will swore to himself. But at least he was now in front. He had only to make sure he stayed there.

For more than an hour Will rode more easily, the knowledge of his advantage boosting him along, but by midafternoon his body was once again flagging and, though he did not want to acknowledge it, he felt another change in Hosanna. Although the horse's pace did not alter, he was gulping and the veins in his neck stood right out in a thick, tangled tracery. He was no longer sweating for while he drank whenever he could, dehydration had set in so severely that his blood was sluggish and poisonous. No matter what Will did to help, the red horse's head sank farther and farther toward the ground and his burgundy mane swept through the mud. More than occasionally, he almost lost his footing entirely.

"I should slow down, I *must* slow down," Will told himself. But every time he tried, he thought he could hear Shihab behind him. He would turn and she was never there, but as his own body began to break down, his mind grew ever more fanciful and saw the silver horse everywhere. Sometimes she was flying. Other times she was swimming in the river. Still Will pushed on. The cold, clear logical part of his brain told him that this punishing pace was going to kill Hosanna yet he could not slow down because, through the clatter of hooves, he could hear Richard's death rattle.

When the early evening bells rang out, Will was moaning aloud. "Will we never be there?" He felt as if he had been flayed and the dagger mark on his face pricked and cracked. Underneath him, Hosanna's heart was now missing every other beat but still the great horse plugged on, his hooves scraping ground over which they would once have eagerly sprung. Though his crusading wounds were dripping blood, Hosanna had ceased to be conscious of pain. Indeed, he was hardly aware of anything except the need to move in a straight line. But though neither wanted it, their pace was finally slowing.

In the gloaming, with Mainz almost within sight, the road grew busier. Blinking away the glazed shadow that was spreading over his eyes, Will helped Hosanna to plow his way around wagons and groups of men bearing the imperial coat of arms. Neither horse nor rider was aware that people fell silent when they saw them staggering and weaving. Nobody offered assistance. Both horse and knight looked beyond anybody's reach. Even the large group of nuns who passed him just crossed themselves.

It was strange, when he had been longing for the moment for so long, but Will did not notice when Hosanna eventually passed into the city. He could think of only one thing now and that was Richard's face. It had become imperative for him to see it. If Richard would just turn toward him, all would be well, for everything would be explained and everything understood. Will tilted forward, almost falling as a new terror assailed him. What if Richard had moved on again? How could Will follow him then? Even if God himself asked, Hosanna could go no farther. Will picked up his reins and choked out his horse's name. He got no response.

The streets leading to the cathedral were brightly lit, with torches flaring over the thousands of men-at-arms jostling for space. Will's way was constantly blocked and in the general melee, Hosanna was pushed and hustled, kicked and scratched as he blundered through. In the square, the crowd was so thick that the horse was almost carried. He objected to nothing. All he knew was that he must keep moving until his beloved master told him to stop.

Will could hardly breathe now. The builders' scaffolding turned the unfinished cathedral walls into the corpse of some enormous, half-eaten animal. Every moment he expected to see Amal spurring Shihab on, still smiling in that half-apologetic way he had. But though no silver horse appeared, even when Will reached the steps of the cathedral he did not dare to pause, just pushed Hosanna straight up and through the open doors. He never knew why nobody challenged them for he could not see himself as he appeared to others, a sight of almost mythical pathos.

Once inside, it took Will's eyes a while to adjust, but through the arching dark he at last made out globes of light at the far end. He strained and strained to see what he was looking for, and then, finally, he found it. At the top of the nave, a throne and a chair had been specially illuminated. On the throne sat the emperor and on the chair, with his head uncovered and his back ramrod straight, sat Richard. He was undoubtedly alive because he was talking to somebody.

When Will saw the familiar figure, his cry of relief galvanized Hosanna into his last and greatest effort. People fell back as the red horse picked up his head and struggled down the length of the church, the crowd opening up like the Red Sea before Moses. When Hosanna reached the chair, he stopped at last and those closest to him heard the smallest of sighs. Will slid off. "My king," he said. His parched throat was almost closed and he wondered if he had even made any sound, for nobody moved. He tried again, grinding out the words as if sawing them from wood. "I am your loyal servant, sire," he wheezed, "and I have come a thousand miles to tell you that. You must beware. The Assassins—" Will spluttered, and Richard got up. This was not how Will had imagined it. Almost drunkenly, he knelt down, dizzy and disoriented. Richard did not seem to be listening. Will could say no more. In despair and confusion he crawled back to Hosanna and pressed his forehead against the once proud neck. He looked at the king's feet. "Sire," he entreated, but could not go on. Beneath his fingers he could feel Hosanna's pulse winding down. Slower and slower came the beats as Hosanna lowered himself onto the flagstones. When he reached the floor, Will slid down and took his head in his arms. He did not cry out. There was nothing more to say.

Then, "Will, Will, Will," he heard. He frowned before his brain, now sluggish as porridge, recognized the voice. Hal. He sighed. He was obviously dead. Hal was greeting him in Heaven. There was no need to answer. But then another voice, higher and more piercing, broke through. "I knew it! I knew it! Didn't I just know it, Hal? I told you we should have faith in Mistress Ellie's necklace!" Elric pitched himself forward, so overwhelmed with relief that unwanted tears poured down his cheeks. Holding on to his hopes had been so hard, especially when, having rushed as quickly as possible to the king's side, they had not been greeted as heroes but as unwelcome messengers bearing awkward news. For the worst week of Elric's life, he and Hal had been imprisoned in a cell, before Richard asked for them to be released. On pain of death, they were forbidden to leave the court. Worse, when they told their story, the king had appeared unmoved! Now Elric refused to be shushed. "We couldn't find you," he cried, "and then nobody would listen!" With unusual roughness, Hal pushed him aside. "For God's sake, Elric! Look at Hosanna! Just look at Hosanna!"

Will roused himself, "Yes, Hosanna . . ." But Hal was already pulling off the saddle and shouting for water. Carefully taking the red horse's head from Will's arms, he was fierce. "We'll not let him down, sir. But be careful—" At once he and Elric were pushed away and now Will found himself staring straight into the royal eyes. He tried to get up, but then, in a moment of dreadful clarity, he also saw somebody else bearing down on him. He shook his head. It could not be. He had been so sure. He searched again for Richard and found the king's eyes as chilly as marble. Will looked again at the man by the king's side. Now there could be no mistake. Standing in front of Will, shaved and dressed like a senior imperial servant, his skin no longer gray, but pale, easily disguising his eastern origins, was Amal. He had taken a risk, abandoned the road for the river, and was now so close to Richard that he could have stabbed him with a needle.

Will opened his mouth. He formed words, so many words, all the words he had dreamed for so long of saying. He tried to force them out. Clutching Richard's legs, he would not let go, not after everything he and Hosanna had been through. He could not fail now. Surely he could not. But Richard did not help him and before anything more than a crackle could emerge, Will passed out.

19

In Speyer, Ellie was carried straight off to bed by the nuns. Now that she was completely in their charge, they were happy to fuss over her. Even Hersende, after she had consumed a belated breakfast, joined in. At first Ellie was too shattered to sleep and tossed and turned, filled with terrible fears. Petronilla did not leave her until she dozed off and then she slept the sleep of the dead for half a day. After that, she half woke several times, momentarily confused as to where she was. She tried to pull herself up, but her body would not respond and once again she found herself sinking down, this time falling into waking sleeps, in which Will's voice was calling her, and then Kamil's, but when she answered they could not hear her. At last, hours later, Ellie woke properly and found that she had thrashed about so much she had pulled down the old hangings surrounding her bed and her face was speckled with gold leaf.

She got out of bed and saw Petronilla sitting by the fire. When Ellie refused to get back under the covers, Petronilla did not argue but summoned a laundress who brought Ellie's clothes, newly washed and aired. "Now that you are awake," Petronilla said, full of practical authority, "you must eat."

But Ellie was not listening. "I must get to Mainz," she said, pulling on her clothes as fast as she could. "I have already delayed too long."

"The man you were with said you were to remain here. And besides, even if you are not in bed, you need to rest."

"I have already rested and I know what he said." Ellie was just as firm as Petronilla. "I am going to Mainz."

Petronilla did not bother to argue. "Well, you are in luck," she said placidly. "Your brave horse may not be able to carry you—we have had to put poultices on her poor legs because she is quite worn out, like you—but a group of nuns has arrived. They have come down through Mainz and some of them are to return there. I shall go, too. It seems that there is trouble afoot with far-fetched stories about thieves running off with your king's ransom. The emperor has need of our prayers. You can travel in a wagon."

Ellie pulled on her cloak as if she might run to Mainz.

Petronilla pursed her lips. She should have said nothing. She tried to distract Ellie with Sacramenta. "Never mind about that for now," she said. "Men are always making things up. Now, I am sure your nice horse can be led on the journey. That shouldn't tax her too much. Calm down, my dear, or you'll collapse and make yourself truly ill. All will be well. Go and see your horse."

Ellie tried to walk but her muscles were stiff and she was light-headed. She tried to ask again about Mainz but Petronilla refused to be drawn.

"We leave in half an hour," she said, "and before we go you must eat. If you don't eat you can't come. Here is bread and beer. Take it." Ellie began to refuse. It would choke her. Petronilla crossed her arms and then, because her expression was just like Old Nurse's, Ellie did as she was told. Next, the nun produced a jar of liniment and made Ellie sit as she rubbed it into her legs and then she inspected the arrow wound. The scar was lumpy but the color was good. "It seems to me that you have been very fortunate," Petronilla said. "Now, you must promise me something. You must promise that you won't take one of our horses and ride to Mainz on your own." Ellie's heart sank. Petronilla had read her mind. She fiddled with crumbs of bread. "Promise," Petronilla insisted gently. "It's for your own good. You are not fit." And she would not leave until Ellie reluctantly nodded.

As soon as Petronilla allowed it, Ellie hurried to Sacramenta. "I know just what you feel like," she murmured, looking at the mare's legs and caressing her ears. Then she badgered the nuns to start the journey. It was unbearable not knowing what was happening to Will and Hosanna.

To her relief, the nuns caught some of her urgency and began to mount on mules and palfreys but as Ellie exhorted them not to delay, she heard the unmistakable sound of squabbling. One of the covered carts was rocking and many of the sisters crowded around it were giggling. Ellie frowned and walked closer. She knew that voice. Pushing her way through, she pulled away some sailcloth hangings and found herself face-to-face with Marissa.

They stared at each other blankly. "What are you doing here?" Ellie couldn't help herself. Marissa stopped midkick. "You!" She was momentarily taken completely aback. Then she grabbed at Ellie. "Will? If you are alive, is he? Is he? Oh, tell me. Tell me now."

"He's gone to Mainz," Ellie said quickly, and watched as Marissa sank down to the floor. "We've just been in Mainz," she muttered, "we must have passed him."

"But you didn't see him?" Ellie shook her arm. "And you didn't hear anything? Marissa, I'm so afraid." Ellie bit her lip. She was not used to confiding.

Before Marissa could say anything more, the nun attached to her, thankful for some respite, sighed and rubbed her shins. "I don't know who you are," she groaned, "but if you know this demon, maybe you can take her. We caught her as a runaway. She said she was coming to a convent here, but nobody knows her at all so my abbess decided to take her back to Mainz where the archbishop can decide what to do with her. Good luck to him."

Ellie had no time to say anything before another nun disagreed. "You keep her with you," she ordered. "Offer your bruises up to the Virgin Mary. The girl's got to be punished."

Marissa did not hear either of them. She was staring at Ellie's hair. What on earth had happened to it? Had Ellie cut it off to prove something Marissa could not even imagine?

Ellie swiftly climbed into the wagon just as it began to roll. Amid the noise of the wheels, the two girls remained silent until Marissa's jailer, now that her charge was quiet at last, was rocked to sleep by the wagon's motion and began to snore.

213

It was then that Ellie told Marissa all that had happened. She restricted herself to the plain facts, trying hard not to reveal any of the deeper things that had passed between herself and Will. Marissa remained expressionless, revealing nothing of her own tale until Ellie spoke of Amal and the Old Man of the Mountain. Then she jumped.

When they stopped for the night at a convent on the road, Ellie fretted. How many miles had they covered in the day? Ten at most? Directly after supper she went to the stables, hoping to find that by some miracle Sacramenta's legs were cured and the mare was ready to speed away. But there was no such miracle. Instead, under the light of the lanterns, Sacramenta was lying down and seemed disinclined to get up even when Ellie called her name. Ellie left her to rest.

It was on her way to her own straw pallet that she heard Marissa hissing. All the nuns lay in a long line, close together, and the girl was lying on her back, her jailer still tied like a millstone to one arm and one leg. "We've got to get away from these people. Are Sacramenta's legs really too bad to ride?"

"Yes."

Marissa tussled with herself. "Untie me."

"Oh, for goodness' sake, Marissa!" Ellie had no time for this.

"Do you care about Will?"

"Of course I do," Ellie exploded. "You know that."

"Then untie me. I can help him."

"You?"

"Yes."

"How?"

214

But Marissa shook her head. "If you don't untie me, I won't tell you anything."

Ellie did not know what to do. It seemed inconceivable that Marissa could help Will, but if Will really was in trouble over the ransom, could she take that risk?

She hovered. She could see Marissa tense as a strung bow even though she was pretending not to care. "If your help involves stealing horses, I promised I wouldn't," Ellie said.

Marissa turned, her eyes full of scorn. "Well, if that's the way you want it." She raised her foot to kick her jailer awake. She needed somebody to fight.

"No!" cried Ellie suddenly, and then dropped to her knees, praying that she had not woken anybody. "I'll do it, Marissa, I'll do it, but if it is just a trick, I'll never forgive you, never."

"You'll need a knife," was all Marissa said.

Ellie wasted no more time and soon Marissa was free, exultantly attaching her jailer to the next nun in the row. She and Ellie did not exchange another word until they had crept into the stables, found the least sleepy-looking horses, and were peering out of the barn door. The grooms were busy warming their toes, so it proved surprisingly easy to slip across the yard. Once behind the buildings Ellie, hoping that she would be able to justify breaking her promise to Petronilla, helped Marissa to mount and then vaulted on herself. I'm not breaking my promise to Will, she said to herself. Or at least not really. He told me to stay with the nuns, and Marissa is a nun. Then she concentrated only on getting away. It was several miles before Marissa slowly told Ellie of her visit from Hal and Elric and, through

215

the dark, she could feel Ellie's tears, half of joy that they were alive and half of anxiety as to what had happened to them since. Then Marissa slowly revealed something else and when she had finished, it was gratifying to find that her great rival for Will's affections was absolutely astonished.

20

Hunger brought Will around at last and he had no idea how long he had been unconscious. He had been brought to a small room with a rush-strewn floor and a pallet for a bed. He was unwashed but blankets kept him warm and at his feet, now bare, somebody had placed a smooth stone that had clearly once been warm. He woke up quite slowly and stretched out his hand, thinking it would touch Hosanna. When his knuckles hit a clammy wall, his eyes jerked open and he tumbled off the pallet, making for the door. It was locked but through the window he could see straight out into the yard below and the sight was not reassuring. Hal was standing by the water trough and his expression was so grim that Will's heart crashed. Hosanna was dead. He was sure of it. His sense of loss was overwhelming but he fought it. He must get to Richard even though he too could be dead by now, for it was quite possible that Amal had done his work in the night. Ignoring the food placed on a table in the corner, Will banged on the door until he heard soldiers shouting at him to shut up. This made him bang all the more and he quieted down only when they thrust spears through the bars. But he could not sit still and eventually, hating himself, he wolfed down the food, choking as he suddenly heard Richard's name. The king was dead. He felt it. He threw the remains of the food away.

When the door at last opened, Will was prepared for anything except for the sight he now saw. Richard himself came in, shrouded in a cloak. Will dropped to his knees at once, but when the king lifted a warning finger Will got up again and waited until the door slammed to pay his homage. Now Richard pushed back his hood. In the daylight, his hair was a little grayer and his cheeks a little fuller than Will remembered, but when Will's hand was clasped, he found Richard's grip had lost none of its strength. The king, however, was still as remote as he had been in the cathedral.

The key turned in the lock. They were alone. Still the king gave no gesture of warmth and Will's heart sank. "Am I a prisoner?" he asked. He was not sure what else to say.

Richard walked to the window. "We are all prisoners," he said pleasantly enough, but as if Will were a stranger. "I can wander about the emperor's court more or less at will but I am not free since the ransom is not paid. My mother will arrive tomorrow, but it seems we will wait in vain for the wagons in your charge."

Will went cold. The reason Amal had not yet killed Richard was clear. If Richard died before Queen Eleanor's part of the ransom was delivered, she would turn straight for home, for Richard's subjects would not be happy to exchange their silver for a corpse. Only once the Queen's silver was safely in the imperial vaults would Amal strike. But now something else began to agitate at the back of Will's mind, to niggle.

"So much silver," the king continued, his tone almost whimsical, "is surely a temptation for any man. Our mutual friend Kamil, where is he now, Will? Your squire and your boy arrived with a very garbled story. Then, just yesterday, one of the emperor's servants told us how the imperial soldiers were set upon by your men and how he followed you and watched as ships sailed from southern ports taking my ransom to Saracen coffers. It seems that Kamil was not quite the man of honor we thought he was. That is a pity, but perhaps nothing better can be expected of such people. But you, Will . . ." He stopped and looked Will straight in the eye. "I am told that you have been corrupted by visions of untold wealth and the power that wealth brings. I am told that you are here now only because Kamil double-crossed you and took not just his share of the silver but yours also before abandoning you. His treachery seems to know no limits." Richard paused. "And yours, Will? How far does that stretch? Let me guess. I think you are here now either with some preposterous fairy tale of your own or simply to beg my forgiveness. Frankly, I don't know which would be worse."

Will flushed with anger. "That is what you were told," he said, "and you choose to believe it?"

Their eyes locked and Richard came very close. "The thing is, Will, it doesn't matter what I believe. It matters only what the emperor believes, for he has the key to my prison door. Without the silver in your charge, I must remain here at his pleasure."

Will's whole face blazed. He wanted to shake

Richard. However, he would not beg the king to believe him. He would not stoop to that. He would say what he had to say and the king must judge for himself. Will was acutely conscious that he barely looked like a knight, wrapped in a blanket and with a face streaked with filth. Nevertheless, he would remember his father and bear himself like a de Granville. "Sire," he said, knowing he had only one chance, "I ask only that you hear me to the end. Then you must decide whether I am to be trusted or not. The imperial servant you speak of is not German at all. He is a Saracen called Amal. He sought us out at Hartslove, saying he was sent to deliver the horse you gifted to my brother, Gavin. You must remember the horse, said to be the fastest in the world? If you look, I expect you will find her in the imperial stables. We took this man for a friend, never suspecting that he would turn Kamil into a conspirator. Some of what he told you is true. Kamil did wish to steal the ransom because Amal persuaded him that he could stop it from being used to pay soldiers to kill his own people. Surely that is something you can understand?" Richard made no movement at all. Will went on, more urgently now. "Kamil's actions were treacherous. They were. But he himself was a victim of treachery. The ship waiting for the ransom did not belong to Saladin's followers but to Saladin's enemy, the Old Man of the Mountain, who bears a grudge against Kamil. It's neither the Saracen leaders nor the emperor who is Amal's true master, but the head of the Assassins." Richard crossed his arms. His eyes were still cold as marble.

Will chose his next words very carefully. "And there is deeper treachery even than that, sire, treachery that goes against every grain of Christian chivalry." It was an effort to speak quietly for his veins ran hot, but nobody except the king must hear him now. He spoke very distinctly so that there could be no misunderstanding. "I wondered why, sire, when soldiers disguised in the imperial colors helped Kamil to commandeer the ransom, there was no pursuit. Why did we see nobody? But now I know the answer. The soldiers who helped Kamil were not *disguised* as imperial soldiers: They *were* imperial soldiers." Richard caught his breath and Will pressed on. "It's so obvious, sire. If the ransom vanished, then the emperor could keep you his prisoner and you could do nothing about it. You would be powerless. The truth is that the Old Man and the emperor are in this together." Will found it harder and harder to keep his voice steady. "But there is something worse, sire, something that even the emperor does not know about, for the Old Man keeps his darkest secrets to himself. You are not to be kept a prisoner. Once the queen's silver has arrived, you are to be found dead with Kamil's dagger between your ribs. The Old Man knows that the emperor will be angry, for you are of much more value to him alive. But what does he care? You see, the Old Man wants Kamil to be thought of as a murderer. With his dagger stained with your blood, Kamil's name will be blackened. It will be assumed that he slipped in silently and carried out the Old Man's orders, like every other good Assassin. I suppose the Old Man reckons that the ransom silver will soon dry any tears the emperor sheds on your behalf." Richard frowned. Will spoke faster and faster. "Sire, you must see. Your death will complete the Old Man's revenge. By using Kamil's

221

knife to kill a king, he can ensure that Kamil's name will be denounced among all honorable men, whether Christian or Muslim, until the end of time. It will be said he betrayed everybody, that he was a man of no value and no quality: that he belongs only among the damned. That will be the Old Man's final triumph."

Will fell silent though his eyes still burned fierce and bright. Richard's expression, however, was unaltered and when he spoke, his voice had a steely rasp. "Will you swear on the life of your red horse that what you say is true?" He made Will face him directly. "Will you swear?"

Will felt as if the king had struck him. He had lost his father and his brother in the cause of the king. He had broken Hosanna in the cause of the king. Everything he did was in the cause of the king. To be doubted by the king was intolerable.

"Swear, Will, swear," Richard's voice commanded him.

Will sank back onto the pallet, completely deflated. The king had certainly changed. Once, Richard could have judged a man's character with only a look. Now he demanded oaths and weighed up the word of a knight with whom he had fought in the field against the word of an enemy he scarcely knew.

And Will resisted. He could not—would not—swear on Hosanna's life. Even if the horse still had a life to swear on which Will, in his heart, scarcely dared to believe, it would be entirely wrong. Worse than wrong. If the king could not believe him without an oath, the trust between them was at an end. He tried to find some form of words that would not be insulting but gave up.

"I will not swear on Hosanna's life," he said dully. "I will not swear to you. I will not swear at all. If we are reduced to oaths of loyalty, then there is no loyalty left." He put his head in his hands.

There was a short silence, then, "How like your father you look now," Richard observed, sitting down beside Will and taking his hands from his face. The king's eyes had lost their glacial gray and now shone green and quizzical. It took Will a moment to adjust. "I miss him, you know," Richard said.

Will could hardly think straight. He sat with his jaw half-open. Richard studied his fingernails. Only slowly did Will begin to understand that he had passed some kind of test. Richard allowed him time to close his mouth before touching him lightly on the shoulder. "In times like these men swear oaths easily," he said. "I have found it better to depend on the man who won't swear." Relief flooded Will's entire body. He put his hand between the king's cool palms and, looking up, found that they understood each other very well.

They spoke at length and when Richard finally got up to leave, Will begged that he would guard himself with vigilance. "From what you say, I should be safe until the queen's silver arrives," Richard replied, trying to reassure.

But Will could not be content with that. "There may be others here in the Old Man's pay. Try and keep Hal with you, sire," he pleaded. "He would die defending you, and Elric, too."

"If they can be spared from that red horse." Richard gave a faint smile.

Will shook his head, trying to hide his overwhelming distress. "I saw Hal from the window earlier," he said. "I think Hosanna is beyond human care now."

"Oh?" said Richard. "Before I came up here, he was still worth saving. That boy—Elric, is that his name?— well, he is quite clear that Hosanna is going home. He tells the horse so all the time, and Hosanna won't want to disappoint him."

"Hosanna would have been happy to die for you, too," Will said when he could trust himself to speak, and Richard did not laugh at such a thought. He was not a sentimental man, but he knew something of the bond that could grow between a knight and his destrier. He half envied Will his attachment. Sometimes the king thought that the only thing to which he was truly attached was war. On a sudden impulse, he walked swiftly over to Will and embraced him with the embrace of a father. Then, just as quickly, he left him.

The day dragged on and now Will allowed himself to rest. Hosanna would pull through. Richard knew everything and Richard believed him. Hal would foil the Assassin's knife and the king was clever. When the door next opened, it would be to announce that they were all on their way home. That night, Will slept. In his dreams, Ellie was riding Sacramenta. They were just about to meet. Ellie was smiling. Then Will was shaken awake by a terrible clattering.

At first he thought it was just the rest of the ransom rolling in and he paced up and down, anxious for reassurance that Hal was alert at his post by Richard's side. But the wagoners also brought news that they shouted out with glee. Richard's lands were under fierce attack from the king of France. The queen had brought with her not only the ransom silver but long lists of knights openly in revolt against their absent lord. At once the wagoners found themselves surrounded by cheering imperial soldiers and Richard's powerlessness was openly mocked. He would need to get home quickly, they catcalled, or he would find he had no home to go to. Will kicked his door with impotent fury.

It was not until midmorning that, without any ceremony at all, he was hauled out and frog-marched, still barefoot and filthy, along dark corridors reeking of damp. This was not the release he had hoped for. Then the dark gave way to light and he found himself being hurried right into the middle of the great hall. Will blinked, almost blinded by the flickering of hundreds of candles. With no time to collect himself, he was being stared at by a great and distinguished gathering, all crammed close together on benches, their fine furs and silks shimmering as wax dripped from above their heads. A public gallery had been erected at one end, for the emperor liked his subjects to witness his justice, and people from the town had flocked in, men and women jostling for space.

Will was bewildered by the sea of faces. Some of the people he recognized. Most he did not, but through them all he focused on only three. Directly in front of him were Richard, the emperor, and Amal. He was so relieved to see the king still alive that he did not need to see anybody else, not even Queen Eleanor, who sat directly behind her son. All her seventy-two years were written over her face but still she sat upright.

The emperor raised a hand and the company fell

silent except for a continuous murmur from the public gallery. Will's chest tightened. Was this Richard's moment of freedom? He could not tell. Added to that, the emperor was much younger than Will expected. Dressed in green velvet, with the imperial crown balanced precariously on his head, he sat nervously on an ornate throne set on a dais between two pillars. Amal hovered behind him looking sickly. Life at the imperial court, with its rich food and bawdy jokes, did not suit an old spy used to the harder life of the Syrian mountains. He was more emaciated than ever and his bright tunic only accentuated the depression rooted in his face. Richard sat below the dais and Will was comforted to see that Hal was at his shoulder.

It was soon clear that this was no joyful scene of reunion and freedom but a trial, and to his alarm Will found himself the defendant. Yet even as two soldiers stationed themselves on either side, his alarm diminished. Will could not see the king's face but Richard seemed to be sitting easily, his legs splayed out. Occasionally he addressed his mother and her expression too was encouraging. If the king and Queen Eleanor were relaxed, Will need not worry.

The emperor began to speak and the translators took deep breaths for the emperor spoke quickly and in German, to stamp his authority. The charge against Will was treason, both against his king and against the imperial majesty. Will had conspired with his friend Kamil, so the emperor declared in tones that were entirely reasonable, to steal Richard's ransom and thus to prevent the emperor from doing his Christian duty and releasing a holy and respected crusader. He could not, naturally, release Richard with the ransom unpaid since that would send out a signal that the empire was weak and the emperor's reputation would be sullied. With regret, therefore, without the ransom entrusted to William de Granville, Earl of Ravensgarth, he must keep Richard locked up.

Will looked at the king but Richard said nothing.

A man unknown to Will was summoned to speak in his defense. Will signaled that he would defend himself. The request was denied. The defender did not even look at his client but puffed out his chest. Will was just a young knight, he said, easily led astray. The fact that he was here now, having come voluntarily to throw himself on the mercy of the king and the emperor, should speak in his favor. He would not be treacherous again.

Will surged forward, restrained only by the soldiers. Surely Richard would speak up? But still Richard said nothing. Will clenched his fists and tried to keep his temper under control. *There must be some reason for the king's silence,* he thought. *He will speak soon.* He could see Hal tense.

Now Amal was summoned to bolster the case for the prosecution. "I wish everybody to see that this is a fair trial," the emperor said again and again. "We do not condemn without evidence."

With his perfect German, Amal was the perfect witness. He spun his tale in sorrow, not anger, and he told it so well that the audience was moved almost to tears. They stared with hostile eyes at Will. How shocking, they muttered, for a knight to be seduced by the lures of a false Saracen friend and the promise of easy money. What price Christian chivalry now? They shook their heads even as they licked their lips like prowling foxes scenting blood. Amal warmed to his theme, his crackling voice bleeding Kamil's reputation dry. The audience shuffled their feet. Some called out "Shame!" others something worse. Richard shifted slightly. When he had finished, Amal bowed his head and slid back behind the throne.

The emperor cleared his throat. "It is a dreadful thing," he said, and the French interpreter relayed his words in a voice scratchy as a quill, "that a crusader hero like Richard should not be able to return in triumph to his own lands. How much it pains me to see him still confined. Yet the terms of the ransom that King Richard himself agreed to, a ransom which was to make up for all the king's shortcomings, have not been honored. What can an emperor do in such circumstances? If there has been wrongdoing, somebody must be punished. That is the law." He coughed.

Now, Will thought, *now Richard will stand up and this charade will be over.*

But still nothing. Only Hal was on his feet, staring wildly from Richard to Will to Richard and clasping his sword. He too could not believe what was going on. A groan began to swell through the crowd. They knew what was coming next and it made them rustle their cloaks in anticipation.

The emperor flapped his hands until the swell died down. He sank his head into his chest as if he was debating. Then he sighed and began again. "This knight's betrayal," he gestured in the direction of Will, "has been terrible indeed. But," he paused for effect, "I have decided, in my own way, to be merciful." Will held his breath. "I have decided that Richard, Duke of Aquitaine and King of England, should not be required to remain here until more wagons of silver can be gathered and delivered." To Will's surprise, Richard's expression did not change. "I ask for only two things in exchange for his freedom," the emperor continued. "He must swear allegiance to me"—at this Richard looked genuinely surprised and horrified, and Queen Eleanor leaned forward and spoke quickly to him, which the emperor pretended not to notice—"and he must oversee the punishment of this wicked knight, William de Granville, Earl of Ravensgarth, who, despite his youth, must pay the heaviest price for his treachery. That is my decision. Freedom for the king and death for the knight. It is simple and, I believe, fair. Does King Richard agree?"

Will lurched backward. He had eyes only for Richard now. It was clear what had happened. Despite all Will had said, the king had struck a deal with the emperor, a deal in which each would get what they craved most: the emperor Richard's homage and the legal execution of the only knight who knew of his hideous pact with the Old Man, and Richard the ability once again to exercise his kingship in more than name. The logic was as perfect as it was deadly.

At last Richard got up and walked heavily toward Will. In his face Will read his fate. Half of the king's mind was weeping for a young man who had been more loyal than any son. He did truly love and respect him. But the rest wept only for his benighted kingdom and his wounded lands, consolidated so carefully and now pulled apart like a sheep mauled by wolves. Will could follow the king's thoughts as if they were his own. Richard's subjects had given all they had for the ransom. If they did not get their king in return—and soon—the spring fields of England and France would be speckled not with wildflowers but with blood, and the dull rattle of sword against sword would drown out the cries of newborn lambs. It was clear to Will that to avoid this Richard would have sold his own mother, and Will was hardly that. There had been no better bargaining tool than the information Will had provided and it was this that had sealed his fate. He was to die a traitor's death to save both his king and the imperial honor.

At first, a sense of appalled horror and indignation engulfed him. Will's whole self revolted against such a calculation. He wanted to cry out and denounce a king who would condone such black injustice. But when Richard approached and looked Will fearlessly in the eye, not begging, not apologizing, but simply regarding him as an equal, a different feeling entirely overtook him. Though the king did not speak, Will knew he was being asked to understand the dilemma and to weigh up the situation dispassionately. Richard was asking his most trusted knight for the greatest sacrifice he could ever make. Will's life for a king's freedom. Will's life for a kingdom's safety. Will's life for the good of countless others who were defenseless without their lord and crying out for peace. Will's life could deliver all that.

Richard's eyes were hard as flint, but below them, the edges of his mouth were creased. Will could not take his eyes from those creases. They called to him. They told him that the king could not do what he needed to do on his own. Richard might not beg but he needed Will as he had needed nobody else. At that moment, Will held the king in the palm of his hand.

Slowly, then like an onrushing tide, Will's indignation was swept away. He half wanted to cling on to it. He half wanted to scream and shout that the king was a monster. But instead he found himself possessed by a mad bravery. It overtook him with such force that he could not resist it and within moments he stopped trying. Breaking away from the king's gaze he stood straight as a spear. He, Will de Granville, Earl of Ravensgarth, would save the king and the kingdom. Maybe he would save the world. He could already see himself approaching the scaffold, head held high. He could see his body being cut down and Ellie crying and tending his grave as tenderly as she tended Gavin's. *She will love me forever now*, Will thought. *To her, I will always be a hero. I shall never disappoint her.* The thought was momentarily thrilling. It filled him with power and the audience was astounded to see him smile, one brilliant, glorious smile, which even the dirt smeared on his face could not disguise.

But just as quickly this reckless bravery gave way to reality. What was he thinking? Whatever Ellie thought and whatever the truth, forever after the de Granvilles would be known as the family who had nurtured two traitors, himself and Kamil. People would talk about their friendship and nod their ignorant heads as if they had always seen this coming. Moreover Ellie herself would be besmirched by association. How could Will allow that? Suddenly, he felt her kiss and saw again the look in her eyes when he had left her. His smile vanished. What use was all that to a dead man? Was he really going to throw away their future together, just when he had really begun to believe that it was his for the asking? And yet he was the king's servant. He must help the king. He gripped his arms to his sides.

Richard saw all Will's inner turmoil and did not flinch from it. Part of him even rejoiced to see, reflected back at him, a vision of his own youthful, better self, when his head was hot with similar heroic visions and not cold with grubby considerations of statesmanship. He wondered, humbly, how many kings could boast of a knight who believed it a matter of honor to be dishonored for the sake of the kingdom? When he had cut his deal with the emperor, he had been certain that Will would not let him down, for Will *was* the finest man he knew. Yet now, with the young man's unblinking eyes boring into his, his barefoot stance still proud, and his mouth never betraying for an instant the terror he must now be feeling in his heart, it was Richard who hesitated. A trick of the light meant that the king thought he could see Sir Thomas and Gavin standing at Will's side. Their expressions were not friendly.

He took a step back, almost crashing into Hal, and his hawk-eyes circled the whole hall. He had to speak but he had no idea what he was going to say. All he knew was that he must say something to put off the dreadful moment when he, with his own mouth, would condemn Will to death. That moment would certainly come. There was no other way. But not quite yet. "I thank the emperor." Richard knew his voice sounded much too loud. He began again. "I thank the emperor." Then he saw Amal and hatred bubbled up in him like oil boiling in a barrel. The hatred was useful. Its heat could help the king finish this terrible undertaking. His voice hardened. "A man who plots to betray a king deserves to die. It is the ultimate in treachery."

The emperor did not want Richard to speak further. Executing Will was all very well in theory but in the flesh Will looked too young and fresh for such a sacrifice. The sooner this business was over, the better. But Richard did not stop. "Do we all in this hall believe that?" he asked, glaring at Amal as a man glares at a rat. "Is a person who, in league with a Saracen enemy, betrays a Christian king, worthy to live?"

"No, no," the people shouted back, enjoying themselves.

The emperor twitched. This was getting a little close to the knuckle.

"Whoever he is and whatever his rank?" Richard was psyching himself up. Soon he must point to Will. His finger trembled at the thought.

The crowd was baying. "Whoever he is and whatever his rank." Some began to point at Will themselves. Several leaped forward, rolling up their sleeves, waiting only for Richard's nod to begin a public lynching. Richard did not dare to look at Will but now braced himself and raised his hand, his finger pointing to the ceiling, ready to snap down. The crowd's bay became a bellow until a commotion in the public gallery distracted them. A cry, loud and high pitched, demanded a hearing. "Let me through! Let me through! I WILL get through. I have something very important to say. If you don't let me through, may God have mercy on your souls, for your families will be cursed forever."

Will, who had hardly been aware of breathing at all, found himself breathing very fast. So hard was the blood pounding in his ears that he could hardly hear the voice and when he did, he could not believe it, for it was a girl's voice, and not one he either expected or wanted. Those peremptory tones could only be Marissa's. But how could it be her when she was shut up at St. Martin's? Yet there she was, elbowing her way to the front, tolerating no obstruction.

Will's mind began to race. He did not want her here. If he was to sacrifice himself, he did not want her to see. Nor did he welcome a delay. It must be done now or all his courage would desert him. In desperation, Will turned to Richard. "Get her out," he cried. Richard gestured to the emperor, who summoned his guard. They ran to the gallery and seized Marissa, pulling her into the hall, trying to stop her still calling down curses if she was not allowed to have her say.

Now Queen Eleanor was frowning. Her family had been cursed, with terrible results, over many generations. It had made her very superstitious, and she did not want them cursed any more. The girl might be simply a troublemaker but what harm could it do to hear her speak? She made up her mind and sent a message via a servant to the emperor. "Let the girl speak."

The emperor did not know how to refuse.

Marissa never knew that she had the queen to thank for giving her a hearing. All she knew was that this was the moment for which she had been waiting. For just a minute she who was so powerless would be all-powerful.

Now that Marissa was so near him, Will began to sweat. What could she know? She would just humiliate herself and him. She was going to mess everything up. Couldn't she see? Will *must* die a traitor so that Richard could go free. He tried to talk to her but she took no notice. She concentrated only on the emperor and the crowd. "It may not be customary but it is surely right," she said in a voice as piercing and clear as Elric's, "that the defense should be able to question the prosecutor." Nobody denied it. "In that case I would like to call that man there"—she pointed to Amal—"down onto the floor again. He spoke so eloquently. We should hear some more."

Amal shook his head but the audience had become intrigued and Marissa reeled them in. He was forced down and shrank in front of her, a blighted crust against a smooth young sapling. But still, he had the emperor behind him. There was nothing this girl could do to hurt him. Why, she had barely seen him since they crossed the sea months ago. He stood up a little taller and tried to turn from abject crow into confident raven.

"Ah, Amal," Marissa said to him, "I greet you." Amal bowed, then, crucially, realized his mistake. Marissa had spoken in Arabic. She had learned the words from Ellie as they rode. At the imperial court, his name was not Amal and he was supposed to speak only German. Quickly, he righted himself. The emperor gave him a glassy stare. With increasing satisfaction Marissa circled him like a cat. She hoped Ellie had heard her perfect pronunciation from where she was standing in the gallery.

"I wonder at you, Amal," Marissa purred, now in Norman French, "that you find it so easy to live among us." One of the translators came to stand by Amal's ear but Marissa courteously dismissed him. "You needn't bother with that," she said. "Amal speaks perfect Norman French. Just translate for the emperor and for the audience." The translator looked confused and sat down. His fellow translators, when the emperor did nothing, scattered themselves about the hall and did as Marissa had told them.

"Now," Marissa said, "I think, Amal, you should tell the emperor who your real master is." Amal tried to look at her pleasantly but blankly. Why had he been so frightened? This girl could never beat him, a spy of the Old Man's. He would just stare at her like this, with no apparent understanding, and eventually the crowd would grow weary and she would have to withdraw.

Marissa hardly hesitated. With absolute confidence, she told her own tale. She told of Amal's arrival at Hartslove, his infiltration of their hearts and minds and of all the good things he had done. Then she spoke of his treachery and his allegiance to the Old Man of the Mountain. She warmed to her story, spinning, weaving, drawing in listeners who were soon hanging on her every word. It was as if Marissa had been born for the role. Nor did she spare Kamil. Only when she told of his end did she relent, and the audience groaned in sympathy.

When she had finished, Amal neither blinked nor frowned, only resolutely retained his look of patient confusion. Now a new murmur arose. Marissa had certainly spun a good yarn but there seemed no reason to believe it was true. And there was Will's blood to be spilled. They would not be denied that now, when it had been promised.

The emperor found his hands sticky on the arms of his throne. He needed to take control for he had no idea how much Marissa knew of his part in the Old Man's plot or how much more she intended to say. He could not think where she had come from or who on earth she was, but he knew now that he should have snubbed Queen Eleanor and never have let her open her mouth. Yet still, he reminded himself firmly, she had no proof of anything. His hands grew less sticky as his mind raced. "As I am sure Queen Eleanor will agree, you are an excellent storyteller," he observed loudly, making sure to sound kindly. "You are to be commended, young lady, for your skills—and also for your love." Marissa flushed, her composure rattled, and the emperor was immediately reassured for it confirmed something useful. "Yes," he continued, "your love, for I can see that it is your love for this knight, William de Granville, Earl of Ravensgarth, that brings you here now to save him. Yours must be a great romance. But alas, my poor servant"—he indicated Amal—"cannot be sacrificed even in the face of such passion." The crowd began to snigger and Will, caught between pride at Marissa's courage and fury at her interference, wanted to punch them.

He pushed toward her but was held back. "Look." Richard gestured with his head. "Look." From out of the crowd, Ellie now emerged. Will shook violently and strained even more. No, not Ellie, too! Why hadn't she stayed in Speyer? However, she was not looking at him. She looked at only Amal and she held out something toward him, something so small and tattered, something that was barely a book, more a collection of dog-eared pages, but something that Ellie raised as if it were the

Bible. Queen Eleanor stood up. The crowd did not know how to react. Not so Amal. When he saw what it was that Ellie held, the confident raven lost even the little stuffing he had left. "Oh," he cried before he could help himself, "Oh," and his arms could not be stopped from holding themselves out in supplication. "My book, my precious book! Oh, you wicked Christian! You stole it! You stole it!" There was no German now, nor even French. Amal felt as if his tinder-dry innards had been set alight. For the first time since he had entered the Old Man's service, he spoke without thinking. The image of Ellie and Marissa tracing the names of his children with their fingers, defiling them, was too much for him. He wavered like a thin flame and words sparked out of him, short, sharp, terrible words whose sting Ellie felt even though she had no idea what they meant. She trembled as they scattered about her like shards of glass, but she had to continue. People had to know. There could be no doubt. She had thought that this revenge on Amal would be sweet. Yet the shredding of an old man in the public gaze made her feel sullied.

Nevertheless, she kept her nerve. This proof of Will's innocence could not be wasted for it was the only one they had. Slowly, she held the book to her eyes and read aloud the Old Man's inscription and name that she had painstakingly worked out with the skills Amal himself had taught her at Hartslove. Then she held up the book again to show the painted dagger, the unmistakable mark of the Assassins, and pointed. "This is the guilty man who caused the ransom to be stolen," she said. "This is the man responsible." Amal, his hands still outstretched, denied nothing.

At once the emperor did the only thing he could do, which was to feign horror and stand bolt upright. He addressed Amal directly and had to watch as the old spy teetered as if on the lip of an abyss, before, as final proof of his traitorous allegiance, he fell to his bony knees and with thin, painful cries begged Allah to avenge him.

Marissa and Ellie stood together now, holding on to each other. The sight of Amal, completely undone, was horrible. Then Will called out and opened his arms. For one, wild moment, Marissa thought they had opened for her and prepared to fly into them. But only for a moment. For though she knew she was included in Will's embrace, she knew immediately, from his expression, that that special place, the place right at the core of his heart, was still reserved for Ellie and only Ellie. Of course Marissa had known it would be so but it was only now that she found the courage finally to acknowledge herself beaten. Yet she could never be beaten entirely. Neither Will nor Ellie could ever forget her. After all, it was not Ellie's love that had saved Will. She, Marissa, had done that. Every moment they were together was thanks to her. She stood back to let Ellie through.

But Ellie never reached Will's arms. As soldiers bent down to hurry Amal away, he sprang out of their clutches and seized her, pulling her close to his ribs with arms like steel wire. In his right hand flashed Kamil's triangular blade, bright and sharp, and he held it directly across her throat. "Get back, get back," he warned. Suddenly, he was terribly tired, but he would not let go.

"Do as he says," cried Will, pushing Marissa behind him. This could not be. It was surely all finished. Wasn't God satisfied yet with all that they had suffered? He lunged but Amal and Ellie were locked together like dancers in some macabre entertainment. It was impossible to separate them. Amal edged his way to the steps of the dais on which the emperor's throne was placed, and as he and Ellie climbed up, the emperor scuttled down to Richard and his mother.

Once at the top, Amal turned Ellie around to face him and they stood, for all the world, like a couple about to exchange vows, with Ellie's back against a pole holding the imperial canopy. With the tip of the blade pointing toward her heart, Amal relaxed his grip on her arms and with his left hand carefully and very politely took back his book. He quaked from top to toe, so desperate was he to feel once again those familiar pages, to see his children's names and read the declarations of affection for the father who still loved them. Although he had recited the memorized sentiments to himself every night since the book was lost, the whispered words could not be compared with seeing those childish letters and touching the paper on which, all those years ago, his children had leaned. The unevenness of the characters, the smudged ink, and the way his daughter had tried to draw a kiss sweetened the gall in his heart. His eyes looked at Ellie but he saw somebody quite different and he smiled.

Ellie saw his smile and guessed what it meant. "You have children," she said, her anger masking her fear, "yet you tortured Kamil, who might have been like a son to you, until he died in a ditch."

His eyelashes were like cobwebs over the mouths of two caves. However, with a jab of the blade, Amal reminded her that for all her youthful vitality, he still had the power to consign her to dust before him. "Better to die alone in a ditch than die with the Old Man as a companion," he whispered, and his voice was the rustle of an antique page.

"Kamil should not have died at all." Ellie's voice was deadly quiet.

"Death," Amal said, almost musing, "is not the worst thing." He gripped the knife with renewed intensity although it seemed an effort. "Death is just the cracking open of a husk. We should not dread it. It will all be over in an instant." He gathered himself together, and she turned so that she should, with her last glance, see Will. She wanted him to know that she was not afraid, even though she was. She also wanted him to know, for always, that she did love him, not with the awkward love she had had for Gavin, nor with the admiring love she had had for Kamil, but with a love so important she could not live without it, yet so unobtrusive that she scarcely felt it. And the best thing about this love was that she knew that Will understood it. He would mourn her, yes, but he would never doubt her and, of course, there was someone else to ease his loneliness. Ellie tried to feel glad that Marissa was there, but though Marissa had proven so stalwart at the end, it was still hard to think of her as Mistress of Hartslove. Ellie decided to stop trying.

She faced Amal directly now for she did not want Will to see her face at the moment when the knife bit in and she could no longer control herself. Only Amal would see her final agony. She hoped it would haunt him. "I shall feel something of what Kamil felt," she told herself. "My death will somehow make his less dreadful." She held her hands tightly together so that they would not let her down by trying to push Amal away.

He seemed to be waiting for her signal and she gave it with a queenly incline of her head. His lips disappeared. His knuckles whitened. Then suddenly his smile was a rictus and it was he who was gasping, not she. Ellie frowned. She felt no pain, but perhaps you didn't when you were dying. Yet there was blood everywhere. It took her a minute to realize that though it ran down her dress, the blood was not hers.

Amal rocked back. "See," he murmured, "I am glad." Indeed, he was jubilant as he showed her Kamil's blade, buried not between Ellie's ribs but between his own. The thin skin had split like old silk. "All my life I have obeyed another," he breathed. "It is good to choose the moment of death for myself." He staggered and Ellie found herself holding him up. "You did not let Kamil choose his moment of death," she cried out. "You chose it for him."

She had to bend close to hear him for he had but a whisper of breath left in his lungs. "Ah, Miss Eleanor," he said, "but I didn't."

"What do you mean?" Ellie seized him harder. "What do you mean?"

But though she tried to shake more words out of him, he could say nothing as froth bubbled from his lips, his tongue lolled, and death rattled in his throat. Revolted, Ellie thrust him onto the emperor's throne. His body was too small to fill the seat and he lay, sprawled, no longer a branch or even a twig, just the ghost of a splinter. The deep red of his blood looked too vibrantly colored to have once flowed through the veins of such a man. Under the throne, the pages of his book flapped as the binding broke.

A great moan arose from the crowd as Ellie stumbled backward down the steps, her eyes on the knife as if it might suddenly leap at her again. The moaning grew in intensity when the people realized what had happened. A corpse on the emperor's throne! It was an omen of the worst possible kind. Queen Eleanor put her hands over her eyes.

Will was with Ellie in a trice. She clung to him. "Was what we did enough?" she asked him. "Was it enough?"

It was Richard who answered, for he knew just what she meant. "Yes," he said. "You have proved Will's innocence. He is safe." He walked swiftly to retrieve the parchment leaves before they drifted away in the draft, and holding them high, he turned to the crowd. He could not look at Will, for they both knew only too well that had Marissa and Ellie not intervened, it would have been Will's blood now slowly oozing down the flagstones. The king felt a black smudge stain his soul.

Guards now had to hold the crowd back though what the people wanted to do was unclear. The emperor held his ground proclaiming that he knew nothing at all about Amal except that he had seemed a good servant to the empire. Had he known the man's real background and intentions he would have had him flayed alive. The emperor had no idea if anybody believed him and Richard let him sweat before going to stand beside him in a gesture of solidarity. This was hardly the moment to claim moral high ground since the actions of his captor had been no more contemptible than his own. And anyway, Richard calculated, to shame the emperor publicly would not be shrewd. It was shaming enough to have a dead Saracen dressed in imperial colors leaking blood onto the golden cushions. If Richard helped the emperor at his moment of need, the man would be grateful and gratitude could be useful. With Richard towering above him, the emperor had little choice but to concur.

And so it was that Richard the Lionheart, Duke of Normandy and Aquitaine and King of England, finally threw off his role as a supplicant prisoner and reassumed all his God-given authority. Standing at the top of the steps, he commanded silence. "I asked you some moments ago if a treacherous man should be allowed to live," he declared. "The man lying dead on the emperor's throne was such a man. His actions shame himself and his master. Yet we cannot be surprised since his master was the Old Man of the Mountain. Let this miserable corpse remind us all of the importance of loyalty and honor." He paused, then gestured toward Will. "But this man, on the other hand, is entirely innocent. He returns home with me with his integrity intact and any man who utters a word to disparage William de Granville, Earl of Ravensgarth, will not live long." He stopped abruptly, threw Amal's book into the dirt, and dared anybody to gainsay him.

For a moment, the mood of the crowd threatened to turn nasty. Who did Richard think he was, to issue threats? Richard, Will, and Hal formed a barrier around Ellie and Marissa, their hackles raised like dogs.

Then, somebody began to cheer, a small sound at first, but it proved contagious. A lynching or an unofficial crowning, what did it matter? Both were good spectacles and it was not as if there was no corpse over which to gloat, even if a man dying by his own hand was not as satisfactory as a man dying by theirs. The small sound grew larger until Richard, sweeping up his mother beside him, was borne out of the hall in a tide of goodwill.

Will, Ellie, Marissa, and Hal were left behind as the hall emptied, Ellie full of Amal's dying words. She wanted to ask Will what they might mean but was afraid to hear the answer. Instead, she began carefully to gather together the fragments of the old spy's book.

"Are you going to take those back to Hartslove?" It was Marissa who spoke first.

Ellie shook her head. "We should burn them," she said. It was good to know something with certainty. "Amal's whole life is in these pages. It doesn't seem right that he should be dead and they should survive. They have served their purpose." She waited for objections and when none came, carried a candle over to the imperial throne. Amal's body was virtually a skeleton already and although Ellie did not want to touch it, she steeled herself to make it neat before she burned the book and scattered the ashes over it. When she had finished, Will pulled down a curtain and threw it over the remains. Nobody said a prayer. They did not know what prayer to say.

Now Ellie could wait no longer. "Will," she began, but was interrupted by a familiar piping voice. Elric burst through and the air was suddenly light again, even though the boy was clearly distressed. Throwing himself down in front of Will, he cried, "Was it my fault? When that man insulted Mistress Ellie, should I have done nothing? Should I, sir? I just couldn't bear it. But then I thought you'd died because of me until we found the green necklace and then we went to Marissa and she said I was wicked and not fit to be a knight but Hal says the fighting wasn't because of me and then I didn't think it was but then I did and—"

"Hush, hush, Elric." Will picked him up and held him close and the boy, so keen to be thought a man, for once didn't object. Will noticed at once the scars on Elric's arms from where he had tried to protect Hal during the massacre and there was now a furrow between the boy's eyes that mirrored a similar furrow between Will's. "The fighting was not your fault, Elric," he said gently, feeling very old, "but you must learn to be less impetuous. It's a hard lesson and even a sad one because it means you sometimes have to seem to accept things that are utterly wrong. But sometimes that's the right thing to do. You should watch Hal. He thinks before he acts. It's a good rule."

"But is it really?" Elric just couldn't give up. "I know that's Hal's way but everybody says Marissa has just been impetuous and she saved you."

Will let him go and shook his head. "Honestly, Elric, have you an answer for everything?"

Elric was momentarily very sober. "Not everything, sir." Then he was back to his usual irrepressible self. "Do you know, when I was coming out of Hosanna's stable, King Richard came past and swung me in the air. Swung in the air by the king! My mother will never believe it!" Elric seemed to have quite forgotten the coldness with which Richard had greeted him and Hal after they had ridden so hard to find the king. Better to forget. Now was not the time to remember.

"Hosanna!" exclaimed Will and Hal together. "You should not have left him." They hurried out of the hall with Ellie and Marissa right behind them.

"Not at all," retorted Elric, skipping alongside, "a nice nun is with him and Sacramenta's there, too. She looks like a horse with four wooden legs! But the nun explained that the things they have wrapped around are to help with the swelling. She seems to know almost as much as you, Hal," he finished naughtily. "I've learned a lot."

Hal gave him a mock swipe across the head. "Though not enough," he observed.

Ellie had another concern. "And Shihab?" she asked. It would be good to see her. "She is here, isn't she?"

"Oh," said Elric airily, "don't worry, she's here and as bad-tempered as ever. She glares at everyone with that blue eye. I'm quite friendly with her groom. He's been teaching me some German. I like him. He asked what on earth we had all been doing and whether all Englishmen ride their horses into the ground." Elric went pink at the memory. "I put him right. I showed him Dargent. Hal has been letting me look after him almost by myself."

Will hurried on, rejoicing in Elric's babble, and when he saw Hosanna, still weak and hollowed out but standing up, his star shining once again, and heard him whicker a greeting, he ran ahead and almost fell over Petronilla kneeling in the straw. Wordlessly he circled Hosanna's head in his arms. The horse sighed as Will crooned his name and hid his eyes in the flowing red forelock.

Ellie watched for a moment. It was a moment just for Will and his great horse. Her moment with Hosanna would come later. She moved on to the next stall, where Dargent was happily chewing strands of hay. Next to him was Sacramenta, who gazed out with wise eyes, and in the stall at the end was Shihab. The silver mare was thin as a wraith and the metallic sheen of her coat had dulled to nothing. Like Will, Amal had not spared his horse. She looked at Ellie and accepted her caress but with reserve, as if she was bestowing a favor. It was impossible not to smile at the mare's unconquerable conceit. She was standing in buckets of ice to reduce the swelling in her legs but still she held herself like a princess.

"You are very lucky, young man," Petronilla observed to Will, stirring the poultice mixture she was creating. "This horse carried you long after most would have given up."

"Yes," said Will. "Long after." He let go of Hosanna's head and began to run his fingers over his flanks, searching, checking, and caressing all at once, finding tender spots and scrapes just healing. Hosanna sighed again and, when Will had finished, licked his master's palms in search of the salty taste he loved. Petronilla deftly applied bandages. "This should draw out any poison from the cuts and then he needs a river," she said. "Cold water works wonders. I'm afraid he'll not be carrying you into battle again." She wiped her hands and looked at Hosanna appreciatively. "Perhaps you don't want the bother of taking him home?" she asked. "I could use a horse like him. Actually, I'm surprised you ever had him as a warhorse. He's really much too small."

Will shook his head. "I could never part with him," he said. "It would be like parting with myself."

Petronilla was amused but she seemed to understand. "Warhorses are more valuable than money, aren't they," she said a little wistfully, and under her veil, her rather precise features softened. "My father told me that when I was a little girl." Then she shook herself and her eye fell on Marissa. "Now," she said kindly but firmly as she disciplined her face back into its usual contours, "our little runaway nun, it's nearly time for Vespers. Shall we go?"

Three small words. But they hung in the air as Marissa hesitated and Petronilla waited for her answer. The atmosphere was suddenly tense again. For Marissa, this was the biggest moment of her life, bigger and more decisive even than the moment she had cut her hair and walked, without a backward glance, into the cloister at Arnhem. Since not even an hour ago she had proven her worth so well that Will could deny her nothing, this was the moment when she and she alone got to choose. Marissa would dictate how Marissa's life would be. And whatever she decided, nobody would dare to question it. She could go where she wanted, live where she wanted, have what she wanted—except, of course, the one thing she really did want. Even at this moment, she could never have that. Will was as out of reach now as he had ever been. And yet, it was so hard.

She moved forward to rub Hosanna's star. The horse was smooth to her touch and the smell of his coat mingled with the smell of the poultice. She heard Shihab shift in her stall and though she could not see Ellie, she knew she was listening. Hosanna's whiskers tickled her ear as he rested his head on her shoulder. She could feel the exhaustion of the world in its weight. His head was as heavy as her heart.

Slowly she drew away from Hosanna and took a deep breath. Looking deep into his wise eyes, she saw her own reflection. Nobody hurried her and in the silence that neither threatened nor forced, she felt a sudden surge of strength. "Yes," she said to Petronilla, slightly surprising herself. Then she looked at Will. She did not have to seek his admiration. It was there and it was all for her. "Yes. We should go." Her voice did not waver although it was far from natural, and she only hoped that now she had made her decision she could sustain it, and that Will, if he could not love her as she wanted, would at least, in the end, be proud of her. And Petronilla, with her kind practicality and quiet authority, was proof that life in the cloister need not suffocate. As she drew herself to her full height, Marissa felt a sense of liberation it took her years fully to understand.

But she would do one last thing, have one last worldly satisfaction. She would make sure that Will would take back to Hartslove a memory that would flash into his mind whenever life with Ellie palled. When they were dull together, or irritable, she wanted Will to wonder what might have been. So she tailored her last look at him with exceptional care. It proclaimed her love and then withdrew it, not as if she was accepting defeat, but rather to remind him that she was choosing her own terms of victory. "I shall return to St. Martin's," she said. "Good-bye, Will." He moved to hug her, but she moved away. "You can hug me when I am abbess," she said with the ghost of a smile, which Will, his heart aching for her, could not return.

Before Marissa finally left, she went to Ellie. "When I took Amal's book," she said, "I also took this. I think you should have it," and she handed over Kamil's little bone comb. Ellie too wanted to hug her but Marissa kept her distance. "Give my love to Marie," was all she said before, with a sigh only Hosanna heard, she took her place at Petronilla's side and obeyed the summons of the bell.

Ellie did not wait. Slipping the comb into her belt, she left Shihab and went straight to Will. He was standing, motionless, with Hosanna. Ellie held out both arms. "Come on, Will," she said, enfolding him and holding him very tight, "it's time to go home."

21

Hartslove, five years later

Voices rang out from the river below Hartslove. It was a boiling June day, and Will and Ellie were standing barelegged in the water while Old Nurse, sitting magisterially in a chair on the bank, was supposed to be minding two small children and a baby. In fact, Old Nurse had fallen asleep and Will was just climbing out to rescue his elder son, who was running in a determined fashion away from his parents and toward the warhorses relaxing under the chestnut tree not far away. Ellie was watching him, reluctant to leave the water that was so cool on her skin. She saw Hosanna raise his head and separate out from the others as little Gavin approached. The horse blew at him just as Will caught up, swept his son into his arms, and plonked him on Hosanna's back. Laughing, the child wrapped his fingers around the long strands of Hosanna's mane and shrieked as the red horse moved slowly forward, indulgent of his small burden. Hosanna's gait was stiffer now but his coat still shone and he still carried himself with pride although his flanks were more sunken and his muzzle was speckled with gray. He nibbled the edge of Will's shirt and, when little Gavin drummed his heels into his ribs, snorted and tossed his head in quite his old fashion. Will softly scolded the little boy and told him to treat Hosanna with respect. They began to walk back to Ellie but were brought up short by somebody shouting Will's name. Will raised his hand in acknowledgment before walking more quickly. "Everything's ready."

Ellie climbed out, shook down her skirts, kissed the top of Old Nurse's head, and checked on the baby dozing in a basket. She picked up her daughter, tidied Hosanna's forelock, and touched his star, smiling up at her son. He looked so comfortable. Will balanced the little girl on his shoulders as Ellie slipped her arm through his, loving the sound of Hosanna swishing the flies from his flank with his heavy tail as he wandered off, making his own way up the field. Neither Will nor Ellie made a move to stop him. Little Gavin had long since learned that nobody would catch him if he let go and his parents had learned that their son was safer with Hosanna than with Old Nurse. The other horses raised their heads as Will greeted them. He still missed Sacramenta, who had died shortly after their return from Germany and whose memorial stone shimmered in the heat. Shihab was standing apart from the others, as she preferred, ready as ever to take offense even as she dozed. Hosanna made his way past them all and as he did so, faithful Dargent took his usual place behind him. Will watched them. Nobody had horses like the Hartslove horses. He glanced at Ellie and knew she was thinking the same. They did not hurry.

Outside the castle walls, at the top of the road, a little group had gathered. In the center was a young man, clearly foreign. He was holding a colt, unbroken and skittish, shining red in the sun. Ellie's grip on Will's arm tightened. "Do you really think we can trust him?"

"I think so," he said gently. "After what he brought you."

Ellie felt at the pouch in her belt. Once, a similar pouch had held her green jasper necklace but she wore her necklace now. This pouch held a small, beautifully carved bone comb. Three weeks before, the young man now holding the colt had turned up. He spoke no English himself but had produced a small package addressed to Ellie. When she had opened it, both she and Will had become very still. Inside had been a comb, an exact match of the little comb that Marissa had stolen from Kamil all those years before. Surely only one person could have made a comb like that but it was only when Ellie had brought out the original comb and laid out the two together that she had dared to breathe, "Kamil."

After Richard was freed and they had left Germany, both the king and Will had sent messengers far and wide to try and find news of Kamil, but none had been successful. The men had brought other news, however. Although Ellie had been glad to hear of the Old Man's death, she could not give praise for the storms that had sunk his ship. Though the English silver the Old Man had coveted now rested with the fish and he himself had last been seen a bloated corpse, Ellie's plait wrapped around his neck and empty-handed after the waves had prized Marissa's ruby brooch from his fingers, Ellie would rather he had made it back to his mountain hideout if it meant that Kamil too was somewhere alive and happy. But there was no news. None at all.

For some months, Ellie had believed that Kamil would turn up for her wedding to Will and had almost persuaded Will to believe it too. However, though they had looked for him amongst the revelers all their wedding day, longing for him to share their happiness, he had never appeared.

After that, Ellie had tried to put Kamil out of her mind and had succeeded most days, particularly after the children were born. Then, suddenly, out of the blue, their unexpected visitor had arrived. Everybody had been so suspicious of the messenger boy to start with. Constable Shortspur had openly accused him of being another Amal and Elric, now Will's full squire, had followed him around like a persistent terrier. But the messenger had been patient. In halting English, he said that he was Kamil's servant and revealed what his master had told him and what Amal had kept to himself—that the old spy, despite his fear of the Old Man, had found himself unable to cut Kamil's throat. Instead, after Kamil had fallen from Shihab at the river, Amal had pulled the arrows out and covered him with leaves. Nobody had gone to check, particularly when Amal had emerged from the wood covered in Kamil's blood. To the Old Man's soldiers, Kamil was Amal's business. Nevertheless, it had been a long time before Kamil finally felt it was safe to send the messenger with the comb.

When Will and Ellie reached the road, Hosanna was waiting. Little Gavin wanted to get down. Ellie lifted him off and Marie, who was visiting with Hal—or Sir Hal as he had become when he was dubbed to knighthood—took him and his sister to play with their own little sons. Elric, though pretending to be far too grown-up, was joining in their game of tag with huge enthusiasm and had all the children yelling with delight. Hal was standing near the colt's head. He grinned at Will. "We'll employ Elric as a nurse if he's not careful. He's got a real way with him."

Will laughed. "You'll have to fight Ellie for him," he said. "He's rescued Gavin from the moat at least three times even though he can't swim himself. I'm glad we haven't made him completely sensible. He's a good squire, Hal. I suppose he should be. He had a good teacher."

Hal blushed and changed the subject. "Just look at this colt!" he said. "He's got the best bits of each parent. Hosanna's bravery and beauty and Shihab's elegance and speed." As if glad to be the center of attention once again, the colt lifted four slim legs one after the other, quivering impatiently. "He is a fine present, Will." Hal stood back as Ellie moved forward.

Will watched her as she stroked the colt's neck and whispered in its ears. The sight made him forget Hal and Elric as a familiar specter shimmied up to haunt him. Suddenly, he wanted to tempt fate. "Do you want to deliver him yourself?" he asked. "Do you, Ellie? You always wanted to see the desert."

Ellie stood completely still. In her dreams, she often saw herself walking up a dusty track with Kamil at the end of it holding out his hand. She never knew what happened next because she always woke. Now she considered what Will said very carefully. She looked first toward the river where Old Nurse was snoring beside the baby. Next she looked at Gavin's grave, then at Sacramenta's, and then to where her son and daughter were playing so happily. She looked at the horses in the meadow, then at Hartslove, so lovingly built by Sir Thomas de Granville, and finally she looked at Will. "No," she said, and gave him a look of such certain love that the last of the tiny pricks of fear that had shivered in his heart since he was old enough to love her were finally stilled. Now he really began to believe that Ellie was truly his, not because Gavin was dead or because Kamil was gone, not even because of her wedding vows, but because it was to him that she had chosen to belong. The new clarity of this knowledge made him curiously giddy, and he was glad to feel Hosanna at his back. As the horse rubbed his head on his master's shoulder, Will felt an overwhelming surge of pure happiness. He gave the foreign boy his final instructions. "Once over the sea, make for St. Martin's at Arnhem," he said. "Ask for Marissa. She will make sure you have food and shelter, and give her this." He handed over a parchment scroll on which Ellie had written, under Will's dictation, all the Hartslove news. At the bottom, as Marissa had requested in her missive to him, he had attached a lock of each of the children's hair, marked with their names: Gavin, Mary, and Baby Thomas. Then Will patted the colt and wished him and the boy Godspeed.

Ellie herself dallied a little at the colt's head, plaiting and unplaiting his forelock. She waited until the last moment, then, as the messenger finally set off, she gave him something of her own. Even then she was not entirely satisfied and followed the colt as he jostled and pranced his way down the road. Only when he settled to a steady jog did she stop and raise her hand in a final farewell. Then she turned and seeing Will and Hosanna watching from the drawbridge, she waved, picked up her skirts and ran all the way back to them.

Six months later, in a small settlement near the River Tigris, a solemn-looking little girl was sitting on a hillock watching a boy toiling toward her. She watched until the boy came quite close and then got up and ran to a house set among orange and lemon trees. A man in full Arab dress emerged when he heard her calling. "What is it, Ella?" he asked gravely, for his daughter was a serious child and liked to be addressed in a serious manner. The little girl pointed and Kamil followed her finger.

He was suddenly alert as a hawk. Yet still he waited, long after another man might have run forward. He had learned to be cautious. Nobody could have detected any change in his expression, but his daughter was aware of a slight trembling in his hands. Her father was not expecting what he was seeing.

Since his return to the land of his ancestors, Kamil had worked hard to build a new life for himself. He had never forgotten Amal's face as the old spy found that he could not deliver the deathblow. Something had passed between them as Kamil lay, utterly helpless, and while Amal covered him with leaves, both men had been praying. After many hours, Kamil had dragged himself back to the river to drink and had been found, in the end, by a peasant come to the river to find fish. The man had, with some reluctance, half carried Kamil to a village and dumped him on a kind woman who had looked after him until he could at least stand unaided. He had left Germany only after hearing of the Old Man's drowning, begging passage on a boat. Now, surely it would be safe for him to return home. As he had sat, watching the shores of Europe vanish, he had thought a great deal. His trust in Will was absolute. Will would explain to Ellie that he was no follower of the Old Man and that though he had caused the deaths of Hartslove men, he was no traitor. Kamil did not, however, know if Ellie would believe him and he found that this mattered to him, mattered very much.

The boy on the road came closer and salaamed. It was late and he was tired and dirty but he still walked with purpose, keeping up well with the colt, still sprightly at his side. When they reached Kamil, the horse shook himself for his coat was dusty and he regarded his surroundings with interested disdain. Despite the dust, between the colt's eyes a small star gleamed like a pearl. Kamil could not take his eyes off it. The boy handed over the colt's lead rope without a word and headed for the servant's quarters. Then he turned back. "Oh," he said, "there's a message."

"A message?" Kamil did not look, just held out his hand. Into it the boy dropped a silken purse. The feel of the embroidery was familiar. It was the purse in which Kamil had packed the comb he had made. He forced himself to look away from the horse, but then kept looking back as if it might disappear. Only when it licked his hand did Kamil begin to breathe again. He looked at the purse properly now and opened it. In place of the comb he had sent was a plait of red and silver hair and a piece of parchment. Kamil fingered the plait, then took the parchment out and slowly unfolded it. On it, Ellie had written, in tiny but perfect Arabic letters, the names *Hosanna* and *Shihab*. He read them again and again.

A tugging at his shirt made him look down. Ella wanted to see. He crouched and they looked at the plait and the parchment together. Then the horse moved and the little girl grew nervous. Kamil slipped the paper back into the purse and picked her up. At once, the horse sniffed her hair and she laughed. More confident now, she put out a hand and began to sweep the dust from his coat. "What color do you call this?" she asked.

Kamil put her down and hung the new plait from his belt, alongside the rope of Hosanna's hair he was never without. "It's blood red," he told her. Then he took the colt's halter and began to lead it toward the stables. He looked back as he turned the corner. Ella was waiting, expectant. Kamil stopped, full of things that he wanted to say but could not. The colt waited beside him and sighed. He wanted his supper.

And finally Kamil knew that there was only one more message to give. It was a message for his patient wife, the girl who had nursed him back to health and in whose eyes he had found the kind of peace he thought would never be his. He would send her a message that said everything and he knew that she would understand it, not quite as Ellie would, but enough. "Go and tell your mother," he said as the colt rubbed his head against his new master's chest, "that at last I have a blood red horse." And as the little girl repeated the message so that she would not get it wrong, Kamil looked west, toward the setting sun. He touched the plait and felt the parchment, and though he sighed as deeply as the colt at his side, in the quiet of his heart he rejoiced.